A CATERED
MURDER

A CATERED MURDER

ISIS CRAWFORD

KENSINGTON BOOKS
http://www.kensingtonbooks.com

Longely is an imaginary community, as are all its inhabitants. Any resemblance to people living or dead is pure coincidence.

Library of Congress Card Catalogue Number: 2003108426
ISBN 1-57566-710-X

First Printing: December 2003
10   9   8   7   6   5   4   3   2   1

Printed in the United States of America

I'd like to dedicate this book to my editor,
John Scognamiglio,
for his unfailing kindness and support

Acknowledgments

I'd like to thank Kathy Feeley for her editorial acumen and her cultural references.

Larry for reading my book.

Linda Nielsen for her cooking advice and support in all areas of my life, dog and otherwise.

Amy Zamkoff for kindly donating her recipe.

And Ann Marie Grathwol and Kathy Verbeck for their contributions.

Chapter 1

Back in Longely again, Bernadette Simmons thought as the Lincoln Town Car she was riding in sped up Oak. Could be the title of a song. Only this time she wasn't coming home for a vacation. She was coming to stay. At least for a little while.

She tried not to think of that whole *You Can't Go Home Again* thing as she took a sip of her coffee and looked out the window. At five forty-five in the morning, the shops on Oak Street were shuttered. A calico cat trotted towards an alleyway. It was the only thing moving.

"Works for me," Bernie muttered to herself.

As far as she was concerned, the fewer people around to witness her less than triumphal return, the better. Bad enough to have to explain to her sister without repeating the explanation to friends and acquaintances. That would come soon enough.

"Stop," she told the driver, pointing to a store on her right. "No. A little farther up. Yes. Here. In front of the place with the green-and-white-striped awning."

As the driver pulled up to the curb, Bernie peered at the shop through her sunglasses. It looked perfect. As always. She drained her coffee cup and crushed it in her hand. The geraniums in the planters on either side of the shop door provided just the right splash of color against the dark green storefront. The display windows gleamed.

There was even a robin perching on the arm of the wrought iron and wood park bench outside the store. It was all so . . . so . . . Bernie rubbed the cluster of stars she had tattooed on her forearm while she searched for the correct word. So quaint. So early 1900's, she decided as watched the driver adjust his turban.

"You will be giving me $213.35 now," he announced, turning towards her.

"I have to get it," Bernie told him.

"You don't have this money?"

"I will," Bernie told him.

The driver scowled.

"Where I come from, people do not hire someone if they do not have the means to pay," he huffed.

Bernie leaned over and patted the man on the shoulder.

"You see. That's what makes America so great. We borrow."

The driver threw his hands up. He was still muttering when Bernie opened the door and stepped out onto the pavement. The sweet smell of the early June morning mingled with the faint odor of the river a mile away, but Bernie didn't notice as she marched—with a slight wobble since her wedges were four inches high—towards the store. She didn't even flinch the way she usually did when she saw the gold letters spelling out *A Little Taste of Heaven* on the shop door. She was too busy thinking about what she was going to say to her sister.

She took a deep breath and knocked. It would just be her luck that Libby had slept in. That she wasn't baking in the kitchen. Which meant she'd have to go around to the side entrance and chance waking up her father.

She should have kept the store and house keys on her key chain, not put them in a drawer so she could fit all her stuff in that evening bag. She knocked again. A moment later she heard footsteps. A few seconds after that she saw the outline of her sister through the door shade and listened to the sound of the lock clicking.

As Libby opened up, Bernie couldn't help noticing that her sister was looking decidedly matronly. She'd gained at least fifteen pounds and stopped streaking her hair since Bernie had seen her at Christmas. There were smudges of flour on her cheeks and along the front of her T-shirt.

"Oh, my God," Libby cried, putting her hands up to her mouth when she saw who it was. "What are you doing here?"

"I'm paying you a surprise visit."

"What happened?"

Bernie grimaced. "I'll tell you later. I need two fifty-five for the car."

"What car?"

"That car." Bernie gestured towards the Lincoln Town Car parked outside.

Libby's eyes widened. "You took a limo from Kennedy?"

"It's not really a limo. Strictly speaking."

"It's close enough." Libby rubbed the corner of one of her eyes with her knuckle. "You could have taken Metro North. Or called me. I could have gotten someone to pick you up and saved that money. I mean two hundred fifty-five dollars . . ."

"Look, Libby," Bernie said, cutting her off. "I'm tired. I've slept about two hours in the last twenty-four. Can we not discuss this now?"

"But . . ."

"Really. The driver's waiting for his money."

Libby sniffed. Her mouth pursed in that expression of disapproval Bernie knew so well.

"I hope I have it."

"This is why God invented ATMs. And don't worry, I'll pay it back."

"Right," Libby muttered just loud enough for her sister to hear.

"I will," Bernie insisted.

As her sister went back inside the store, Bernie turned and waved at the driver. *One more minute,* she mouthed. The driver didn't wave back. Libby returned a moment later with a fistful of one, fives, and tens in her hand. All of the store's petty cash, Bernie presumed as she took the bills and paid off the driver.

"No luggage?" Libby asked when Bernie returned.

"The airline lost it," Bernie lied.

"Lost it?"

She nodded. She was too tired to go into it now.

"That's terrible."

"I've got my mascara," Bernie quipped. "What else does a girl need?"

"A little common sense."

"That was a joke," Bernie said as her sister put her hands on her hips.

"I know what is was, but what I really want to know is when are you going to tell me what's going on?"

"Can we go inside first?"

Libby gave a half bow and put out her hand.

"Be my guest."

"How's Dad?" Bernie asked as she stepped into the store.

Libby closed the door behind her.

"The same."

"He'd probably do better if he went out."

Libby made a face.

"You try and convince him of that," she told Bernie. "I've given up."

Bernie sighed. "And how are you doing?" she asked.

"Good. Of course, it would be easier if I had some reliable help, someone who had a stake in the shop," Libby said, staring straight at Bernie, who got busy studying the sink. "My God," she said, noticing the tattoo. "When did you get that?"

"Two months ago."

Libby shook her head.

"Why?"

"Because I felt like it."

"I just don't get it," Libby said.

"I know you don't." Bernie laughed and changed the subject. "Everything looks great. As always." And she indicated the cooler by the counter and all the shelves stocked with high-end goods with a wave of her hand. "How's the catering coming?"

"I have a big job this evening."

"I can help if you'd like."

Libby put her hand over her chest. "Be still, my heart."

Bernie could feel herself flush. "Do you think we could maybe not fight?"

Libby looked chagrined. "I'm sorry." She gave Bernie a hug. "This catering job is driving me crazy." Then she put her hands on Bernie's shoulders and held her at arm's length while she studied her face.

"What?" Bernie said. "What's the matter?"

"Joe's the reason you're here, isn't it?" Libby said.

"Can I get a cup of coffee before we get into this?"

"Of course."

Bernie followed Libby into the kitchen. It had always been her favorite room. Her mother had set it up when she'd opened the store. Bernie fingered the kitchen witch hanging from the window. It had been there for as long as she could remember. So were the pictures of her mother's mother and father on the far wall. When Bernie was little, she'd thought they watched over her.

The kitchen was compact, without an inch of wasted space, yet two or more people in here could turn out a picnic for two hundred without stepping on each other's toes. A kitchen designer who'd come in had offered her mother a job with his firm, but she'd refused, telling him she preferred to be available to her family.

Now, all the counters were piled high with food in various stages of preparation. "So what's the event?" Bernie asked as she poured herself a cup of coffee out of the carafe sitting in the corner and took a sip. Whatever else you could say about Libby, she made a good cup of coffee. Fresh ground beans. Water at the proper temperature. Unlike the coffee Joe made, which despite his name, was barely drinkable.

"Ethiopian?" she asked appreciatively.

Libby smiled.

"Nice, isn't it? My supplier gave me a sample. I'm going to serve it at the reunion tonight and see what people think."

"What reunion?"

"The Seventeenth Annual Clarington High School Reunion."

Bernie grimaced. "God, is it that long ago?"

"It is for me. Depressing, isn't it?"

"Scary. *The Breakfast Club* was on TV the other night." Bernie sang a few of bars of "Don't You Forget About Me." "Remember? That was my prom theme."

"How could I forget? You went around singing it for three months straight."

"Let's not exaggerate. So how come you got this job anyway? Usually you do smaller stuff."

"Bree Nottingham."

"Working with her must be fun."

"Oh, it is." Libby folded her arms across her chest. "It's just wonderful. Like taking a field trip to the ninth circle of hell. And it gets even better. The guest of honor is Lionel Wrenkoski, aka the great Laird Wrenn."

Bernie groaned. "He's such a . . ."

"Believe me, I know, but what I really want to know is why you're showing up here at five forty-five in the morning with no money and no luggage."

"I told you the airline lost it."

"You expect me to believe that?"

"It happens all the time."

"Not to someone who makes a fetish of never checking her bags through."

Bernie took another sip of her coffee.

"Can't a person change her mind?"

"No."

"All right then. How about because I wanted to see my dad and my sister?"

Libby rolled her eyes. "Spare me. Oh, my God." A look of panic crossed her face. "You didn't kill Joe, did you? You didn't kill him and run away?"

"Don't be stupid," Bernie snapped, although she'd certainly felt like it. "It's nothing that dramatic. We just had a fight, that's all."

"It must have been one hell of a fight."

"Why don't you like him?"

"I already told you. He's a sleaze."

"How do you know that?"

"Because I do."

"That's not an answer."

"Sure it is. I felt that way about the last guy you were dating too, and I was right. You know, the one that went around yelling *Olé* and clicking his heels."

"Of course he yelled *Olé* and clicked his heels. He was a flamenco dancer."

"He was a bigamist from Boise, Idaho."

Bernie started to giggle. "So he was a little absent-minded."

Libby giggled too.

"When the police arrested him he tried to climb over the stone wall in back of my apartment—in those tight pants of his." Bernie laughed. "They ripped down the middle. And then my neighbor's Maltese ran out and started pulling at the cuff. And Frank was trying to shake him off and the Maltese just stayed on." Bernie wiped a tear from her eye. "The police had to pry the dog off."

"I wish I'd seen it."

"I wish you had too. His first wife came down and bailed him out. Go figure." Bernie stopped laughing and picked up a sprig of coriander that was lying on the counter and sniffed it. "It's amazing how you either love this stuff or hate it. In Mexico . . ."

Libby held up her hand. "Bernie, tell me what happened."

Bernie shrugged. "It's not a big deal really. I just walked into the apartment and found Joe in bed with Tanya."

Libby put her hands to her mouth.

"But you know the worst? You know who Tanya is?" Bernie asked and then went ahead before Libby could answer.

"My supposed friend. The woman I've been working with on the shoot for Pillsbury. The one who was doing me the favor"—Bernie made a quote sign with her fingers around the word—"of letting me work late when all the time she was in Joe's apartment getting her rocks off . . ." Bernie took a deep breath. "I will be calm. I will be calm. I will be calm. That's better.

"No. I'm sorry. Let me correct that. That wasn't the worst. The worst was that I gave up a perfectly good apartment with a walk-in closet to move in with Joe. I don't get it. Tanya's got a lousy body. A big ass and no boobs. And on top of everything else, she's dumb. She thinks pâté is a sauce, for God's sake." Bernie slid a thin silver and onyx ring up and down her finger. "So I took a taxi to LAX and here I am."

"I'm sorry."

"And you know the next worst thing? On top of everything else, I just loaned that no good sonofabitch three thousand dollars. So I have no money. Maybe I should have gone back and stabbed him. Or her."

"You faint at the sight of blood, remember?"

Bernie made a face. "I think I could get over that." Then she pointed to a pan of skinny white cookies. "They look like fingers."

Libby smiled. "They're supposed to. I made them with cooked egg yolks, raw egg yolks, butter, sugar, flour, and powdered sugar."

"Like the Christmas cookies Mom used to make."

Libby nodded. "Exactly. What about your jobs?"

"What jobs?" Bernie bit at her cuticle. "They're cutting my column from the paper. A cost-saving measure. They're getting rid of all the freelancers because advertising is down by a third."

"And the food styling thing?"

Bernie shrugged. "One company I do stuff for is filing Chapter Eleven on Wednesday, and as for the other one . . . If I see Tanya, I'm going to stab her with her carving knife. Listen," she said. "Don't tell Dad what I told you. It'll just get him upset."

"So what do you want me to say?"

Bernie chewed on her lower lip for a second while she thought. "I don't know. How about that I had some time off and I decided to come home for a visit. Which is true."

"Without your clothes?"

"I'll tell him what I told you. The airline lost my suit-case."

"And after a couple of days?"

"It shouldn't be a problem because I'm going to tell Emily to pack my closet up and send everything to me."

Libby looked dubious.

"Will Joe let her in?"

"He'd better," Bernie growled. "Or else I'll . . ." She stopped. Or else she'd what? Good question. Then she brightened. "What the hell. I can use a new wardrobe anyway, and speaking of which, I figured that as long as I'm here we can do a little redecorating. Spruce the place up a bit. Maybe paint the rooms upstairs. Heaven knows, they need it."

"They're fine."

"They haven't been painted since Mother died."

"So?"

"It'll make all the difference in your and Dad's attitude. You'll see. There's this great blue-gray slate color called Innuendo. We could paint your bedroom in it." And Bernie wagged her eyebrows up and down. "Is that a name for a bedroom or what?"

Libby couldn't help laughing. As annoying as Bernie could be, she couldn't deny missing her.

"And I found this great red called Ruby Lips. It's a deep, dark red. Almost crimson. We could use that for the sitting room."

"That sounds as if it's going to be really dark."

"You'd think so, but it isn't," Bernie was saying when the intercom over by the door squawked and spluttered. A second later her father's voice floated out.

"Libby, do you think you could bring me something to drink?"

She went over and yelled into it. "Be right up, Dad." She looked at her watch. "He's early."

"Let me go up," Bernie said. "I might as well get it over with."

"Be my guest."

Ten minutes later Bernie was climbing the stairs to her father's bedroom carrying a tole tray containing a pot of coffee, a pitcher of cream, fresh-squeezed orange juice, two scrambled eggs, a side of toasted walnut-raisin bread, pots of butter and strawberry preserves, and a vase with a daisy in it.

"Look, Dad," she said as she opened the door. "It's your little girl home from Sin City."

"So what mess did you get yourself in this time?" Sean Simmons asked from his wheelchair, trying to sound gruff and failing miserably.

"Why do you say something like that?" Bernie protested as she put the tray down and gave her father a big hug. "I'm not in a mess."

He chuckled.

"Sure you're not, and I was never the chief of police."

MENU FOR RECEPTION HONORING
LAIRD WRENN

COCKTAIL HOUR

Bloody Marys
Port wine cheese and white water crackers
Mixed marinated olives
Red caviar mold

DINNER

Appetizer: Tomato Aspic in heart molds served on
white or black plates

Crusty peasant bread

Salad: Mesclun lettuce and goat cheese salad with blood
oranges and toasted almonds

Entrée: Midnight Beef (Blood-rare black pepper-crusted
tenderloin) with au gratin potatoes and asparagus tips

Dessert: Devil's food cake and finger bone cookies

Coffee and selection of Romanian brandies

Chapter 2

Libby parked the van as close to the rear entrance of the Clarington High School cafeteria as she could get. This was the part she hated most about catering—loading and unloading.

"Okay," she said to Bernie as she swung open the van doors. "Let's get to work."

Her sister glanced at the nicked windowsills and dented garbage cans. "I don't remember the place looking this bad."

"That's because when we went here we came in the front entrance." Libby plonked two cartons filled with produce in Bernie's arms. "Put these on the counter next to the sink." Libby was turning to get another two when she heard, "Miss Simmons. Miss Simmons."

She turned around. A thin lady with frizzy red hair wearing a suit and high heels came running towards her followed by a man strung with cameras.

"Are you Libby Simmons?" the woman asked in a breathy voice.

"Yes," Libby said cautiously.

"The Libby Simmons that's catering the reunion dinner for Laird Wrenn?"

"Yes."

"Good." She turned to the man in back of her. "Fred. Take the shot."

Fred stepped forward and raised his camera.

"Wait," Libby cried.

"Don't worry. It's for a story we're doing for Laird Wrenn's fanzine," the woman said as Bernie came out. "Are you helping her?" the woman asked, gesturing to Libby.

Bernie nodded.

"Great. Both of you scootch together in front of the van. Closer," she said, herding them like a sheepdog.

"But we're not dressed for this," Libby protested, looking down at her shorts and stretched-out T-shirt.

"You look terrific," the woman said. "Now smile."

The camera clicked. A few seconds later the woman pressed a business card in Libby's hand.

"I'll send you a copy. Do you know where Lime Street is?"

"Three blocks and take a right," Bernie answered.

"Thanks. Come on, Fred," the woman cried. "Try keeping up. We've got places to go."

Libby looked at the card. "Ms. Griselda Plotkin. Reporter at large."

Bernie whistled. "Can you imagine what life must have been like for her in grade school?"

"Fanzine?" Libby asked her sister. "What the hell is a fanzine?"

"A magazine for fans."

"I've never seen one."

"They're one step above the tabloids."

Libby grunted and glanced at her watch. "Whatever."

At this point she didn't have time to care about Griselda or fanzines. The clock was ticking. All she cared about was getting into the kitchen and getting to work.

* * *

Libby nervously regarded the small mold sitting on the counter in front of her.

"Can we change the music to something other than Depeche Mode?" Bernie asked. "Don't you think it's time you got out of the eighties?"

"Nope." Libby went to the sink, wet the towel over her shoulder with hot water, wrung it out, and draped it over the mold. "My job. My choice of music." She tapped the mold with the bottom of a spoon. "And don't touch that box," she warned.

"I wasn't going to," Bernie replied even though she had been. "The least you can do is get a decent system. They have much better stuff on the market these days."

"I like this one."

In Libby's view there was a lot to be said for things that just kept going. She put the towel on the counter, took a deep breath, and lifted the mold up. It was perfect. Thank goodness. Sometimes the aspic stuck for reasons she had yet to ascertain.

"What do you think?" she asked her sister.

Bernie stopped chopping parsley long enough to glance over at the shimmering tomato aspic heart in the center of the white plate.

"We've already discussed this."

Libby's mouth tightened.

"Leaving the historical dimension aside . . ."

"You can't."

I might as well be suggesting child sacrifice, Libby thought, looking at the shocked expression on Bernie's face.

"Accuracy is important," her sister pontificated. "Especially in a themed dinner. For openers, tomatoes, let alone tomato aspic, didn't exist in Dracula's day in Romania. Tomatoes originated in South or Central America and weren't introduced into Europe until the early 1500s.

Dracula—well, not really Dracula but Vlad, one of the sources of inspiration for Bram Stroker's literary character—was born in 1431, so you can see the problem."

Libby almost got the words "not really" out, but she wasn't fast enough and Bernie continued steamrolling along.

"And when they were first introduced," she said. "They weren't eaten. They were used as ornamental plants in Europe. People thought they were poisonous because they come from the nightshade family, but I'm sure you know that."

"Doesn't everyone," Libby muttered.

Bernie pretended not to hear.

"Ergo any dish made with tomatoes is—in my humble opinion—a bad choice. That said, I have nothing against tomato aspic per se. It's even kind of interesting in a retro fifties way. I just thought it might have been more interesting to serve the kind of food people ate back in Transylvania during Vlad's time. That's all."

"That's enough."

When Libby had first heard the phrase, "That's more than I need to know," her sister had immediately come to mind. If Bernie had her way, they'd be serving blood soup to start and boiled beef heart hash as the main course at the high school reunion dinner. That would certainly go over well with the alums.

For sure the inhabitants of Longely—bottled water guzzling, yogurt eating, health obsessed yuppies to the core—would not be appreciative of the fact that they were eating an authentic six-hundred-year-old Transylvanian recipe—give or take a hundred years one way or another. Few people would. But in the unlikely event she'd ever have to cater a dinner for a pack of medievalists specializing in Carpathian culture, she'd be all set.

Libby spread out the damp towel to dry on the edge of

the kitchen counter and smoothed out the edges. Even when they were kids, her younger sister always had an annoying mania for authenticity.

Libby clicked her tongue as she remembered the incident with the beeswax candles and the beehive in the oak tree out back.

"Your sister has no common sense," Libby remembered her mother saying as she'd dabbed Calamine lotion on Libby's stings. "She takes after your father's brother."

Did she ever, Libby thought, recalling the time Uncle Jack had, despite warnings, decided to wash Fluff n' Stuff, the family's Persian cat. He'd emerged from the bathroom with rivulets of blood streaming down his chest, a sadder but no wiser man.

Even though the menu was already done, Bernie had insisted on going onto the Web to look for old Romanian recipes from Transylvania. "Just for kicks," she'd said. Amazingly, she'd found some. Most of them seemed to involve boiling parts of animals Libby didn't want to know about for long periods of time. Granted, beef heart hash would fit in with the Dracula theme, but it sounded horrible and probably tasted worse.

She was taking enough of a chance serving rare beef tenderloin as it was. Her clients would eat seared, raw tuna but they wouldn't eat bloody meat. Go figure. But it was hard to come up with a themed vampire dinner that featured poultry. No. It was impossible. And God only knows, she'd tried. The pressed duck actually would have worked but you needed a duck press for that—something not even Williams Sonoma was making.

Libby was wondering if anyone did as she watched Bernie put her knife down and wipe her hands on the dishtowel she had tied around her waist in lieu of an apron.

"Working here, I can see why institutional food is really bad," Bernie mused.

"Why?" Libby asked, glad for a change of subject.

"Look at the color of the walls." Bernie indicated the school cafeteria kitchen.

Libby snorted.

"Color is important," Bernie continued. "These walls are beige. So was most of the food we ate, if I remember correctly. Whadayathink? Could there be a correlation?"

Libby rolled her eyes. Bernie put her hands on her hips.

"You don't think that color influences people?"

Libby carefully placed a sprig of mint on the tomato aspic. "In some ways."

She wasn't going to get into another New Agey discussion with her sister, not when they had so much work left to do. If she weren't careful, they'd be talking about Feng Shui next and why the current arrangement of the furniture in the living room blocked the flow of energy.

"It's a well-known fact," Bernie said as she went back to chopping. "Red makes people hungry, blue calms people down, and yellow cheers people up."

"What about puce? What does puce do to people?"

"Makes them redecorate."

As Libby watched her sister's brow furrow, it occurred to her that living with Bernie was like living with a talking encyclopedia, an encyclopedia that followed you around, bombarding you with facts you had no desire to know.

"I believe," Bernie said, "the word puce comes from the French by way of Latin and means flea-colored."

Libby felt like slapping her.

"That is enough."

"Sorry." Bernie reached for the last bunch of parsley. "It's not my fault if I have a photographic memory."

"Go on one of those game shows. Make some money."

"Don't think I haven't thought about it, but all those people . . . I'd get so nervous I'd blank out."

"Pop a beta blocker."

"I'll stick with tranqs."

"Whatever," Libby said as she put the aspic in the cooler and began washing the celery under the faucet. She preferred to hide in her kitchen, but she never thought of Bernie, the belle of Clarington High, the person who had dyed her hair bright blue, as shy.

For the next minute or so the women worked in silence. The only sounds in the kitchen were the thunck of Bernie's knife on the cutting board, Depeche Mode coming from the CD player, and the sound of water as it hit the sink basin and swirled down the drain.

"I can't believe that reporter," Libby said.

"Why not?" Bernie answered. "Laird Wrenn is big business. According to a friend of mine at Willie Morris, he just signed a contract for two books at three million each."

"But they're horrible," Libby protested. *"Damned to Hell* was unreadable."

"Someone's reading them. I don't know why. His vampires can even walk in the daylight. Where's the fun in that? And on top of everything else, he's such an asshole."

"He's probably worse now," Libby said. "Fame doesn't usually bring out the best in people, that's for sure. And changing his name from Lionel Wrenkoski to Laird Wrenn?"

"That was Lydia's idea." Bernie grinned. "Maybe we should call him Lionel when he shows up."

Libby was just about to remind her sister that you never insulted the guests when she heard a tapping on one of the windows.

"Is that Tiffany Doddy?" Bernie asked, looking at the face staring at them through the panes of glass.

"Yeah."

"I thought you told me she was moving to New Jersey."

"She was there for two months and came back," Libby said. "Let me see what she wants." And she hurried outside.

"Is that Bernie?" Tiffany asked when she saw Libby.

"She came in early this morning." Libby took a closer look at her friend. Her eyeliner was smeared, her eyes were red, and there was a coffee stain on her T-shirt. "Are you all right?"

"I'm fine." Tiffany sniffed. "Really. It's just that something's come up."

Libby gestured towards the kitchen.

"Come inside and we can talk while I work."

Tiffany shook her head and took a step back.

"No. It's all right," she reassured Libby. "I should have remembered you'd be busy."

"If it's really serious . . ."

"It's fine. Honestly."

Then, before Libby could say anything else, Tiffany got in her car and sped off. For a minute Libby thought about going after her, but then she thought about how much she had left to do and changed her mind.

"What was that all about?" Bernie asked Libby when she came back in.

"She wanted to talk to me."

"About what?"

"She wouldn't say."

Bernie wiped her chopping knife off on her apron.

"It was probably nothing. You know the way Tiffany gets."

Libby bit her lip. "I think she's started drinking again."

"Oh, dear." Both sisters were quiet for a moment; then Bernie said, "You know what? Let's change the subject to something a bit less serious. Let's talk about nail polish and whether you should get your hair streaked."

"It's just . . ."

Bernie shook her head.

"Drop it. If it's that urgent, Tiffany will come back. She always does."

"I suppose you're right," Libby said doubtfully.

"You know I am." Bernie paused for a second, then said, "Lionel's last three books topped the *New York Times* best-seller list." She picked up the metal bowl sitting next to her and swept the mound of chopped parsley into it with the edge of her knife. "Which just goes to prove that the masses have no taste. Did you know that the vampires we see in the movies are a strictly literary invention? That folklore vampires are usually bloated and ruddy, not thin and gaunt?"

"Sounds like Lionel to me," Libby said getting into the spirit of the conversation. "Okay, he's fat, not bloated, and he's kinda pale. At least he was the last time I saw him."

"Actually," Bernie continued, warming up, "today's vampires—the aristocratic vampire—hark back to the eighteenth century Gothic revival. Some people think Lord Rutherford is based on Byron . . ."

"Fascinating," Libby interrupted, hurriedly changing the subject before her sister got going. "I've been thinking," she said, "that I should start doing Moroccan salads in the store. They'd make a nice change for the summer. Like the carrot one with the lemon juice and cinnamon and the baby beets with cloves."

"How about something with couscous?" Bernie suggested. "There was a salad they made out at Ahmed's that everyone in Brentwood loved. It had raisins and almonds and slivers of orange and lemon rind and chopped coriander with just a little oil to moisten it all. I think I can recreate it if you're interested."

"I'd love it," Libby said. As she watched a smile creeping over Bernie's face, she made a vow to herself that she'd work on being more patient with her younger sister.

"Great. What do you want me to do next?"

Libby consulted her list. They still had to prepare garnishes for the aspic and finish cutting up the blood oranges for the salads and toast the almonds. The potatoes had to be sliced and peeled as did the asparagus. They also had to arrange the cheese and fruit platters, plate the olives, and peel the celery stirrers for the Bloody Marys. Fortunately, dessert was pretty much done. The devil's food cakes were baked and sliced and the finger bone cookies were in their baskets.

Three hours to count down and so far they were on schedule. Knock on wood. The one thing Libby had learned about catering was that Murphy's Law absolutely held. Anything that could go wrong would.

She glanced at the clock on the wall. Amber and Stan, two high school students who helped Libby out on her bigger jobs should be there any minute to help with the last-minute stuff. *Seventeenth Annual Clarington High School Reunion, here we come,* Libby thought as she touched the underside of the kitchen countertop three times.

For some reason, doing this event was making her more nervous than the fancier parties she'd catered down in New York City. She'd once heard a famous author say that nothing made his stomach flip-flop like giving a reading in his hometown. Well, her stomach was certainly moving. For sure. She knew why she felt that way too. Because her old boyfriend, Orion Clemens, was coming.

Orion. Her stomach had definitely clenched when she'd seen his name on the acceptance list. Thank God Bernie hadn't seen it. Libby closed her eyes for a second. She wondered what Orion looked like now. She hoped he'd gotten fat and bald and lost all his teeth and smelled bad. Suddenly she was aware that Bernie was talking to her.

"Why do you always do that?" Bernie was asking her.

Libby shook her head to clear it. "Do what?"

"Touch things three times."

"Do I?"

"Yes, you do."

"It's a habit."

"It's OCD."

"I'm not obsessive compulsive."

"You're borderline. Have you thought about getting treatment?"

Libby pointed a finger in Bernie's direction.

"Show me a caterer who isn't slightly OCD and I'll show you a bad one. Catering is all in the details," Libby said as she walked out into the cafeteria and surveyed the scene in front of her. "You should know that."

"So is everything else," Bernie said, trailing after her. She could tell, though, that Libby wasn't listening to her. She was studying the room in front of them.

And Bernie had to admit, given the constraints Libby was operating under, she'd done a good job, even though she privately thought that themed dinners were incredibly tacky. So were theme restaurants for that matter. If there was one thing she'd learned as a restaurant reviewer out in L.A., it was that palm fronds and tribal masks on the walls spelled bad food on the plates.

Libby ran her eyes over the cafeteria. Last night she and Stan and Amber had spent almost four hours getting it ready. They'd set up the guest of honor table, then moved in large round tables and covered all of them with black tablecloths. Next they'd done the place settings— white china—and arranged tableaux of little skeleton men playing instruments, eating food, and riding on donkeys on each table. Libby had gotten the figures from a supplier who handled candy skeletons and skulls for the Mexican holiday, *El Dia de los Muertos,* The Day of the Dead.

They'd been an overstock item from last November so she'd gotten them at a good price. But her biggest coup had been the gold foil-wrapped milk chocolate coffins. She was just thinking what a good table decoration they made when the doors to the cafeteria banged open.

Laird Wrenn swept in, trailed by his publicist, Lydia Kissoff. Three men carrying a shiny black coffin followed.

Wrenn looked around the room and frowned.

"And where," he said, pointing to his coffin, "am I supposed to put this?"

Chapter 3

Libby leaned towards Bernie.

"He's kidding, right?"

"Not from what I heard."

"He reminds me of a pigeon," she whispered in Libby's ear as she watched Laird Wrenn and Lydia Kissoff advancing on them.

"A pigeon?" Libby repeated.

"You know—all chest with skinny little legs. And that cape he's wearing doesn't help. No wonder the dust jackets on his books feature head shots."

Libby put her hand up to her mouth to smother a giggle. "Well, he doesn't exactly look like Keifer Sutherland in *The Lost Boys*, does he?"

"I loved that movie. I especially loved the guy with the blond curls. The one that looked like a Botticelli angel." Bernie wound a lock of her hair around her finger. "If I had all the money Lionel has and a body like that, I'd get my shirts tailor-made." She shook her head. "Boy, that cape looks hot. Maybe he has little electric fans in it."

"Stop it," Libby pleaded.

"And get a load of Lydia. I never thought she'd age well."

"Way too much makeup," Libby noted. Then she said, "We shouldn't be bitchy."

"Why not? It's fun."

"Quiet." Libby gave Bernie a poke in the ribs with her elbow as Laird Wrenn closed the distance between them. "Laird," she said when he was about a foot away. "I don't know if you remember me, but . . ."

"Are you the one in charge here?" he barked.

"Yes, I am."

Libby could see the sweat pouring down Laird Wrenn's face. He took a handkerchief out of his pants pocket and mopped his forehead with it. Then he snapped his fingers.

"Yes. Of course I recall you. You're the cop's daughter. The frumpy one who always had her nose buried in a romance novel."

Libby could feel her cheeks reddening with anger, but she couldn't think of anything to say. Especially because it was true.

Laird tucked his hankie back in his pocket.

"What I want to know," he said, "is where do you plan to put my coffin?"

The obvious comment jumped to Bernie's lips, but out of deference to Libby, she said, "How about in the ground?" instead.

Wrenn's eyes drifted over Bernie's body.

"The sister," he said when he'd taken the complete tour. "The party girl with the fondness for tequila. How could I forget?" He leered. "Yes. The Simmons girls. So you two are cooking now. How sweet."

He's making it sound as if we're cleaning out toilets in Motel 6, Libby thought as she took a deep breath and reminded herself that this man was the guest of honor. No matter how much she wanted to, telling him to go take a flying leap would not be good for business.

"I run a catering service out of our store, A Little Taste of Heaven, and my sister writes a restaurant review and food column for one of the L.A. papers," Libby told him through gritted teeth. Which wasn't strictly true—the tense was wrong—but what the hell.

Laird Wrenn stifled a yawn and looked around the room. "How interesting." Then he drew himself up to his full height, all five feet, eight inches of it—that was with the platforms in his shoes—flung one side of his cloak over his shoulder, and scowled. "Surely you know I always travel with my coffin."

"No, I didn't," Libby said.

"Doesn't everyone?" Bernie said speaking at the same time as her sister. "It was so complicated getting mine back from L.A. I almost left it behind, but then I said to myself, 'Now, Bernie you know you're not going to sleep nearly as well without it.' Does yours have air conditioning in it, because I'm thinking of having it installed in mine."

"I was on Letterman," Wrenn said to the girls.

"Now there's a non sequiter," Bernie retorted.

Wrenn glowered at Bernie before turning to Lydia Kissoff.

"I thought you said you were sending the caterer my interview in *People* magazine."

Kissoff's yellowish complexion took on a whitish hue around her eyes and mouth.

"I did."

"Obviously she didn't receive it, because if she had we wouldn't be having this discussion," Laird replied.

"Sorry," Libby said. "I must have missed it."

"I don't see how," Lydia snapped. Libby noticed she had begun peeling the nails on her left hand with her thumb. "I sent you a copy of the article last week along with Laird's special dietary requirements."

"Really?" Libby said as she guiltily thought of the unopened pile of mail on the dining room table. "We've been having trouble with deliveries lately."

"That's not acceptable." Laird patted his stomach. "I have a delicate constitution," he informed the girls. "Always have had. That's what drew me to vampires in the first place. The specificity of their needs."

"The specificity of their needs? Wow. I'm impressed," Bernie said. "And here I thought you were the one that won the pie-eating contest at the county fair when you were a sophomore in high school and then puked all over the judge, but obviously I must have been mistaken."

"You are."

"Bernadette," Libby said.

"What?"

"Don't you have things to do back in the kitchen?"

"Not really."

"You have to string the celery."

"A difficult chore."

"I think you should do it now."

Before she could reply, one of the men holding the coffin coughed.

"Hey, mister," he said. "Where do you want this to go?"

Laird looked around.

"There." He pointed in front of the dais. "Put it there."

The men started forward.

"But we'll have to rearrange some of the tables if you do that," Libby protested. "The wait staff won't be able to walk through."

Laird raised an eyebrow. "That's your problem, my dear, not mine."

"How about putting it over there?" And Libby pointed off to the left side of the room.

The men stopped and looked at Laird. "Keep going," he told them. "Are you seriously suggesting," he asked Libby, "that I deprive my fans of the chance to experience something unique?"

"God forbid," Bernie said.

As Libby glared at her sister, she wondered if she could get close enough to her to kick her in the shins without anyone noticing.

"I think it would be just as unique over to the left," she told Wrenn.

"Well, I don't. My coffin is an integral part of my personality. You're not suggesting I sit in the corner."

"No," Libby said. "But it's . . ."

"Good. It's settled," Laird said as the men set the coffin down and turned and looked at him. "Yes?" he said.

The men shuffled their feet.

"Ah, yes. A tip," Laird said and pointed to Libby and Bernie. "The caterers will take care of it."

Libby was just about to say, "No, we won't," when Bernie reached in her jeans pocket and took out a twenty. "Here you go," she said, handing it to one of the men.

"Where did you get that?" Libby asked. "I thought you were broke."

"Broke is a relative concept."

"And by the way," Lydia Kissoff chimed in as the men were leaving the room, "I hope you have Laird's water on hand."

"Water?" Libby asked.

"Yes. Bottled water."

"Of course we do," Bernie lied. "My sister has clearly labeled each bottle with his name."

"That'll be fine," Lydia Kissoff said shortly.

Libby was just saying, "Good," when the door banged open again and Bree Nottingham, real estate agent extraordinaire and organizer of the reunion, sashayed into the room.

"Oh, Laird," she gushed, heading straight for him. "I'm so excited to have you here. I couldn't wait to come and see Longely's most famous author." Then she turned and air-kissed Lydia Kissoff's cheek. "Darling, you look wonderful," she lied. "Simply wonderful. I love those skull earrings. They're so you."

She turned to Bernie and Libby next. "You two have done such a nice job. The place looks so sweet. Black tablecloths? Halloween in June. How adorable," she said to Libby. "And those little skeleton men. How did you ever come up with those? But I think you may need some flowers . . . something . . . I don't know . . . daisies . . ."

"But . . ." Libby said. "Daisies will . . ."

"No. No." Bree held up her hand. "You're right. Daises would be too . . ." She gazed off in the distance for a second, apparently lost in thought. Then her eyes widened as an idea struck her. Playing to the balcony, Libby was sure her father would have said. "Black roses," Bree stage-whispered. "That's what we want. Half a dozen to a table. And of course a dozen of them on the coffin. It will tie everything together." She put her hands on Libby's shoulders. "Now, Libby, I know how you get, and I don't want you to worry about a thing. I'll have my girl take care of it and charge it to your account."

"What a wonderful idea," Lydia Kissoff gushed.

"Inspired," Wrenn agreed.

Libby took a deep breath and tried to get the situation back under control. "I'll get them," she said. If Bree Nottingham did it, the roses would cost a fortune and the store wasn't turning a profit on this job as it was.

"No. No," Bree insisted. "I feel responsible. You have way too much to do." And she whipped out her cell and called her assistant. "Done," she said as she slipped her phone back in her bag. She looked at the coffin in front of the dais. "Are you going to put it there?" she asked Laird.

He nodded.

"Perfect." She waved her hands in the air. "I want

everyone to have the full Laird Wrenn experience. Don't you agree, Libby?"

"Definitely," Libby said, trying to get some enthusiasm into her voice.

For some reason Bree always made her feel as if she was the last pick at the high school dance. Maybe that was because Bree weighed a hundred and ten pounds. Her hair was always perfect. So were her nails and her makeup. Her pants were never wrinkled; her shirts never got stains. She could probably garden in the middle of a monsoon and she'd look as if she'd stepped out of the salon after the storm passed.

Libby should have been more assertive about the roses, Libby thought. Now they'd be lucky if they cleared a couple of hundred dollars profit for all the work they'd been putting in. You'd think she would have learned by now. Bree had been doing the same thing to her since eighth grade. She watched her point to the coffin.

"It's wonderful," she gushed to Wrenn. "All that black mahogany. I'm wondering if we should move it a little to the right. It would get a little more light that way." Then she turned back to Libby.

"How wedded are you to the tomato aspic?" she asked.

"They're already made," Libby told her.

"Oh. I know I approved the menu, but I was thinking that it might be fun . . ." she began to say when Bernie jumped in.

"You know, they're all the rage in L.A. now."

Libby shot Bernie a grateful look as Bree said, "I didn't know that."

"It's mentioned in this month's *Food.*"

"Then I suppose we should keep them."

"Absolutely," Bernie said. "And anyway, tomatoes were emblematic of Vlad the Impaler. That's why Libby put the dish on the menu in the first place."

"They were?" Laird Wrenn said. "I didn't know that."

"It's true," Bernie said, grinning at Libby. "Isn't it?"

"One hundred percent," Libby replied as she struggled to keep a straight face.

At that moment she could have kissed Bernie.

Chapter 4

The Seventeenth Annual Clarington Reunion Dinner was half over. The salad and the main courses had been served and eaten. The alums were chatting, basking in that pleasant afterglow brought on by red meat and hard liquor at the same time as the catering crew were scurrying around like ants on speed. Almost everyone in the class was there.

The waitstaff had begun clearing tables, while the lone dishwasher was doing the last of the salad plates. Bernie was at her station plating slices of cake and finishing them off with swirls of raspberry puree while Libby was standing in the kitchen doorway making sure that everything went smoothly.

She was thinking that much as she hated to admit it, Bree had been right about the black roses; they did tie everything together. She watched Stan, Amber, and Googie, her new hire, clear the tables. A moment later, Amber swept by her with a tray full of dirty dishes.

"Wait," Libby told her.

Amber obligingly slowed down and lowered her tray so Libby could check the plates. Nothing was coming back. Libby sighed in relief as she nodded to Amber to go on into the kitchen.

Despite some initial problems with the oven temperature, the beef had come out perfectly. The black peppercorn coating had turned out to be a wonderful foil for the slightly bland tenderloin. The potatoes had absorbed all the cream and crisped up just the way they were supposed to.

Even the string beans had turned out well. Actually, they were the hardest to get right. They'd come out bright green, with a slight resistance when you bit into them. But not underdone. Why people thought that vegetables needed to be served practically raw was beyond her. She'd finished the beans off with a squirt of lemon and a sprinkling of sea salt. Perfection.

Several people had congratulated her on the dinner and asked for her card. Told her they didn't know that she did big affairs. Needless to say, she hadn't told them this was the first one she'd ever done. Two people had asked her to call them about weddings they were planning. Not bad. This affair was turning out to be worth the considerable hassle.

Even Laird Wrenn had had something nice to say. He'd complimented her on the goat cheese salad with blood oranges on a bed of spring greens. Which had been very good, if she did say so herself. The tart taste of the oranges and the crunch of the toasted almonds was inspired.

People had even liked the tomato aspics. They'd found them charming. Now, if they got through dessert and coffee without any disasters, Libby was thinking she could uncross her fingers and toes and count the evening a success, when Bernie came over to her.

"I think Marvin still likes you," she confided.

"That was in the tenth grade."

"He was talking to me about you."

"He's probably interested in you. Everyone always is."

"You have to stop thinking like that," Bernie remonstrated. "He's a nice guy."

"He's helping his father run his funeral home."

"So what? Someone has to do it. Unless, that is, you'd rather have another go-around with *him.*" And Bernie gestured to the back of the room.

Libby squinted but she couldn't see anything.

"Who are you pointing to?"

"Orion. Last table on the left. Third seat in."

Damn, Libby thought. She swallowed.

"I didn't see him come in."

"He came in late. Look, he's getting up. I think he's coming this way."

"He's probably going to the bathroom."

"I don't think so. Libby . . ." Bernie hesitated.

"What?"

"Let it go."

"That's funny coming from you. Anyway, I just . . ."

"You are such a bad liar."

"I'm just going to talk to him," Libby protested. "Where's the harm in that?"

Bernie shook her head.

"I give up. I'll be in the kitchen if you need me."

Libby nodded absentmindedly as she watched Orion approach. Suddenly she was acutely aware of the weight she'd gained. Unlike him. He still had an athlete's body. And that cleft chin. God. What had her mother said when she'd brought him home? "Handsome is as handsome does."

Although his hair was thinning slightly on the sides and top. And he did have a few more wrinkles in his face since the last time she'd seen him, but, much as she hated to admit it, he looked better than ever. Which, unfortunately, was more than she could say about herself.

"Hi," she said. "Long time no see."

Brilliant, she thought.

Orion smiled.

"About ten years."

"You've gotten your teeth capped," Libby blurted out. "That little gap is gone."

She felt like disappearing into the floor.

Orion's grin grew wider.

"I'm flattered you remembered." He indicated the room with a sweep of his hand. "Very impressive. The food is great, but then it always is. I still remember the cake you made for our wedding."

"Coconut," Libby said mechanically. Everyone had told her how good it was. The odd thing was that she couldn't remember making it. "How *is* Sukie?" she asked.

Orion's smile disappeared.

"We're separating."

"I'm sorry to hear that," Libby lied.

"Me too. So what's going on in your life?"

Libby tried for a nonchalant shrug.

"You know. Same old, same old."

"No Mr. Right yet?"

"Several . . ." Libby let her voice trail off. She hoped she sounded convincing.

Orion planted his hand on the door frame and leaned over her.

"We should have a drink sometime. Catch up on old times."

"Definitely," Libby agreed.

"Good then. I'll give you a call."

"You're staying in town?"

"With my parents until this thing with Sukie gets settled." Orion straightened up. "Got to go catch a smoke outside before dessert."

Libby tsked-tsked.

"You still smoking those awful cigarettes?"

"Just started again. I need something to get me through this. By the way, loved the chocolate coffins. Where'd you get them?"

"From a funeral museum in Austin. They even have a mail order catalog."

Orion reached over and squeezed Libby's hand. "Trust you to find something like that. I'll give you a ring."

Libby nodded because she didn't trust herself to say anything else. Orion was almost at the door when Bernie materialized next to her.

"He is good-looking. I will give you that."

"He and Sukie are separating."

"I heard."

"You were eavesdropping."

"Oh, don't look so outraged," Bernie told her. "You'd be doing the same thing."

Libby fiddled with the collar of her white shirt.

"You don't think I should have a drink with him, do you?"

"No, I don't."

"Why?"

"Because he broke-off his engagement with you, for God's sake, and then got married to someone else two months later, and if that wasn't bad enough had the nerve to ask you to make the wedding cake."

"I offered."

"Well, he should have refused." Bernie slipped her shoes off and massaged first one foot and then the other. "At least I make the same mistake with different guys."

"What's that suppose to mean?" Libby asked.

"Figure it out."

Libby looked around the room again.

"We have to get the desserts going."

"Okay," Bernie said. "But you can't have my pills when you have a nervous breakdown."

Libby laughed as Googie came sailing by the two women with a tray piled high with dirty dishes.

"Coming through," he yelled.

"Hey." Libby took half a step back to avoid a collision. "Slow down. This isn't the Indiana 500."

"You mean the Indianapolis 500," he threw over his shoulder.

"Whatever." Libby folded her hands across her chest and frowned. "That kid gives me an ulcer. Oh-oh," she murmured.

Bernie followed her gaze. Tiffany was coming towards them.

"She's wobbling," Bernie said.

"It's the heels," Libby answered.

"You wish," Bernie countered as Tiffany reached them.

Libby reflected that while Tiffany had changed her clothes, her eyes were still red and puffy.

"Nice do," Tiffany said.

Libby smiled. "So far so good."

Tiffany took a strand of blond hair that had fallen across her eyes and tucked it back in the mass of curls on the top of her head.

"Sweetie, I'm not feeling very well. Do you have anything I can take?"

"I've got some aspirin," Bernie offered.

"That's not what I had in mind." Tiffany leaned in close enough for Libby to smell the alcohol on her breath and indicated the glass she was holding with a nod of her chin. "Do you think maybe I can get another vodka?"

"Shouldn't you . . ."

"Screw AA," Tiffany told her.

Libby opened her mouth, closed it, and finally said, "If you give me a minute . . ."

"No, no. I don't want to bother you." Tiffany slurred the word *bother*. "Just tell me where the bottle is and I'll fix myself a drink."

"Stan," Libby yelled. "Where'd you put the bar stuff?"

"In the green cartons by the door."

"Thanks." Tiffany patted Libby's arm and tottered off.

"I don't think I could walk in four-inch heels sober let

alone drunk," Bernie said as she and Libby watched Tiffany go.

"I never could," Libby said.

"How bad does she get?" Bernie asked.

"Bad enough."

"Isn't she seeing . . . ?"

Libby shook her head.

"She broke it off."

"Mike's a nice guy."

"Yeah. He is. Unlike Lionel."

Bernie snorted. "I guess when it comes to men, we're all a bunch of idiots."

"You got that right." Libby readjusted the towel on her shoulder. "It's not the same with Orion."

"I never said it was."

"Lionel keeps stringing her along. It's painful to watch."

The two women stood there for a minute, then Libby said, "We need to get the third course going."

"I'm on it, boss man."

And Bernie hustled off to finish up the cake. As she walked through the kitchen, she thought of the time when her father had given her the beta fish he'd won at the State Fair. She'd been about eight and enchanted with its iridescent blue and red coloring.

The fish had come in a little glass bowl and she'd insisted on getting a five-gallon fish tank and putting it in there, even though her father had warned her that it was a waste of money. The fish would keep swimming around in its little circle no matter where it was, because that was what it had been conditioned to do. And her father had been right.

Were we like that with men? Bernie wondered as she picked up the mustard bottle filled with raspberry puree and began swirling the puree on the next piece of chocolate cake. Were we conditioned to repeat our mistakes over and over again? Forever swimming around in a tight little circle like that beta fish? God, she hoped not.

Maybe what she needed to do was go out with men she wasn't attracted to because that way she'd meet someone nice. And after Joe, she was ready for nice. And speaking of nice, there was Marvin. Who'd liked Libby since high school. Who gave his word and kept it. Unlike other people she could name. People whose first names started with O.

Maybe fish couldn't change, but she was damned if she believed that people couldn't.

If Bernie was thinking about men, Libby was thinking of everything that still had to be done. She was in the middle of mentally assigning everyone tasks when Googie materialized next to her and pointed to Laird Wrenn.

"The funny-looking guy with the cape said to tell you he wants his bottle of water."

"It's in the back with his name on it. Go bring it out to him." Libby gave his hand a light slap. "And stop twisting that nose ring."

Googie dropped his hands down to his sides. "Sorry. You want me to get the water or put cookie baskets on the rest of the tables?"

Libby thought for a second. "You do the cookies and I'll do the water."

Then she promptly forgot as everyone converged on her for instructions. For the next twenty minutes, Stan, Amber, and Googie ran back and forth from the dining room to the kitchen serving the cake, and distributing coffee cups while Bernie and Libby went around with coffeepots filling the cups up with decaf or regular.

Libby was making her fourth trip back to the kitchen to refill her carafe when Lydia Kissoff appeared before her.

"Laird is waiting for his water," she said.

Libby put her hand to her mouth. "I'm sorry."

Lydia Kissoff sniffed.

"That doesn't help Laird. This wouldn't happen in Manhattan, I can tell you that," she said.

"I'll be right back," Libby said and took off for the backroom.

Bernie glanced up from the coffeepot she was filling. "What are you looking at?" Lydia Kissoff demanded.

"Nothing. You just seem a little tightly wound."

"What I am is no concern of yours," Lydia Kissoff snapped.

Bernie screwed the top of the coffeepot back on. "Maybe you should think of taking up yoga. I understand it's very relaxing."

Two bright spots of color appeared on Lydia Kissoff's cheeks.

"If I want advice, I'll go to a doctor," she said to Bernie as Libby appeared at her side with the bottle of water.

"Sorry I took so long," Libby apologized, handing the bottle to Lydia, who grabbed it and marched off. "She doesn't look happy, does she?" Libby said to her sister.

"Nope," Bernie agreed. "She doesn't, but then, if I worked for Laird Wrenn, I probably wouldn't be happy either."

"True," Libby said. "She really hovers around him. Not something I'd want to do. I wonder what Tiffany sees in Lionel?" she mused. "Because whatever it is, I'm sure not getting it."

Then she ran off to check on Stan's whereabouts, since he was supposed to be packing up the glasses and was, at the moment, nowhere to be seen.

Five minutes later, out in the dining room, Nigel Herron, the master of ceremonies, stood up and tapped on the microphone. Everyone in the room turned towards him. He straightened his tie and slicked back his hair with the palm of his hand.

"I'm not going to waste any time introducing my old classmate and friend Laird Wrenn," he said. "He's Clarington's most famous alum, and I'm sure you're much more interested in hearing what he has to say then in listening to me introduce him."

Someone in the audience yelled, "Damn right we are," as Herron extended his hand to indicate Laird Wrenn, who was sitting on the right of him.

Laird nodded at Nigel Herron, then flicked his cape over his shoulders and stood up as everyone clapped wildly. When the applause died down, he began to speak.

"I can't tell you how much I owe my dear friend, Nigel Herron."

More wild applause, although Libby reflected that Nigel Herron had a strange expression on his face. She just couldn't decide what it was.

"And the school. After all, you"—he indicated the audience—"are where I get my inspiration from. The events that happened here have given me the stories I've written about. Who would think that Longely holds deep, dark secrets? But it does. And I want to thank you for sharing them with me—willingly or not."

And he brought his lips into an unpleasant grin and laughed.

More clapping, but now it was tentative.

"My friends," he continued. "As my character, Count Catal Hayucuk, would say to you: Welcome, welcome. You and I have much to experience together and little time to do it in." Laird Wrenn's cape spread out as he opened his arms wide. "Being here for the first time in more years than I want to remember awakens old hungers and old memories.

"Did you know that blood has always been seen as the currency of life? There is blood and there are the creatures that feed upon it. Thus it was and thus it shall be. This was true in Mesopotamia and it is true now. We like to think we've left all of that behind." Here Laird leaned forward. "But we haven't," he confided in a stage whisper. "We haven't at all. There is evil . . ."

"Right here in River City," Bernie whispered to Libby.

"Shut up," Libby hissed back while giving Bernie a vicious jab in the ribs.

Laird Wrenn continued. "That is why people read my books. Because they are hungry for the truth. Hungry to know about lives outside of their own stunted existences that consist of mowing lawns and driving children to soccer games."

People exchanged uneasy looks.

"Hungry to experience the exquisite fulfillment of pure desire. I have been lucky in that sense. I have been lucky that my talents have brought me to this place. I have been lucky to have met Count Catal Hayucuk."

Laird stopped, picked up the bottle of water Lydia had given him, unscrewed the top, poured some into a glass, and gulped it down. In Libby's dreams the drinking went on and on. In reality, it just took a few seconds.

Laird put the glass down on the table. An odd expression played over his face. His eyes widened. He put his hand to his throat and opened his mouth. A strangled noise came out.

Libby thought she heard the word, "Oh, no." Or maybe it was a name. She couldn't be sure.

Then he toppled over onto the dais.

This is not good, Libby thought as she watched Lydia Kissoff and Nigel Herron leaning over Laird's body. *This is not good at all.*

"Bernie," Libby said. "I think he's dead."

"At least he brought his own coffin," her sister replied as she watched Griselda Plotkin, followed by Fred the photographer, run towards the dais.

Chapter 5

"'Get the shot, Fred, get the shot,'" Libby mimicked Griselda Plotkin as she ran towards the dais at the reunion dinner. "Who the hell invited them anyway?"

Sean Simmons looked at his daughter. He didn't think he'd ever seen her this upset. It was a little after nine in the morning. Sunday in Longely. Except for the churchgoers, the occasional jogger, and the hum of the lawn mowers, no one was out. Most of the townspeople were eating their breakfasts and reading the morning newspaper and, Sean thought, talking about last night's event.

He followed the progress of a black and white neighborhood cat that was crossing the side street outside his bedroom window while he considered what he could say that would calm Libby down.

"Lionel probably had a heart attack," Sean suggested, covertly glancing down at the *New York Times* crossword puzzle. Given the circumstances, doing it would seem callous, he decided.

Libby rolled the pencil under her palm for a few seconds before speaking.

"I hope so, but he didn't grab his chest. He grabbed his throat."

"One thing doesn't preclude the other." Sean conveyed

a piece of egg to his mouth. "People do strange things in times like that. Believe me. I know. In my job I've seen them all. At least they won't have to buy a coffin for him."

"That's what Bernie said."

Libby and Sean sat in silence for a minute. He reached over and speared a small piece of potato with a shaky hand.

"I understand your old flame was at the reunion."

"Bernie told you?"

"She mentioned it." Sean lifted the fork to his mouth. "How is he?"

"Orion's good," Libby said.

"I think I can still get someone to beat him up and run him out of town if you want."

There had been a moment when Orion had left Libby that he'd seriously considered doing just that before common sense and his wife prevailed.

Libby laughed and went over and kissed her dad on the top of his head.

"Thanks, Dad. Not every girl has a father that would make an offer like that, but I think I have everything covered."

"Just so you know." He squeezed her hand. "You look tired," Sean said, studying his daughter's face as she moved away.

"I can't understand why," Libby told him.

Tired didn't even begin to cover it, Libby reflected as she took a sip of orange juice. Even though she'd squeezed it herself not more than a half hour ago, it tasted tinny. She reflected that this morning everything seemed to have a funny off taste. Maybe it was because she hadn't gotten any sleep.

It had been eleven-thirty before the police had let her and Bernie go. One o'clock before they'd finished talking to their dad. Then she'd eaten half a pan of brownies and that certainly hadn't helped. She'd spent the rest of the night tossing and turning.

Between thinking about what had happened to Lionel and thinking about seeing Orion again, she hadn't been able to close her eyes. And then, when she finally had dozed off, Mrs. Randall's cats had started fighting underneath her window and that had been it.

Sean carefully swallowed the potato and put the fork down.

"I remember Lionel. Short, fat, pasty-faced kid. Ran around in a black Mustang until he got his license yanked. Always had an opinion, whether you asked him for it or not. I pulled him in twice for trespassing. Once at the school and once at that big keg party down by the docks the first week in September. Remember that one?" Sean coughed. "There must have been over two hundred kids there. At least. I had to get a couple of school buses to take everyone we caught down to the station."

"My God, how could I forget?" Libby made a face. "I heard about it for weeks. It was so embarrassing."

Sean studied his daughter's face.

"That job paid for your college."

"I know."

"That's good because sometimes I get the feeling you wished I had been something else."

"Well, it wouldn't have hurt if you'd sat at your desk like a normal person," Libby blurted out. "You didn't have to go racing around in a patrol car."

"You're right. I didn't have to." Sean coughed again to clear the phlegm out of his throat. "But your grandfather always taught me that if you want to find out what's going on, you got to get out there and get your hands dirty."

"With what? Skateboarders? Keggers? The occasional speeder down Oak Street? Nothing ever happens in Longely," Libby said.

"Plenty happens," her father retorted. "Your mother just wouldn't let me tell you about it."

Libby tried another sip of orange juice, made a face, and put the glass down. It still tasted bad.

"Anyway," her father continued, "what I wanted to say before we got sidetracked is that there was something off about Lionel. Something not right. Most kids, they get into trouble, it's because they're not thinking, but with Lionel you always had the feeling that he was weighing everything. There were rumors about him. Nothing I could pin down, but to be honest, I wouldn't have been surprised to see him land up in jail."

"Instead he made the *New York Times* best-seller list."

"This is true," Sean allowed as he watched his daughter get up from her seat.

She began to pace around the room while she ran her fingers through her hair, trying to calm the tangle of black curls. Finally she stopped and faced him.

"I can't believe he died at my dinner," Libby said.

"I admit that was inconsiderate of him," Sean said. "But I'm sure no one is going to hold that against you."

Libby kept twisting her curls around her finger.

"You wouldn't know that from the way the police acted. They made me leave everything behind. All the dishes. My pots. My knives. The leftover food. Everything. They told me they'd call me when it was all right for me to pick everything up."

"They were just being extra cautious," Sean explained again. "I would have done the same thing in their place."

"You know how it looks?" Libby made another circuit around the room. "It looks as if my food is at fault."

"Don't be ridiculous. People understand about procedure."

"No, they don't."

Sean watched a squirrel running across a telephone line.

"You know I'm right," Libby said when he didn't reply. "That's why you're not answering."

Sean grunted. "What does your sister say?" he finally asked.

But before Libby could answer, the downstairs doorbell went off. Sean heard voices. A moment later he heard footsteps on the stairs and Bernie popped into the room. She had a worried look on her face.

"Libby," she announced. "Clyde Schiller is here. He wants to speak to you."

"Great." Libby blew a strand of hair off her forehead. "Just great."

"Tell him to come up," Sean said.

"Dad," Libby began, but Sean cut her off before she could finish her sentence.

"No," Sean said. "I'm not having my girls speaking to an officer of the law by themselves even if he is an old friend of mine."

"You didn't want to see him before," Libby pointed out.

"Well, I do now."

"You don't have to do this. We can take care of ourselves."

Sean looked at his daughter for a moment before saying, "Oh, yes, I do."

Libby tried to deny the surge of relief flooding through her.

"If that's what you want."

"It is."

"I'm on it," Bernie said and went out the door.

"This isn't good, is it?" Libby asked her dad while absentmindedly pulling at the hem of her shorts.

"It may be nothing," her father told her, but he could tell from the expression on Libby's face that she really didn't believe him.

Chapter 6

A moment later Bernie reentered Sean's bedroom with Clyde Schiller in tow.

"Don't trip on the books on the floor," Sean warned his old friend, fighting the embarrassment of being seen in a wheelchair.

"I'll try," Clyde told him as he came over and grabbed Sean's hand in his two big ones and gave it a vigorous shake. "Wouldn't want to have to sue ya."

Sean snorted.

"Be my guest. Still skinny as ever, I see."

Clyde released Sean's hand and patted his ample midsection. "Pretty amazing, isn't it? Considering the way that Janey cooks, I should weigh a hundred and forty."

Sean smiled. His friend looked like an overweight, genial kinda guy, the kind who sat in front of the TV with a remote in one hand and a beer in the other. In reality, little ever got by him.

"What has it been? Three years? You should get out more," Clyde told him.

"That's what I've been telling him, too," Libby observed.

"How's life down at the station with old Lucy?" Sean said, shifting the focus from himself. He was still old-fashioned enough to believe that a man's problems were his own business.

When the Longely police department had imploded in a political scandal and Sean Simmons had lost his job and two officers had been forced to retire, Clyde Schiller had managed to stay on. To this day Sean wasn't sure how he felt about that.

Clyde Schiller grinned.

"Life with the redoubtable Chief Lucas Broad is fine, thank you very much."

"Good to know. Now tell me and my daughters what this is about."

"Well," Clyde began. "I've got some questions I got to ask your girls and I'm thinking maybe it would be better if I did it downstairs and let you rest a bit."

Sean suppressed a smile.

"You mean, you'd feel more comfortable talking to them out of my presence. Well, that's not going to happen."

Clyde thought for a moment and said, "Okay, Cap. If that's the way you want it."

"It is."

He plucked at a button on his uniform before continuing.

"It seems that the heart attack Laird Wrenn, aka Lionel Wrenkoski, died of was precipitated by a concentration of cyanide . . ."

"Cyanide!" Libby brought her hand up to her mouth.

"Libby, please let Clyde finish what he has to say," her father instructed, but she kept right on going. It was, he thought grimly, like trying to divert a runaway horse.

"It was in the water he poured out of his bottle, wasn't it?" she asked.

As he watched Clyde's expressionless face, Sean knew what his friend was thinking, because in his place he would have been thinking the same thing.

"How'd you know that, Libby?" Clyde asked gently.

Bernie took a step forward. *She's like a tight end running interference for her sister,* Sean thought proudly.

"What do you mean, how does she know that?" Bernie said. "It's obvious. Lionel poured water from the bottle into his cup, took a drink, put the cup down, and grabbed his throat. What else could it have been? The wine?"

"See." Clyde looked at Sean reproachfully. "This here behavior being exhibited is the reason I'd like to speak to your daughters separately."

"You mean we're suspects?" Libby cried.

"Is there a reason why you should be a suspect?"

"I didn't say it, you did," Libby pointed out while her sister and father exchanged looks.

That's my daughter, Sean thought. In times of trouble you could always count on Libby to talk when she should shut up and to shut up when she should talk.

"No, I did not," Clyde said.

"Are you talking to everybody?"

Clyde didn't say anything.

"Why me?" Libby demanded.

"We're talking to you among others," Clyde corrected. "And I'm talking to you because not only did you have access to the water—"

"So did half of Longely," Libby replied.

"But," Clyde continued, keeping his eyes firmly fixed on Libby and away from his former boss, "because it has come to my attention that you and the decedent, Laird Wrenn, had a disagreement earlier in the day."

"What are you talking about?"

"He means the coffin, Libby," Bernie said.

"That's ridiculous. I just asked him to put it off to the side and he refused."

"So you didn't say that you hoped . . . Let's see . . ." Clyde consulted his notes. ". . . that he died?" Clyde asked.

Libby put her hands on her hips.

"What I said was I'd like to kill him. And I didn't say it. I muttered it under my breath. So what?" Libby said. "People say things like that all the time when they're annoyed. It's not a crime."

"You're right. It's not." Here Clyde paused. "If that's all you did."

"Get real," Bernie said.

"We have to check out all possibilities," Clyde Schiller said defensively.

"Bree Nottingham told you, didn't she?" Libby asked Clyde.

"Okay." Sean put up his hand. "I've heard enough." Everyone turned towards him.

"Tell Lucy," he said to Clyde, "that my girls will be down at the station with their lawyer to give their statement tomorrow morning."

"You really want to do that, Cap?" Clyde said. "Makes them look bad."

"Don't try that line on me," Sean snapped at his old friend. "I invented it."

Clyde colored slightly and shifted his weight from one foot to the other.

"This is a small place," he observed stubbornly. "People are gonna talk."

"Not if you don't say anything, they won't."

"I'm not the one you have to worry about."

"Maybe, he's right, Dad," Libby said. "Maybe . . ."

"Libby, really. Let me deal with this." He turned back to Clyde. "You tell that boss of yours that I hear one word about my daughter being a suspect . . ."

"Suspect?" Libby cried.

Her father shot her a look.

"Okay," she said. "I get the message."

"About time. As I was saying," he continued. "I hear

that rumor going around this town and I trace it to Lucy, it will be my pleasure to sue him for libel. And you'd better believe I will. Lord knows, it's not as if I have much else to do these days."

Clyde nodded. "I'll relay the message. Don't bother," he told Libby and Bernie as he turned to go. "No need to go down those stairs again. I'll show myself out."

"Oh, my God," Libby cried when she heard the door slamming shut. "I can't believe this. No one is going to set foot in this store ever again. I might as well go over to Burger King and fill out a job application right now."

"You're a possible suspect in a murder investigation and that's your major concern?" Bernie asked.

"It would be yours too," Libby snapped, "if you'd spent years working here, building the business up, just to see everything go down the drain. I just knew something was going to go wrong. I could feel it."

"Nothing is going to go down the drain," Bernie said.

"Yes, it will. People aren't going to buy anything if they think I poisoned someone."

Bernie shook a finger at Libby.

"That, my friend, is where you're wrong. If you gave people food poisoning, you'd be right. You might as well close the door and padlock it. No one would set foot in the shop ever again. But cyanide . . . now that's a different matter entirely."

Libby looked at her sister incredulously.

"You really are nuts."

"Excuse me. Everyone came to Lucrezia Borgia's table, didn't they, and she poisoned people all the time."

"They were summoned."

"Not all of them." Bernie pointed a finger at Libby. "You wait. People will be lining up to get in. People always want to come to someplace notorious. Right, Dad?"

Sean nodded. "She's correct. It's sad but true. People

visit murder scenes all the time. They find murderers fascinating. Think of all the books that are written about them and the movies that are made."

"But I didn't kill anyone!" Libby yelled.

Bernie patted her on the shoulder.

"I know that, but you were there when it happened and that's almost as good."

"L.A. has fried your brain."

"I'm just trying to explain why you shouldn't be worried about the business. In fact, if I were you I'd do some extra baking for tomorrow morning because, trust me on this, you are going to be selling a lot of scones when the store opens tomorrow. Everyone is going to want to talk to you."

"I hope you're right," Libby said dubiously.

"Of course I am. Nothing this exciting has happened in town since 1880 when the sheriff caught his deputy climbing out of his wife's window and filled his backside full of buckshot. Right, Dad?"

But this time Sean didn't answer. He was scowling at the squirrel. Finally, he pulled his gaze away.

"All I know," he said, "is that if Lucy thinks he can play around with this family, he has another think coming."

"He wouldn't do that, would he, Dad?" Bernie asked.

"Yeah, he would. And he'd enjoy it too."

"You think that's what this is about?"

Sean began wheeling his chair towards his bed.

"Not entirely. But it certainly is playing a part."

"Why do you call him Lucy anyway?" Libby asked.

"It's short for Lucifer."

"He's really that bad?"

"No. He's just your average, incompetent, bumbling, grudge-holding petty bureaucrat. Other than that he's fine."

Libby curled a lock of her hair around her finger. "Calling him Lucy probably doesn't make him feel any warmer towards you," she observed.

"I know."

Libby and Bernie watched a quiet smile of satisfaction creep over their father's face.

"Then why do you do it?" Bernie asked.

"Because it drives him crazy, and because I can. Now," Sean said, "how about you two start from the beginning and tell me everything that happened last night, and I do mean everything."

Bernie and Libby had just gotten to the part about Tiffany wanting a drink when the phone rang.

"Let the answering machine pick it up," Sean told them

"No." Libby moved towards the phone. "It could be Tiffany."

But it wasn't. It was Orion.

Chapter 7

Libby couldn't believe she was out this late. Usually by nine o'clock on Sunday night she was home folding laundry as she watched TV. Instead she was sitting in the front seat of Orion's car watching the lights flicker on the Palisades and smelling the sweet scent of honeysuckle floating in the air.

"You know, my father offered to beat you up," she told him.

"And what did you tell him?"

"I'd think about it."

"That was nice of you." Orion draped his arm over the back of his seat and turned towards Libby. "I guess he doesn't like me very much."

"Would you if you were in his place?"

"No," Orion conceded. "I wouldn't like me at all."

They were silent for a few minutes; then Libby said, "This place hasn't changed much since we used to come here."

Orion sighed.

"I wish there was a do-over button for your life."

Libby leaned back in her seat. Orion's Infinity was new and still had that fresh-leather smell.

"I thought . . ." Orion began.

"That Sukie was glamorous and I was this chubby
hometown girl . . ."

"Something like that," Orion admitted.

Libby kept her eyes straight ahead.

"She's really been hell to live with," Orion said.

"And I'm supposed to feel sorry for you?"

"No. That's not what I meant."

"Then what did you mean?"

"That I made a mistake."

Libby decided not to dignify that comment with a re-
sponse as she watched the lights of a plane going overhead.

"What are you planning to do now?" she said instead.

"I make glass beads."

Libby turned to stare at him.

"Since when have you turned into a crafts person?"

"Since my therapist suggested I find a hobby. I've been
making the beads and selling them on the Internet for six
months now. See." And Orion dug into his pocket and
came out with two glass beads. "Here." He turned on the
interior car lights and handed them to Libby.

She weighed them in her palm. "Pretty colors," she said.

Orion nodded.

"They're a lot harder to do than they look."

"What do people do with them?"

"They make bracelets with them or use them for deco-
rative purposes. I'm beginning to sell to interior designers.
And I have a design for a plate I'm working on. Here."
Orion folded his hand around hers, enclosing the beads in
the palm of her hand. "Take them. Consider them a small
sign of how badly I feel."

Libby smiled at him.

"Okay."

"Good."

Orion looked at his watch and clicked off the car lights.

"And now I'd better get you home before your father
does make good on his promise."

"It feels weird both of us living with our parents again," Libby observed as Orion put the car in gear and backed onto the road.

"Tell me about it. But if you want to talk about weird, let's talk about Saturday."

Libby groaned. "Clyde Schiller was at our house. Evidently someone put cyanide in Lionel's drinking water."

"So I heard. That wasn't very sporting, was it?"

"Definitely not." Libby shot him a quick glance. "You don't seem exactly broken up about his death."

Orion made a right on Ash.

"I'm not and I'll wager no one else is either. Not if they're honest."

"Except for Tiffany," Libby said.

"That's still going on?" Orion asked.

"Was," Libby corrected. "Was going on."

Chapter 8

Monday morning and the thermometer was showing eighty-five degrees, unseasonably warm for early June. It was, as Bree Nottingham, real estate agent extraordinaire, would say, a glorious day in Longely. The smell of bridal wreath and early blooming roses hung in the air. The morning scrim of commuters rushing to catch their trains into the city had abated. The streets were quiet with the kind of hush that money brings.

On Oak, shopkeepers were getting ready for the new day, hosing off the sidewalk outside their shops, rolling down awnings, and opening up registers. All was serene except at A Taste of Heaven, where people were lined up two deep in front of the counter waiting to be served.

"Where are they all coming from?" Libby whispered to Bernie as she went by her on her way to the back of the store to get some more scones. "I've never seen half of these people in here before."

"Told ya," Bernie replied. "Trust me. A little crime never hurt anything."

"Too bad I didn't know sooner. I could have arranged to have a murder staged every week. Then I could have sold the concept to the Cooking Channel and be hosting my very own show. How does Homicide and Hummus sound?" Libby nibbled at her nail. "Or maybe Murder and Madeleines."

"Why not Crime and Crumpets? Or Battery and Butter? Alice B. Toklas has a chapter in her book entitled *Murder in the Kitchen* where she talks about suffocating a pair of pigeons."

"Oh, I could never kill an animal."

"Just a person."

"The world would be a better place without some of them."

"Speaking of which, how did your evening with Orion go?"

"Good," Libby said.

Bernie scrutinized her for a minute and then said, "I think you're making a mistake."

"At least it's something," Libby said.

"Marvin is something. Orion is a dead end."

"Don't you believe that people can change?"

"Hummm." Bernie put her finger to her cheek. "Let me think about that. No, I don't." She picked off a speck of flour that had landed on her T-shirt.

This afternoon, Bernie told herself, come what may she was going shopping. The alternative was wearing Libby's clothes, and she wasn't ready to play suburban matron yet.

"Well, I do," Libby informed her while she hurried off into the back room and Bernie went to help Amber with the customers.

"I know," Bernie called after her. "That's your problem."

From the doorway Libby could see Googie carefully removing the scones from a baking sheet and transferring them to cooling racks while his body swayed in time to the music he was listening to on his Discman.

She wondered if Orion would call tonight as she tapped

Googie on the shoulder. He jumped. "I need you out front at the register."

Googie straightened up and saluted.

"Yowza, boss woman."

"Stop calling me that and leave your Discman on the shelf," she told him as he began heading out the door. "It's inappropriate when you're waiting on customers."

Libby watched as he reluctantly took the Discman off and put it next to a stack of plastic containers.

"People have worked to music for thousands of years," he grumped. "I'm following a long, honorable tradition."

"You're in retail, you're not unloading a barge." Libby pointed to the front of the store. "Just go," she told him.

Googie clicked his heels together, bowed from the waist, and left.

One of these days I'm going to kill him, Libby thought as she picked up the spatula Googie had been using and carefully continued removing the scones to the cooling rack. Of course, then she'd just have to find someone to replace him.

The timer rang and Libby went over to the oven, opened the door, and breathed in the aroma of fresh-baked scones. As she took them out, she noticed that their tops were nice and rounded, just the way they ought to be. Her scones were pretty good if she did say so herself.

They contained heavy cream that she'd gotten from a farm ten miles away and grade AAA butter, not to mention fresh fruit in the spring and summer and dried fruit and nuts in the fall and winter. And she never made too many at once, because they weren't as good the next day. Like all goods of this kind, they staled quickly. That was another secret to the shop's success. Always having absolutely fresh, top-rate merchandise on hand.

Following in her mother's footsteps, at the end of the day she took the scones and muffins that were left over and donated them to the All Sinners Church food kitchen, as her father liked to call the place. But the way they were selling, it didn't look as if there were going to be any left today, thought Libby as she carefully piled the scones on the tray she'd brought in and went back out front with them.

As she reentered the store, Bernie came over and whispered in her ear. "Susan Andrews wants to speak to you."

Libby groaned.

"Is she still as crazy as ever?" Bernie asked.

"Crazier since her husband died. I told you. She's turned into this fiber person. All she talks about is weaving. And this will get you." Libby shifted the grip on her tray. "She's weaving her French poodle's hair into things."

Bernie shuddered.

"Here she comes," Libby said as Susan Andrews began calling out her name and pushing her way through the crowd. "Take these." She gave the scones to Bernie. "I'll see what she wants." Libby wiped her hands on the apron she was wearing and stepped out from behind the counter.

Susan ran over and hugged her.

"Oh, Libby," she cried. "I just had to make sure you're all right."

"Why shouldn't I be?"

"After Saturday night." Susan put her hand on Libby's cheek. "What do they say? In life we are in the midst of death."

"Something like that."

"My heart is still thudding. Here. Feel it." And she clasped Libby's hand in hers and pressed it to her bosom. "See?"

"Absolutely." Libby hastily worked her hand free.

"I hardly got any sleep at all. I went into my workshop and spun until I calmed down. You may find this odd, but working at my spinning wheel helps me realize the hand of God is in everything."

"That's wonderful. It really is." Libby gestured to the people by the counter. "Susan, I'd love to talk to you, but as you can see, I'm really busy right now."

"Of course. I just wanted to tell you how much I and everyone at my table admired the way you kept your composure."

"Well, thank you," Libby said. "Now if you'll excuse me." And she started to walk away, but Susan grabbed her wrist.

"I just have to share this with you. Before we sat down to dinner, Laird was telling me that when he died he wanted me to put a stake through his heart, so he couldn't rise again. At first I thought he was joking. But he wasn't. He wanted to protect his friends from himself. Wasn't that considerate?"

"Very," Libby said.

Bernie was signaling to her. She had to go, but for a small lady Susan Andrews had a powerful grip. She wondered if wrenching her arm away would be considered insufferably rude and decided it would be.

Susan shook her head. "He believed. He did. The thought of becoming one of *them* terrified him. But his saying that." Susan choked back a sob. "It was as if he knew."

Libby almost said, If he knew, then why the hell did he go ahead and drink the water? But she managed to restrain herself.

"Who would do something like that to him?" Susan asked as she released Libby's wrist.

"I'm sure the police will find out." Libby held up her hand, indicating she'd be with Bernie in a second. She had to get back behind the counter. More and more people were coming in the store, not that Susan seemed to notice as she dabbed at her eyes.

"I certainly hope so. Well, I can see how busy you are. So if you could just give me two of those wonderful strawberry scones of yours, that will be fine. Then tonight you can tell everyone all about everything and don't forget about the cooking lesson."

"Tonight?" Libby asked. "Cooking lesson?"

A look of concern passed over Susan's face.

"Dear, don't tell me you've forgotten," she cried. "You're catering the dinner party Nigel Herron is throwing in my honor. Remember? I'm having a private showing of my fiber art pieces."

"Of course. How could I forget anything so special?" Libby lied. "It's written on my calendar in big red letters."

Susan fingered one of her earrings.

"And I'm so excited about Julie Chang."

"Right." Now Libby remembered. Susan had arranged for a Chinese cooking lesson with Julie Chang at her house tomorrow. It had seemed like a good idea at the time. Now she wished she could cancel.

"Everyone will be there." Susan sighed. "Such a shame Lionel couldn't see my work. That was one of the reasons Nigel was having this get-together. I'd like to think that he would have enjoyed them."

"Who wouldn't?" Libby replied.

"I'm thinking of donating a piece to place in his coffin."

"That's very generous of you."

"Why, thank you," said Susan as she watched Libby put her scones in a white bag and hand them to her. "I think it's important that a part of Bebe will be with Laird forever."

"Ah, yes," Libby said. "How is Bebe?"

"Wonderful. I know you think she's just a dog. No . . ." Susan put her hand up. "Don't protest. But she's brought a great deal of comfort to me and I hope she'll do the same for Laird's soul."

Libby searched Susan's face for a sign that she was joking and decided that she wasn't.

"Don't you believe in an afterlife?" Susan asked.

"I'm not even sure what this life is about," Libby replied.

Susan patted Libby on the wrist again.

"Don't worry. You will. It took me a long time to see it too. You have to lose your sense of practicality, of the everydayness of life, and immerse yourself in the great beyond."

Susan sighed.

"It wasn't until after my darling husband died and I became involved in past life regression that I came to believe in reincarnation. I realized that we all circle endlessly around one another. No one is ever truly lost. We all come back in different forms. For example, Bebe could be Bud's brother returned to comfort me. In fact, I'm sure he is."

Libby looked at the number of people in front of the counter while Susan chattered on and felt like screaming. She had to get back to work.

"That's wonderful," she said to Susan. "And I'd like to hear all about it sometime. But . . ."

"Yes, yes." Susan waved her free hand in the air. "The tyranny of the commonplace. I know. You have customers to wait on. I'm sorry to be taking up so much of your time."

"No problem." Libby kept smiling until Susan Andrews went out the door; then she ran over to Bernie and pulled her away from the customer she was in the middle of serving.

"We have a problem," she told Bernie. "A big one."

Chapter 9

Four hours later Libby was in the store kitchen forming the crab cakes for Nigel's party and mentally going over her to-do list when Tiffany walked through the door. Libby took one look at Tiffany's face and told Amber to take over.

"I'm making you a chicken salad sandwich," she told Tiffany.

Tiffany put her hand to her throat. "I can't eat."

"Oh, yes, you can."

And while Tiffany watched, Libby took two pieces of peasant bread, spread them with honey mustard, and then put on a layer of chicken salad, which was composed of poached chicken, homemade mayonnaise, chopped walnuts, and halved green grapes. Then she wrapped the sandwich up and grabbed a bottle of water. At least Tiffany wasn't drunk, she thought. Or not so she could notice.

"We're going to the pond."

"You're busy."

"I can use a fifteen-minute break. My back is killing me. Anyway"—Libby gestured to Googie, who'd just come in the door in answer to her call—"I have three people working. It'll be fine."

"If you say so," Tiffany said, repeating the tag line of one of their old jokes.

"I do."

The pond was officially called the Spenser Durant Swan Pond, and Libby and Tiffany had been going there since they were in junior high. Libby watched Tiffany out of the corner of her eye as the two women walked down the street. She looked as if she was fighting back tears. But she didn't say anything, and Libby managed to contain herself until they got to the pond.

"Where the hell have you been?" she demanded once they reached it. "Don't you check your messages?"

"I was at a motel near Wyckoff. I just needed to think."

"Well, next time you do that, think to call me first."

"Sorry." Tiffany twisted the gold chain around her neck. "I've always liked it here," she said as she watched the swans gliding on the water. "Especially when the lilacs are blooming."

"It is nice," Libby agreed.

Libby sat down on a bench, and Tiffany did the same. For a moment all of Tiffany's attention was taken up watching a little boy and his mother throwing bread crusts to the swans.

"Three kids wouldn't be bad to have," Tiffany said as the boy and his mother left.

"It's not too late." Libby unwrapped the sandwich. "You have to eat something."

"I'll eat half if you eat half."

Libby groaned.

"You're killing me. I had half a turkey sandwich a couple of hours ago."

"That's the deal," Tiffany said. "Take it or leave it."

Libby unwrapped the sandwich, handed half to Tiffany, and bit into her half. "There. Happy?"

"Yes." Tiffany took a bite. "I wish I could cook like you."

"And I wish I could do hair like you."

"Well. Not today," Tiffany gestured to her head.

Libby smiled and handed her the water bottle. "I still remember the first thing I cooked by myself. It was some kind of liver and eggplant pate."

Tiffany made a face.

"It looked so disgusting I threw it in the garbage without even tasting it," Libby reminisced.

"I went to an AA meeting last night," Tiffany said.

Libby reached over and squeezed her hand. "That's good."

"Remember when Orion broke off your engagement?"

Libby nodded. She didn't think she'd ever forget.

"And you couldn't get out of bed for a week."

"I felt as if someone had kicked me in the stomach."

"And you were too embarrassed to leave the house."

"And you practically dressed me and made me go out to dinner with you."

"Well, before Lionel . . . you know . . . died." Tiffany swallowed. "He told me he was getting married."

"That's terrible."

Libby hugged Tiffany.

"He said it was just this PR thing, but I didn't believe him. I told him . . . well . . . I told him awful things. I feel so horrible." Tiffany burst into tears. "Those were the last words I ever said to him."

"Ssssh." Libby stroked Tiffany's hair.

"And now I can't even think of anything else," Tiffany gasped. "I blew off my appointments. Even old Mrs. Randall."

"She'll manage," Libby said as she rocked Tiffany back and forth.

Finally Tiffany quieted down.

"So," she said, wiping her eyes with the back of her hand. "Not to change the subject or anything, but what did Orion have to say?"

"He's separating from Sukie."

Tiffany patted Libby's hand.

"Be careful."

"I intend to be." Libby moved her neck one way and then another, working out a kink in it. "He gave me some glass beads that he made."

"What is a glass bead?"

"It's like a large marble."

Tiffany shifted around in her seat. "Personally I think you deserve a diamond ring."

"I like these better because he made them."

Tiffany rolled her eyes. "You really are hopeless." Then she turned her attention back to the pond. "What happened to the black swan?" she asked Libby.

"He died. Which reminds me." Libby consulted her watch. "I was supposed to be down at the police station ten minutes ago."

Chapter 10

"And I thought doing food styling was grueling," Bernie said to herself as she arranged mini crab cakes on a bed of watercress. Here it was seven o'clock at night and she, Amber, and Libby were in Nigel's kitchen getting ready to serve dinner when she should have been relaxing with a martini. In the TV studio, someone served her food, not the opposite way around.

"At least the kitchen is air-conditioned," Bernie observed, trying to be positive.

Libby grunted and turned up the heat under the sauté pan.

"And we got our stuff back from the police."

Libby nodded and kept her eyes fixed on the pieces of chicken she was sautéing.

Bernie studied her sister for a moment. Libby had been acting preoccupied ever since they'd gotten their stuff out of the cafeteria, but then, Bernie reflected, her sister always had been sensitive to pressure and today had been a bitch.

"Are you sure you're all right?" she asked.

"I'll be better after this meal is served," Libby allowed. "It's been a long day."

"It certainly has," Bernie agreed and changed the subject. "Everyone likes the crab cakes."

"As well they should." Libby slid another piece of chicken into the sauté pan on the stove. The store was known for her mother's crab and sweet potato cakes.

Bernie looked around. "How much do you think Herron spent on this kitchen?"

"Fifty thousand. At least," estimated Libby as she eyed the granite countertops, brushed steel appliances, tile floor, and oak cabinets. "Probably a drop in the bucket by L.A. standards."

"It would be triple that amount out there," Bernie said. "Although these days they're doing fifties kitchens. Refrigerators with rounded corners in robin's egg blue. High Tech is out." She absentmindedly slid her onyx and silver ring up and down her finger. "I was thinking that we've come a long way from crouching over a fire roasting a hunk of meat."

"It's amazing isn't it?" Libby replied. "And those people managed to do it without a three-thousand-dollar gas barbecue, a fifty-dollar sable-hair basting brush, and a three-hundred-dollar German slicing knife."

"Feeling a little puritanical, are we?" Bernie asked.

"No." Libby indicated the hundreds of dollars worth of pristine copper and steel-clad pans hanging on the rack above the eight-burner commercial stove. "I just think if you buy something, you should use it."

Bernie tsked. "Libby, Libby. These pans aren't supposed to be used, they're totemic items, strictly for show, a testimony to Nigel's wealth and taste, in the same way that women in the fifties used to carry white gloves as a sign of their good breeding or African women in certain tribes wear all their gold jewelry."

"Silly me, how could I have missed that?" Libby said.

Bernie laughed. "What does this guy Nigel do anyway?"

"Investment banking. Why?"

"Just curious." Bernie picked up the tray. "And Libby."
Her sister turned.

"Now what?"

Bernie pointed to the white shirt she was wearing, her own T-shirt having acquired a grease stain she couldn't get out earlier in the day.

"I just want you to know that come what may, no matter what emergencies occur tomorrow—even if the entire town is wiped out by the plague—I am planning on getting a pedicure and going shopping. This is the last day I'm wearing this."

"What's wrong with my shirt?" Libby demanded.

"Nothing. If you're a size sixteen."

"It's not that loose."

"It certainly is." Bernie took a handful of material and pulled. "God gave you boobs. Why not show them?"

Libby gave the chicken a jab with her fork. "Because I'm more comfortable when my shirts don't fit like a second skin. I take it you spoke to your friend in L.A."

"She called while you were in the shower."

"And?"

"Emily said Joe told her he gave all my stuff to the Salvation Army. The bastard. He knows there's nothing I'm going to do about it from here. You should have seen my Jimmy Choo's." A wistful expression crept across Bernie's face. "They had Marabou feathers and four inch heels that had this little curve inward. They were wonderful and damned if I didn't look good in them. When I wore them I felt as if I owned the room. Have you ever felt that way?"

Libby pushed her hair off her face with her forearm.

"No," she admitted as she took the chicken out of the pan, laid it on a brown paper bag to drain, and started sautéing another batch. "I can't honestly say I have."

"It's fun." And Bernie started for the living room.

* * *

Libby kept sautéing. Considering the little time they'd had, she was pleased at the way she, Bernie, Amber, and Googie had pulled everything together.

The appetizers were simple but good. One, because Libby believed in taking the edge off hunger, not killing it, and two, because she didn't like fiddly little things. They were serving cherry tomatoes stuffed with goat cheese, nicoise olives, tapanade and hummus with toasted pita wedges, crab and artichoke dip in endive leaves, and little crab cakes with remoulade sauce, all of which Bernie had artfully arranged in bowls and platters decorated with fresh flowers and herbs.

The first course was a salad of field greens with strawberries and glazed walnuts tossed with a balsamic vinaigrette dressing, which tasted good and took two seconds to throw together, and while people were eating that, Libby could finish off the second course, Moroccan style chicken sauté with preserved lemons, and reheat the couscous and gingered carrots.

For dessert Libby had had Googie make four different kinds of cookies: shortbread, linzer tarts, chocolate snaps, and lemon crisps. She'd also pulled some double-coffee ice cream that she'd made two weeks ago out of the freezer and was serving it with a simple chocolate sauce flavored with rum, a combination that everyone always liked.

Libby was thinking that she'd have to make some ice cream tomorrow morning, when Nigel Herron came into the kitchen. Tall and gangly, with a tendency to wave his arms about, he always reminded Libby of his namesake, the Blue Heron.

"Is there anything I can do for you?" Libby asked, still keeping one eye on the chicken so she didn't burn it.

"Well, first of all I wanted to thank you for doing this in the light of what happened on Saturday."

"No problem."

"So distressing."

"Homicide tends to be," Libby observed.

Nigel smiled weakly at Libby's remark and rubbed the side of his nose with his knuckle.

"I was thinking about canceling the party, but Susan's worked so hard, I just didn't have the heart. And I think Laird would have wanted us to go on, don't you?"

"Absolutely."

"I had to force myself to go in to work today. Everything seems so unreal. I understand you were down at the police station for most of the afternoon. Do they have any leads yet?"

Libby moved the chicken pieces around in the pan.

"If they have them, they're not telling me."

"Ah . . . I thought they might. You being . . ."

"The former police chief's daughter?"

"Exactly."

"All the more reason not to."

"Ah, yes. I forgot about that unfortunate political contretemps." Nigel rubbed his hands together. "I also wanted to tell you that Lydia and Janet should be here any moment." He sighed. "I should have told them to come a half an hour earlier. I swear the pair of them has never been on time for anything in their lives." Nigel came closer. "That's a lot of fat in there, isn't it?"

"You need fat to brown the chicken," Libby said firmly. She'd been through this before. She knew there was even a nice long Latin word for fear of fat and it wasn't fatophobia. Bernie had told her what it was. She just couldn't remember.

"Oh," Nigel said, not sounding even remotely convinced.

"Olive oil is good for your heart."

"Yes. Well." Nigel smoothed down the lapel on his

brown silk tweed jacket. "I suppose it doesn't matter really, does it. I mean, look at poor Lionel. One moment on top of his game. At the height of his fame. A three-million-dollar book contract. And the next moment writhing on the ground."

Bernie stopped behind Nigel, empty tray in hand.

"If you want to get technical, he really didn't writhe," she observed.

Nigel half turned.

"No, I suppose he didn't," Nigel reflected. "He toppled."

"Good word choice," Bernie said.

Nigel beamed. "At one time I fancied myself a writer. But you know how these things go. Life takes us in different directions."

Bernie gestured around the kitchen.

"This isn't what I'd call a bad direction."

Nigel shrugged and rubbed his nose again.

"I suppose that depends on how you define things."

"And how do you define this?"

"Well, I haven't achieved my heart's desire."

"That's a pretty tall order."

"I suppose it is," Nigel conceded as the doorbell rang. "That must be Lydia and Janet," he said. "Finally. Sometimes Lydia is beyond irresponsible. She was supposed to be here this afternoon to help me pack up Laird's room."

"He was staying with you?" Libby asked.

Nigel regarded her with the tolerant attitude a parent gives to a slightly backward child.

"Well, of course. Where else would he be staying? In a manner of speaking, I'm his literary muse."

"I wouldn't brag about that if I were him," Bernie commented after Nigel had gone to get the door. "Is he British?" she asked Libby.

"No. He spent a semester in Oxford and has never gotten over it." Libby indicated the warming oven with her chin. "Why don't you take out the rest of the crab cakes and pass them around. Dinner will be ready in fifteen minutes."

Chapter 11

"Oh, Nigel," Lydia was cooing as Bernie hovered behind her and Nigel's girlfriend, Janet, tray in hand. "I'm so sorry I wasn't here this afternoon to help you with Laird's effects. I know I said I would be, but I've been on the phone all day with Laird's publisher and the lawyer. You can't imagine what a nightmare this has been. And speaking of nightmares . . ." Lydia's face hardened as she glanced in Bernie's direction. "You didn't tell me the Simmons girls are catering this event."

"Crab cake?" said Bernie, brightly proffering the tray.

Nigel swallowed and loosened his tie.

"Now, Lydia," he began. "This was set up months ago."

"So what? Don't tell me you couldn't have gotten another caterer."

Janet moved closer to Nigel and put her arm through his.

"I'm sure everything will be fine," she said giving his forearm a squeeze.

Lydia favored Janet with a withering glance before turning back to Nigel.

"You should have told me."

"I'm sorry. It never occurred to me to."

"You realize you're putting everyone here in danger."
Janet's chin shot up. "He's doing no such thing."
Lydia snorted.

"Then you're either an optimist or a fool."

"Off your Paxil, are you?" sniped Janet.

Nigel made a calming motion with his hands.

"Ladies, please."

"Fine." Lydia tossed her hair. "All I'm saying is that I don't feel comfortable eating food prepared by the Simmons girls. Given the circumstances, I don't think that's unreasonable."

"We do live in America, you know," Janet snapped. "You have heard of the concept innocent until proven guilty, haven't you?"

"Be that as it may, I'm not putting my life on the line for some abstract principle."

Bernie took a step forward.

"I'd be happy to run out and get you a McDonald's Happy Meal if you want me to."

Lydia eyed Bernie up and down. Then she said, "It's obvious that L.A. has not improved your attitude."

"And New York City hasn't improved yours. And by the way. Weren't you sitting next to Lionel at dinner?"

"What's that suppose to mean?"

"You figure it out."

Bernie lowered the tray she was holding as she watched Lydia storm into the living room.

"I guess this means she doesn't want a crab cake," she said to Nigel and Janet. "Pity, because they really are quite good."

"She's overwrought," Nigel told Bernie.

"Oh. Is that what we're calling it now," Bernie replied before heading into the kitchen to discuss an idea she'd just thought of with her sister.

*   *   *

The chicken had come out well, Libby decided. She'd just gotten through explaining the idea of preserved lemons to the table, of how salt mellows the lemons, turning them soft and silky, and come back in through the door, when Bernie tapped her on the shoulder.

Even though the house was air-conditioned, Libby was sweating. It was from stress. She knew that, but what she didn't know was why she had to sweat on her face. Why not under her arms like everyone else.

Beads of perspiration on her forehead and above her lip were not attractive. That was why she never wore makeup. Because it ended up running down her skin. Not that she'd ever tell that to her sister, who always looked collected no matter what was going on.

"Are we all set for now?" Bernie asked her.

"As far as I can see."

"Everything under control?"

"For the moment. Even Lydia is eating."

"Like she wasn't going to."

"Why are you asking?" Libby demanded.

Bernie tried for casual. "Well, as Nigel might say, since everyone is engaged I thought I'd just pop up and take a quick peek around Laird's room."

"You're kidding, right?"

Bernie smiled.

Libby put her hands on her hips and glared at her sister. "Don't you dare."

"You really need to take meditation classes or something."

"This is not a game."

"I'm fully cognizant of that."

"No, I don't think you are. I don't want you going up there. We're in enough trouble as it is. You heard Lydia. I'm sure she's just saying what other people are thinking. The last thing we need now is to be caught sneaking around someone's house. That would finish us off."

"Us meaning the business?"

"Yes. I've worked too long and hard building it up to watch it being ruined."

"I'm not going to ruin anything, and if I were you I'd stop thinking about your precious store and start thinking about what the chief said at the station about us being suspects."

"He said *I* was the suspect, not you."

Bernie waved her hand in a gesture of dismissal.

"Whatever."

"Don't make things worse than they already are. We have bills to pay."

"I'm aware of that, but jail would be a much worse alternative than having to close up shop."

"Let's not exaggerate."

"Dad would agree with me."

"No, he wouldn't. He's a by-the-book kind of guy. He'd tell you to leave this kind of thing to the experts."

"In this case the experts are tainted. And I can tell you this. I for one am not sitting around waiting to see if you're arrested."

"Nice sentiment, but I'm not going to be arrested because I didn't do anything."

"This may come as a shock to your idealized view of the world, but the police do make mistakes."

"You're just looking for an excuse to do what you want, aren't you?"

"Not at all," Bernie replied, hurrying on. "It's not as if we were breaking into someplace. We're here. In the unlikely event that I meet someone, I'll just tell them I went upstairs to use the bathroom and I got lost. That's not a crime."

"And what are you going to say when they ask what's the matter with the bathroom off the kitchen?"

"I'll tell them it's stuffed up."

"But it's not."

"It will be."

"Don't you dare," Libby said as she watched Bernie pull a large number of paper towels off of the roll on the counter, wad them up into a ball, and march off in the direction of the toilet. "I mean it," she called after her.

Bernie waved an acknowledgment over her shoulder. "I know you do and that's why I love you. There," she said when she returned a minute later. "That should do it."

"You really are crazy," Libby said.

"No, I'm resourceful. Don't worry. I'll be back before you know it."

And then she was gone up the back staircase, leaving Libby to remember why she had been so glad that Bernie had gone off to L.A. in the first place.

Chapter 12

Okay, Bernie thought as she glanced around the room Lionel Wrenkoski, once known as the great Laird Wrenn, had occupied. Now that she was here, where was what she was looking for? For that matter, what was she looking for?

There should be a blinking red light and a little sign with an arrow that said, "This way to the evidence," and in a well-ordered world there would be, Bernie decided as she slid her silver and onyx ring up and down her finger. Now that she thought about it, the police had probably already taken everything worth taking.

Maybe Libby was right. Maybe she was crazy. She herself preferred the term impetuous, which conjured up visions of Rita Hayworth wearing a safari suit and standing in the middle of the African veldt fending off a pack of lions with a bullwhip. Even if Rita did have red hair and Bernie's was blond, that could change with a visit to the salon.

Joe had thought she was stark, raving nuts ever since she'd thrown a pair of his shoes out the window when he yelled at her for buying a Louis Vuitton bag on eBay. But he *had* treated her with more respect after that. At least for a while. The bag was practically an icon, for heaven's sake.

At a thousand dollars, it had been a steal. It wasn't her fault that they were short the rent. Joe should have told her. And he shouldn't have screamed like that. Had she known what he was going to do with Tanya, she would have thrown him out with his shoes.

Her therapist had informed her she had poor impulse control when she'd told him about the shoe incident. Like he was one to talk. She happened to know through a friend of hers that he'd bought the cherry-red Jag convertible he motored around in off the lot on his lunch hour because he'd been driving by and fallen in love with it. At least she just fell in love with shoes. Even if they were the five-hundred-dollar variety.

What she had never gotten her shrinkman to understand was that she did best when she operated on intuition. It was the long-range planning stuff she didn't do too well with. So be it. She stopped fiddling with her ring and took another step inside the room.

"Okay," she asked herself as she took another look around. "What would Dad do in a situation like this?"

Now that was simple. He wouldn't be in it.

But if he was . . .

If she had her cell phone, she could call and ask him.

Hey, Dad. Howya doing? Libby and I have a question for ya. We were talking about what we should be looking for if one of us happened to wonder into Lionel's room. Hypothetically speaking, of course.

Too bad her cell was in her bag, which was locked up in Libby's van.

Even so, she could hear his voice telling her that most people looked, but they didn't see.

Fine.

So she wasn't going to look. She was going to see.

Whatever that meant.

For a moment she felt like Jeff Spicoli in *Fast Times at Ridgemont High*. Totally not there. Maybe she should rent it again, she mused. It was still one of her favorite Sean Penn flicks.

She shook her head. *Bernie, get a grip,* she told herself. She inhaled. Deep cleansing breath. One more. *Yes. Better. You didn't know anything about food styling when you started out either,* she reminded herself. *You learned on the job.*

If she thought about it, she'd never had a job that she'd been qualified for. She'd talked herself into every single one of them. So if there was one thing she could say about herself, she thought as she assessed the room, it was that she was a quick study. And speaking of quick, she'd better stop chatting to herself and do what she'd come up here for.

Bernie decided the room looked like what it was: a guest bedroom. Everything in it, except for the dresser and the night tables, was color coordinated in different shades of blue. Light blue carpeting, dark blue chenille bedspread, and white-and-blue-striped voile curtains. Even the clock on the bed table was blue. Periwinkle. Probably Nigel's girlfriend, Janet, had helped put everything together.

Very nice. Very tasteful, very boring except for the set of fangs lying near the lamp, the black cape across the foot of the bed, and the small coffin on top of the dresser, all of which somewhat marred the effect of tranquility that Nigel and Janet had strived so hard to achieve.

Bernie went over to the dresser and opened the coffin lid. It was a jewelry case. A pair of gold cuff links were nestled inside. She picked them up and looked at them—Tiffany's. Sweet. Good stuff. Nice and heavy. Then she picked up the coffin. It was enameled with a row of small rubies around the middle. On the inside of the lid was an inscription—*May we be together for all eternity. Your slave, Tiffany.*

Tiffany, Tiffany. Bernie shook her head as she put it back down and began to quietly open the dresser drawers.

You're even more screwed up than Libby and I are. At least, Bernie thought, *she'd had the good sense to confine her presents to Joe to things like CDs and cologne. She hoped Tiffany had got this stuff on sale because Lionel was definitely not worth wasting serious money on. Let alone time.*

What is wrong with us? Bernie wondered. *Why do Libby, Tiffany, and I keep dating such losers?*

Instead of thinking about the answer to that question, Bernie considered Tiffany's inscription. Slave. Now that was an interesting word choice. Were we talking metaphorical here? Literal? Bernie decided she really didn't want to know. Either one was bad.

She clicked her tongue against the roof of her mouth as she turned her attention to Lionel's dresser drawers. They were filled with his clothes. The man had certainly brought a lot of changes for such a short stay. By the time she was done Bernie knew that Lionel Wrenkoski had an unfortunate liking for maroon silk underwear and canary yellow socks, as well as a strange need to own five opera capes lined with red silk and carefully folded in tissue paper, all of which to Bernie's eye seemed to be exactly the same.

She closed the drawers and went over and picked up the fangs with the tips of her nails and held them up to the light. They weren't your average Halloween drugstore purchase, she decided. These babies had been custom crafted. One of Joe's friends out in Brentwood, a vampire wannabe, had had a pair made for him for four hundred bucks. These looked as good if not better.

She put them down and opened up the table drawer. In it was a book. She took it out. The cover featured a man chained to a four-poster bed, with a big-boobed vampire lady advancing on him fangs out, white diaphanous dress swirling around her thighs.

The title read, *Heaven in Hell,* by Nigel Herron. She checked the spine for the name of the publisher. It was a

POD—published on demand—book. Which meant Nigel had paid in the neighborhood of three hundred dollars, give or take a hundred, and gotten anywhere from five to ten books.

Guess Nigel is serious about being a writer, Bernie thought as she opened the book to the title page. Perhaps he'd given the book to Lionel hoping that Lionel could help him get it published in hardback or mass market.

On the title page Nigel had written, *Lionel, remember this? I'm sure you do.*

Bernie flipped through the book.

On page 25, she read: *Her breasts heaved as she felt the warm rush of blood stream into her mouth and down her cheeks. She savored the soft, salty coppery flavor on her tongue as if it was a fine wine.*

The vintage was young but she liked them that way. Impudent. It made her conquest so much sweeter. She licked a trace of the vermilion substance off her lower lip with the flick of her tongue. Blood. Her right. Her due. Her father's inheritance.

"You are nothing," she whispered in Stanislaw's ear as she tightened the restraints on his wrists. "Nothing but a vessel for my pleasure."

He whimpered in pain as she drove her fangs deeper into his flesh.

"You go, girl," Bernie said looking up from the page.

Well, one thing was for sure. Nigel certainly had an active fantasy life.

As for the writing, it was way too purple prosy for her taste. Although from the little she'd read of Lionel's books, they weren't much better than the one she was holding in her hand. Personally she preferred nonfiction. History. Philosophy. Sometimes biography. She was about to turn to another page when she heard a noise. She whirled around. The noise was muffled, but it was definitely footsteps. Someone was coming up the stairs.

"This is not good, not good at all," Bernie muttered as her heart started doing the Macarena in her chest.

Okay, she told herself. *Take a deep breath. It doesn't help to panic.* But somehow what she had told Libby about talking her way out of the situation didn't seem like such a good idea now that she was faced with actually doing it.

Bernie looked around the room. There was only one thing she could think of to do. So she did it. Even though it was totally undignified. Joe would be laughing his ass off if he could see her wiggling under the bed, she reflected as the carpet rubbed up against her arms and chest. Bernie was thinking that someone should sweep under the bed—there were enough dust bunnies for Susan Andrews to weave into one of her pieces—when a pair of scuffed, two-inch white pumps appeared in the gap between the bed skirt and the carpet.

"Lydia," Bernie murmured to herself. "Wonderful."

Bernie knew this because she'd noticed the shoes in the hallway when Lydia had come in and remembered thinking that one should wear white shoes only if one's feet were a size five. Otherwise they made your feet look like boats.

"Someone has been in here," Lydia said as Bernie felt a sneeze coming on.

And it's not Mama Bear, Bernie thought as she pressed a finger firmly under her nose to keep the sneeze in. After a few seconds the impulse passed.

"Nigel!" Lydia screamed.

Bernie held her breath. She didn't hear Nigel's feet on the stairs.

Lydia cursed and started out of the room.

"Nigel, I said get up here now."

"Coming, Lydia."

Okay, Bernie told herself, *now you can panic.*

She couldn't get down the steps she'd used to come up

because Lydia was blocking them, and she didn't want to stay under the bed in case, for some strange reason, Nigel or Lydia decided to look under it. The thought of having to explain what she was doing under the bed in Nigel's guest bedroom didn't bear thinking about.

She wiggled out on the other side of the bed and crouched down behind it while she took stock of her situation. She could: A) hide in the closet—a possibility that presented the same potential for embarrassment that remaining under the bed did; or B) she could go out the window.

She crawled over and peered out the second-floor window. The sill was nice and wide. That was good. When she and Libby had pulled up to the house she remembered seeing a trellis with climbing roses about a foot away from the window. Also good.

Theoretically she could get out on the sill and reach over and step onto the latticework and climb down. Hopefully, it was firmly attached to the wall. And if it wasn't and she did fall, she'd land in the peonies, which wasn't terrible.

There was only one problem. She didn't like heights. Really didn't like them. She didn't even like climbing on a step stool to change a light bulb, much less climb out a second-story window.

"Hurry up," Bernie heard Lydia say to Nigel as Bernie weighed her options.

Don't like heights? Face my sister?
Hum. Let's see.

Not even a close contest.

Bernie opened the window and clambered out on the sill. Belatedly it struck her that wedges were probably not the best shoes for climbing, that she should have taken them off, but it was too late for that now.

She reached out and grabbed the trellis. Then she put one foot on one of the side boards, inched over, put the other foot out, and put her right hand on the outside edge.

The trellis creaked. She took a step. The trellis made a cracking sound. It probably wasn't designed to hold a hundred and twenty-five pound person, Bernie decided. A vision of her ignominiously floundering around in the dirt, a piece of lattice around her neck, flashed through her mind.

No. The trick was to think positive. Her guru always said that negative thoughts led to negative results. Very, very slowly she began her climb down.

Chapter 13

Meanwhile, Libby was in the kitchen arranging cookies on one of Nigel's platters and trying not to have a nervous breakdown while Amber washed the cocktail glasses and hors d'oeuvre plates.

"What's happening upstairs?" Amber asked her.

Libby lied.

"I don't know. I'm sure everything is fine."

"Then why did that woman scream like that?"

"Maybe she saw a mouse."

"No." Amber wrinkled her nose. "Something else is going on."

Libby tried to concentrate on getting the lemon snaps to line up.

"Even if there is," she said, "the dishes still have to be done."

Amber turned off the water.

It's nice to see how well she listens to me, Libby thought as she watched Amber's eyes dart nervously this way and that.

"First Laird Wrenn dies and now this," Amber whispered. "Maybe there's a mass murderer in Longely. Maybe he's in the house."

"I doubt that very much."

"Did you see *Scream?*"

"Fortunately, I missed it."

Amber looked mildly disappointed.

"Well, in that movie this deranged killer gets in the house and—"

"Amber, that's enough. Get back to work."

"Okay, but I'm just trying to be helpful. Don't blame me if you faint when someone's head comes rolling down the stairs."

"I'll bear that in mind."

"Maybe the killer has one of those big Samurai swords."

Libby gritted her teeth. Her sister was a dead woman.

"There is no killer."

"You don't know that."

"Okay. There's no killer in this house. Now please peek into the dining room and tell me if I should clear the table."

Amber opened her mouth.

"Now," Libby ordered pointing to the dining room.

"Fine. If that's the way you want to be." And she trotted off. A few moments later she was back.

"No one is in the dining room. They're all in the hallway. Waiting for Nigel and Lydia to come down. Maybe we should call the police."

"Absolutely not," Libby snapped. "It's not our place."

"It would be if someone were dead."

"But they're not."

"You don't know that."

"Amber." Libby took a deep breath. "You are going to finish the glasses and start brewing the coffee while I finish the cookies and bus the table."

Amber shrugged. "Whatever."

As Libby put three more lemon snaps on the plate, she tried not to glance at the back steps, tried not to think of Bernie being dragged down the stairs, tried not to think of the public disgrace. What exactly was she going to say? she wondered as she put a doily on the second platter and arranged more cookies.

Maybe she could use the drug defense. Bernie had just taken a new anti-depressant and had become momentarily crazy. Or Bernie was jet-lagged and had taken an over-the-counter sleeping pill and become momentarily crazy. Or Bernie was in the process of grieving for her lost wardrobe and had become momentarily crazy. Or Bernie wasn't her sister after all. An evil elf had spirited the real Bernie away and left this one in her place.

Libby was thinking that that was a possibility when Bernie came through the back door.

"I got the soda you wanted out of the van." Bernie handed her a six-pack.

"I will never forgive you for this," Libby hissed while she smiled at Bernie for Amber's benefit. "Never."

Bernie smiled back.

"You have to learn to trust in the universe."

"Don't patronize me."

"I wasn't."

Before Libby could answer, Lydia Kissoff came down the steps Bernie had recently gone up. She was followed by Nigel and Susan Andrews. The remaining guests surged through the other door.

"What happened?" Bree Nottingham demanded.

"Someone," Lydia said, holding up the book Bernie had found in the drawer, "tried to steal this."

"That's terrible," Bernie said realizing that she must have dropped it on her way out the window. In her panic she'd forgotten she even had it. "Simply terrible."

"Isn't it though?" Libby agreed.

"The window was opened. They must have gotten away through it," Lydia said. "You didn't happen to see anyone, did you?" she asked Libby.

"No," she replied.

"I was out at the van getting some more soda and I didn't see anyone either," Bernie volunteered.

"Really?" Lydia's eyes rested on Bernie's forearms. "Those scratches look nasty."

Bernie tried for a rueful laugh, but came out with a snort instead.

"They do, don't they? It's what I get for being in a hurry. I tripped on the way back in."

Lydia raised an eyebrow.

"You should be more careful. How did you fall?"

Bernie pointed to her shoes.

"I think I must be developing weak ankles in my old age. I should really start wearing shoes like yours. You know. Sensible. Mine are too high," Bernie said, at which point Libby quickly stepped in front of her.

Nigel looked around unhappily. "I guess I should report this to the police," he said. "But then we'll be here forever. And they make such a mess."

"After all," Bree Nothingham pointed out. "Nothing was really taken."

"True," Lydia agreed.

"It was probably some teenage boys doing it for the hell of it," Bernie suggested.

"They probably wanted a souvenir," Nigel said. "Something from Laird."

"I wouldn't be at all surprised," Bree Nottingham agreed.

Libby didn't say that she thought that Laird Wrenn's fan base was more apt to be female than male. Instead she looked at everyone standing around and thought about how lucky she was—not to mention Bernie, of course.

"Why don't I make everyone a round of iced Irish coffees to go with dessert?" she proposed to the assembled guests. Thank heavens she'd brought extra cream and brown sugar along. And she always had Jameson's and chocolate in her emergency catering kit because, as her mother always said, you just never know. "You guys look as if you could use something that packs a wallop."

Then she forced herself to smile, which is difficult to do when you are harboring homicidal thoughts about your sister in your heart.

Chapter 14

Bebe, Susan Andrews' miniature poodle, danced around Libby's feet, growling and snapping as Susan ushered Libby into her house.

"I thought last night's dinner at Nigel's house was brilliant," Susan told her.

Libby smiled. Compliments were always nice even though she'd rather be hearing them at a different time. At three o'clock on Tuesday afternoon she should have been in the store making Indonesian cole slaw and talking to her suppliers.

"Come in, come in," Susan said as she scooped the poodle up in her arms and planted a kiss on its muzzle. "She's just a little nervous today, aren't you, sweetums?"

Nervous wasn't the word Libby would have used to describe Bebe as the little dog made a valiant effort to jump out of her mistress's arms and go back to trying to bite Libby's ankles.

Maybe it was the haircut that was making her grumpy, Libby reflected. Aside from a little ball of fur on its tail and a little pom-pom on its head, Bebe was practically naked. Not an attractive look on man or beast, Libby thought as she followed Susan into the kitchen.

"This is Bebe's summer do," Susan informed Libby as she entered the kitchen.

Bree Nottingham was already there, sipping white wine out of a glass as she leaned against the counter of Susan Andrews' kitchen. Bree nodded hello to Libby and Libby nodded back.

"Such a sweetie," Bree cooed at the dog who, Libby was glad to see, growled at her too.

"No. No." Susan tapped Bebe on her nose. Bebe tried to bite her finger. "I'm going to put Bebe in her bed," Susan informed them. "She needs a little time out."

She needs a personality transplant, Libby thought as she wondered if Bernie had remembered to make the deposit at the bank.

"Wine?" Bree asked Libby.

"I've got to go back to work."

"So have I." And Bree poured her a glassful and handed it to her. "Last night was wonderful, although I did think the crab cakes were a bit heavy for a summer appetizer. Perhaps next time some hollowed-out perfectly fresh steamed new potatoes with a dab of sour cream and a little caviar on top."

"Good suggestion," Libby said, trying to smile. Of course Bree's suggestions *were* always stellar, a fact that annoyed her no end.

"I'm so glad you could come."

"So am I," Libby lied.

Then she reminded herself that this was good for business, even if Bree had dragooned her into it. Her mother had liked to say: Never underestimate the schmooze factor in bringing in catering business.

And Libby had found this to be true. Bottom line: People liked having people working in their homes that they felt comfortable with and people felt comfortable with people they knew. It was as simple as that, Libby thought as Susan Andrews came back in the room.

"The others will be here shortly," Susan told Libby.

Then she smiled brightly and reintroduced her to Julie Chang, their cooking teacher, who had just wandered in from the garden. Not that Libby was likely to forget her. After all, she'd been here in May.

Bernie would have approved of her, Libby thought as she studied Julie Chang's clothes. Today she was dressed in white silk pants and top and three-inch sandals. Last time she'd been wearing black silk and pearls Libby remembered wondering how she managed to stir-fry and not get splattered with cooking oil.

Libby herself couldn't seem to fry an egg without getting grease all over her clothes. Maybe she'd use an apron this time, Libby thought as she studied the middle island. All the ingredients for the coming lesson were laid out in neat precision on the countertop.

There were deep green Chinese long beans, crisp bean sprouts, bright green bok choy, two heads of garlic, ginger root, already peeled shrimp, a whole sea bass, not to mention sugar, salt, black bean paste, soy sauce, Chinese cooking wine, and sesame oil with chili paste.

"Today I decided to do dishes with ingredients that one can purchase anywhere," Julie Chang explained.

Which was a tad more practical than the stir-fried beef with fresh bamboo shoots, sea slug with cucumbers, and bird's nest soup they'd cooked last time, in Libby's opinion.

"Even though," Julie Chang continued, "I think it is important to expand people's horizons about what is and is not edible."

As the cooking teacher glanced at the kitchen clock, Libby wished she had that kind of latitude in the store. People didn't want the unfamiliar. Hell, they wouldn't even buy a dish made with olives they couldn't recognize.

"We will wait five more minutes," Julie announced. "And then we start."

Bree Nottingham took another sip of wine, broke off a cluster of grapes from the bunch in the bowl next to her, and ate one.

"So," she said to Libby. "How's Orion doing?"

Libby blinked. She'd been expecting people to ask her about Lionel's death, but she hadn't been expecting anyone to ask her about her ex-fiance, although, she reflected, she should have been since everyone had seen them talking at the reunion dinner.

"He's doing fine."

"Howard's playing golf with him at the clubhouse this afternoon."

Libby tried to think of something to say and could only come out with, "Well, it's a nice day for a game."

Bree smiled.

"Now that he's back, Howard is thinking of asking him to come into the firm."

"But he's . . ."

Bree waved her hand.

"Doing jewelry. Yes, I know. He can do both." Bree ate a grape. "You did know he was coming to the reunion, right?"

"He was on the guest list."

"Still. It must have been a shock. This the first time you've seen him since . . ." Bree allowed her voice to trail off.

"Yes, it is."

"That was so unfortunate."

Libby wished she could think of something blindingly clever to say, but she was never as good as Bernie in a clutch so she just kept quiet.

"Howard tells me he's getting a divorce," Bree continued.

"That's what I hear."

"I'm surprised." Bree adjusted her diamond tennis bracelet and ate another grape. "Sukie is such a lovely lady. I saw her in the city two months ago and she didn't say anything. She still has that great body of hers and after two kids."

Libby flushed. "It's nice that she has time to spend in the gym."

Bree took another sip of wine. "One makes time for what's important to one."

Libby was just about to tell her that that was a lot easier to do if you weren't on your feet twelve hours a day when Susan grabbed her arm.

"Would you like to see what I'm working on now?" she asked Libby. "It'll just take a minute."

"I'd love to," Libby said, allowing herself to be led away.

Susan patted her arm.

"Bree doesn't mean anything. That's just the way she is."

"That's because everyone has allowed her to say whatever she wants all her life," Libby told Susan as they walked down the hall.

Susan frowned.

"You're too sensitive, Libby. You take things too personally."

"How else am I supposed to take them?" Libby demanded.

"With compassion and grace."

Libby snorted. "I'm kinda an Old Testament person myself."

"Meaning?"

"I believe in an eye for an eye."

Susan reflected for a moment.

"I suppose there are situations in which that's appropriate," she conceded as she stopped in front of a door on the left. "Here we are."

Libby followed her inside.

"This used to be Bud's office," Susan told Libby. "I

moved my studio in here a month after he died. It makes me feel close to him working here. I know it's a little crowded."

"Cozy," Libby said as she edged her way past Bud's desk.

"I haven't been able to get rid of it yet," Susan explained.

"Maybe you shouldn't." Libby was still using her mother's knives even though they weren't very good anymore.

"I have to." Susan spread her arms out. "There's no room."

"It is a little cramped in here," Libby allowed as her eyes strayed to the copy of *Damned to Death* that was sitting on the desk. "I didn't know Bud read Lionel's books," she commented.

"Oh, he read everything," Susan said as Libby walked over to the picture of Laird Wrenn hanging on the wall. There were three black candles burning on the shelf below it.

"A memorial," Susan explained. "I feel it's important to pay one's respects to the dead."

Libby, who hadn't been to the cemetery to visit her mother since she died because in her opinion dead was dead, walked over to the loom.

"It looks complicated."

"It is." Susan pointed to the small band of cloth on it. "This is what I wanted to show you."

Libby leaned closer so she could see. It looked like a plain black piece of fiber.

"It's very nice," she told Susan.

"Thank you." Susan bent over and traced the weave of the cloth with the tip of her finger. "It's hard to see in this light, but I'm using five different shades of black to make this and then I'm going to hand paint streaks of red and dark blue on it when I'm done.

"Which will take a while because the pattern is so complicated. It's going to be eight by ten. Maybe bigger even. I'll have to see. It's a tribute to Bud. And then I'm going to do one for his brother Josh. I just have a feeling that then their souls can rest."

Libby brushed her hair back off her face. "I remember when Josh shot himself. That was so awful."

Susan shook her head. "I don't think Bud ever got over his brother dying like that. So tragic." She turned to Libby. "I know I must sound crazy to you . . ."

"No, you don't . . ."

Susan Andrews laughed. "Yes, I do. But honestly, doing this"—she swept her hand around the room—"I feel good. I feel as if I finally have closure."

Libby was just about to tell her that she was glad, when the doorbell rang.

"Time to get started," Susan said, as she hurried towards the door.

Chapter 15

Bernie was not happy. It had been a bad morning and a worse early afternoon.

First there had been the burnt scones, then she'd tripped and spilled a pot of coffee on the floor, and she wasn't even going to think of the half-moldy raspberries she'd taken delivery of.

And having to shop for clothes wasn't putting her in a better mood. Far from it. Even though Bernie was trying, she couldn't help dwelling on the clothes she'd been forced to leave behind in L.A. Especially her red leather skirt. And her Jimmy Choo's.

She'd never be able to afford to replace them. The thought of them sitting around in the Salvation Army gave her an actual pain. At least Joe could have had the decency to take them to an upscale consignment shop. She should have killed him when she had the chance, she decided.

And if that wasn't bad enough, here she was reduced to finding something to wear in Longely. In Cara's Dress Shoppe, for heaven's sake. She hated places that had names that included words like Olde and Shoppe. They should be purged by the cuteness brigade.

At least back in L.A., Bernie thought as she walked towards Cara's, finding something wearable wasn't a problem. Unlike here in the land of soccer moms and elastic waists and pastel colors.

All Bernie was asking for was a plain black or white T-shirt and a pair of low-slung, slightly bell-bottom jeans. They had to have something like that, right? And then on Thursday she'd take Metro North down to the city and do some real shopping.

But when Bernie opened the door, she couldn't believe what she was seeing. Everything had changed. The place could have been in Brentwood or SoHo.

Bernie's eyes widened as Nigel's girlfriend, Janet, came out from behind the counter to greet her. She was decked out in a prairie skirt, T-shirt, and a knotted leather and turquoise belt that could have come straight out of the pages of *Elle*. The orange suede sandals she was wearing weren't bad either.

"You work here?" Bernie asked.

"I own it," Janet replied. "Libby didn't tell you?"

"Maybe she did and I wasn't listening."

Something that happened more than she was willing to admit.

Janet indicated the store with a sweep of her hand.

"Nice, isn't it?" she said to Bernie.

"Nice? It's fantastic. Where's Cara?"

"She got married and moved up to Alaska. I bought the place from her last year."

"Good change," Bernie said appreciatively. "Very good indeed."

"I like to think so." Janet tucked a curl of dark brown hair behind her ear. "I sold all the old merchandise and brought in new lines. Now I've got Prada, I've got Harrari and Nicole Rozan, Dolce and Gabbana. I've got Robert Clergerie shoes, Carol Little sweaters, Lisa Jenks jewelry."

"How come?"

"I decided to stock stuff like this?"

Bernie nodded.

"I saw an opportunity to fill a niche." Janet gave the word the French pronunciation. "We're getting a lot of Japanese families moving into town and they have—ah, how should I put this—more sophisticated tastes and the money to back them up. This way they don't have to go into the city to shop. It's all right here. Anyway, two boutiques carrying soccer mom clothing in one town are enough. We don't need three. I was thinking of changing the name to Chrysalis."

"Emerging from a cocoon. I like it."

"It doesn't sound too . . . exotic?"

"Not really. Or," Bernie suggested, "you could use the word chrysos, the Greek word for gold from which chrysalis is derived."

"How do you know that?" Janet asked.

"What can I say? I read dictionaries in my spare time," Bernie said as she took in the store's brick walls, polished cement floor, and exposed air ducts, its silk-covered chairs and pots full of Johnny jump-ups and forget-me-nots and Shasta daisies spilling out onto the floor.

"Dictionaries?"

"I've always loved words," Bernie explained. "You know," she continued, "this is a wonderful space and I love the stuff you have," she told Janet. "But I don't think I can afford you. My ex-boyfriend threw out my clothes. I'm starting from scratch."

"I'd kill him."

"I would if I were there."

Janet retied her belt.

"Nigel would never do anything like that."

Bernie sighed.

"I didn't think Joe would either."

"Men are such a pain in the ass," Janet observed. "Speaking of which, how's your sister doing now that Orion's back in town?"

Bernie groaned. "They went out for a drink."

"That's too bad. I'd hate to see her getting hurt all over again."

"I know. I'm trying to get her interested in Marvin."

"Marvin's a nice guy. She could use someone like him."

"We all could," Bernie observed, thinking of Joe.

Janet laughed and changed the subject. "You should check out the back room," she told Bernie. "I've got great sales stuff. If I were you I'd buy a few really nice pieces and fill in the rest at Old Navy."

Bernie nodded and walked towards the back. A couple of moments later, she returned with an armload of clothes.

"Any dressing room?"

"Whichever one you like. So," Janet said as Bernie closed the door and began to strip, "would you consider staying here permanently?"

Bernie wiggled into a black spandex dress with little holes cut in the side.

"I really don't know."

Nope. Too weird. She took it off and tried on a pair of black straight-cut pants. Yes. These were better. She slipped on a vermilion T-shirt with a heart in the center and the words Havana written across them and came out.

"Not bad," Janet said as Bernie looked at herself in the mirror.

"I don't know. The pants make my ass look too big."

"Men like women with big butts, but if it bothers you, wear a longer shirt." And Janet went to get one. "Here," she said, handing Bernie a white shirt. "Try this on. I bet Libby's happy you're here."

Bernie slipped the shirt over the T-shirt.

"I'm not so sure she is."

"Why? This way she can take some time off. You can help out with your dad and the store."

"That's the problem. She says she wants help, but I'm not sure she really does. I don't think she would know what to do with free time if she had it."

"That's true of a lot of people," Janet observed.

"Not me." Bernie looked at herself in the mirror again. Then she inspected the price tag. "It's a little high."

"Get the shirt," Janet urged. "You can wear it with everything." She moved closer to Bernie. "So who do you think did it?"

"Did what?"

"Poisoned Lionel, of course. Nigel says he thinks Lydia did it. What do you think?"

Bernie frowned.

"I don't know. Why does Nigel say Lydia did it?"

"Two reasons. One, she got him the water."

"Everyone had access to the water," Bernie protested.

"But Nigel overheard Lydia and Lionel fighting downstairs just before they drove off to the dinner."

"What were they fighting about?"

Janet lowered her voice and looked around even though no one was in the store.

"Lionel threatened to turn Lydia in to the authorities."

"For what?"

"Nigel doesn't know. He didn't hear the rest of the conversation."

"Did Nigel tell the police what he heard?"

"It's just his word. And he and Lydia aren't exactly friends. He's afraid they'll think he's trying to railroad her."

"How come?"

Janet waved her hand in the air. "It's a long, complicated story."

"Even so. He should tell them anyway."

"That's what I keep saying to him, but he won't listen. He thinks he's got a line straight to God. I can't tell you what a pain in the ass he's being since Lionel died."

Bernie clicked her tongue against her teeth while she thought. Finally she said, "I'll take the shirt and the T-shirt. I'm still thinking about the pants."

"Marked down from three hundred dollars to fifty," Janet said. "You're not going to do better than that."

"You're right. I'll take them too," Bernie told Janet.

She picked up a large bag. It was yellow canvas in front, leather in back, with the words *Italia Postale* stenciled on it. "How much?"

"Six hundred. It is great, isn't it? I got it in Milan."

Bernie nodded and handed the bag back to Janet.

"Who knows," Janet said as she put it back where it had been. "Maybe you'll win the lottery." Janet straightened up. "Anyway, from what I heard, Lydia and Lionel were always fighting."

"Then why did she work for him?"

Janet shrugged. "I imagine the money was good."

"I don't know." Bernie picked up the bag again and slung it over her shoulder. "Sometimes famous people pay worse than anyone else," she said, thinking of the time she'd worked for a famous chef. "They think it's a privilege to work for them. What I'm wondering about is what was Lydia doing in Lionel's room."

"She said she wanted to show us Lionel's fangs. Did you know she's planning on selling them and his capes on eBay?"

Janet shook her head as Bernie handed the bag back to her.

"I don't know who's worse," Bernie said as Libby walked through the door. "The people selling or the people buying."

Chapter 16

As Libby looked around Cara's Dress Shoppe, she was suddenly aware of the soy sauce under her fingernails and the grease spot on her linen shirt, not to mention the way her hair was curling up and that she probably smelled of Chinese food. She should have washed up and changed before she came over.

"This is certainly different," she observed.

"Yes, it is," Janet told her. "Can I help you with something?"

Libby shook her head. "I just need to talk to my sister."

Bernie turned.

"How was the cooking lesson?"

"Let's just say I could have put my time to more profitable use," Libby said, "although I was thinking maybe we could give cooking lessons in the store. It might make us some extra cash."

"We need a hook."

"Cook like Mom. Comfort food is all the rage these days."

"That's not a bad idea," Bernie conceded. "Not bad at all." She picked up the bag again. "What do you think?" she asked Libby.

"It's okay."

"Just okay?"

"Well, really, it's kind of weird."

"Screw it," Bernie said to Janet. "Put it on layaway. I'll pay it off somehow."

"How much is it?" Libby asked as Janet took the bag.

"Trust me. You don't want to know."

"One hundred?"

"Not even close."

"They have nice tote bags in the L.L. Bean Catalog. You should look at those."

"I'll do that," Bernie said and changed the subject. She wasn't getting into this now. "So what's up?"

"Can you go take the van in for an inspection? I just realized it's past due and I don't have the time."

Bernie grinned as an idea occurred to her. "Maybe." She looked around, then walked over to one of the tables near the front of the store, snatched a black T-shirt off it, and held it up.

"Only if you try this on."

"It's the size of a postage stamp," Libby protested.

"It stretches," Janet said.

"No."

"Just try it on," Bernie urged.

"It's too small."

"No T-shirt, no inspection."

Libby grabbed the T-shirt out of Bernie's hand.

"Fine," she said as she stomped off towards the dressing room. "But you really are a pain in the ass."

"And proud of it too," Bernie called after her.

A moment later Libby emerged from the stall.

"I told you it was going to be too tight."

"I think it looks great," Janet said.

"I agree," Bernie said.

Libby studied herself in the mirror. "No, it doesn't. It makes me look fat." She grabbed a roll of fat around her waist and pulled. "See."

"It makes you look thinner. Baggy clothes make you look heavier. It's a common misconception that loose clothes slenderize. They don't."

Libby pursed her lips.

"I feel so . . ."

"On show?" Janet supplied.

"Exactly."

Bernie and Janet watched Libby turning this way and that as she studied her reflection in the mirror.

"It's only thirty bucks," Bernie said. "I bet Orion would like it."

"You think so?" Libby said.

"Definitely," Janet agreed.

"After all," Bernie pointed out, "when you put food out to sell, you want to make it look as attractive as possible, don't you? You don't just dump it on the plate. You arrange it. Presentation counts."

"I am not a plate of pasta."

"I never said you were. I'm just making a point."

"I think you're wrong."

"No, I'm not." Bernie was just about to explain why when the door opened and Bree Nottingham came in followed by Griselda Plotkin and Fred the photographer.

"Have you heard?" Bree asked the three women standing there.

"Heard what?" Janet said.

"They've arrested Tiffany for Laird Wrenn's murder," Griselda said.

"You're kidding," Libby cried.

"Not at all. Howard called to tell me." Bree went over to the counter and took a Tootsie roll out of the bowl by the register. "And I have to say," she said, unwrapping it, "it doesn't surprise me one single bit."

Chapter 17

Libby turned her head away from the rising cloud of steam as she poured the pot full of boiling water and partially cooked red new potatoes into the colander set in the sink. After the water had circled down into the drain, she lifted the colander onto the cutting board on the kitchen counter and began slicing the hot potatoes up with her paring knife for French potato salad.

The skins of the potatoes burned the tips of Libby's fingers but she didn't mind. She'd always loved the purity of this salad, loved mixing together the olive oil, tarragon vinegar, chopped onion, salt, and freshly ground pepper with the potatoes and watching the mixture mutate into culinary gold, as Bernie would say.

She was thinking that her mother was right, that sometimes the simplest things are the best as well as the hardest to do properly, when the side door opened and Tiffany came running in and grabbed Libby's arm. Libby gasped when she saw who it was.

"I thought they arrested you," Libby told her.

"They tried." Tiffany hugged herself so hard the skin around her fingers turned white with the pressure. Libby could see beads of sweat around Tiffany's hairline. "I saw them coming up the walk," Tiffany cried. "And then I heard one of them asking Lois, the receptionist, where I was, and I just dropped everything and ran out the back of the salon and came over here."

Tiffany shook her head.

"I know I shouldn't have run like that," she continued. "I know it was wrong. But I was so scared, I just didn't know what else to do. And then I was out on the street and I couldn't breathe. I thought I was dying and I didn't know where else to go." Tiffany touched Libby's arm. "I would never . . . ever . . . do what they said I did. You know that. I loved Lionel even though he was going to . . . that was just for show. Lydia . . . God, I'd like to kill her. . . ."

"Shush." Libby put her finger across Tiffany's lips.

"Libby," Tiffany said. "Please. They're going to put me in jail. You've got to help me." And she started to cry.

Libby bit her lip. She knew the right thing to do was to tell Tiffany she had to turn herself in. But she just couldn't. Not when she was in this state.

"Just go in the bathroom," Libby told her.

Tiffany blew her nose.

"Why?"

"Because I don't want anyone coming in and seeing you. And don't come out until I tell you it's all right."

Tiffany gave Libby a little smile and did as she was told.

I'm crazy, Libby said to herself as she wiped her hands on a towel. Really nuts. *The police are going to be looking for her.* But that didn't stop Libby from cutting a wedge of Brie and putting it in a bag along with half a loaf of French bread, a couple of peaches, two chocolate chip cookies, and a bottle of water, never mind that the last thing Tiff probably needed right now was food.

"Let's go," she said, knocking on the bathroom door.

Tiffany opened the door and stepped out.

"What's happening?"

Libby handed her the bag.

"Something for you to eat. It'll make you feel better.

Come on. I'm just going to take you somewhere safe while I talk to my dad."

After all Libby reasoned, who knew the ins and outs of the legal system better than her father.

"I don't want you to get in trouble because of me," Tiffany said.

"I wouldn't."

Tiffany's eyes misted over. More tears spilled out onto her cheeks, carving paths in her foundation. "I just didn't know where else to go. Everyone else . . ."

Libby put her finger up to Tiffany's lips.

"Don't worry," she told her. "It's going to be fine."

Sean Simmons looked at his two squabbling daughters and sighed. He'd forgotten how much bickering went on when they were both home.

"We should stay out of this," Bernie was saying to Libby.

"How can you say something like that?" Libby demanded. "Tiffany's a friend of mine. She needs help."

"You've been bailing her out of trouble since you were twelve years old. Enough is enough."

"That's a terrible thing to say."

"It's true, Dad, isn't it?

"Well . . ." Sean began, but Bernie didn't give him a chance to finish before she started talking to Libby again.

"What she needs is a lawyer."

Libby practically stamped her foot in frustration.

"You think I don't know that? She can't afford anyone. She doesn't even have health insurance. Do you know how much a homicide defense could cost? It could run . . ." She turned towards her father. "What?"

"A hundred thousand dollars easy," Sean answered. "Probably more like two hundred thousand depending who you need to put on the stand. Just to start she'd need forty thousand dollars for a retainer."

"I don't think she even has two thousand dollars in the bank," Libby said.

"Then the court will appoint a lawyer for her," Bernie replied.

"Those people are horrible," Libby protested.

"Not all of them, but let's say you're right. Let's say she's in a bad situation. It's unfortunate, but there's nothing we can do."

"You thought there was when you went up to Lionel's room. Otherwise you wouldn't have gone," Libby pointed out.

Sean's eyes widened.

"What the hell were you doing in Lionel's room?" he demanded of Bernie.

"She was checking things out," Libby answered for her sister.

"Bernie, I thought you were smarter than that," her father told her.

Bernie flashed her sister a murderous look. "It wasn't a big deal."

"That's because you weren't caught," Libby retorted.

Sean looked at both his daughters and shook his head.

"Don't tell me any more," he said to them. "I don't want to know."

Bernie leaned against the wall and crossed her arms over her chest. "Works for me," she said.

Libby blinked back tears. "Tiffany didn't do this."

"Kill Lionel? How do you know?" Bernie demanded. "What makes you so sure?"

"Because I know her. She'd never be able to do something like that."

Bernie rolled her eyes. "I bet that's what Ted Bundy's friends said too."

"This is different."

"No. It's not."

"How can you say that?"

"Tiffany and Lionel's relationship."

"What about it?"

"I've heard enough," Sean said, giving his daughters the same look he'd used to silence them when they were fighting in the back of the car on the way to the beach when they were little. "Where is Tiffany?" he asked Libby.

"Ah . . ." Libby looked abashed. "Down in the basement."

Bernie leaned forward. "Our basement?"

"Well, I couldn't exactly leave her in the kitchen, could I?" Libby retorted.

"Tell me," Bernie demanded. "Does the term aiding and abetting mean anything to you? You do realize the police will check here as a matter of course since they know you're a friend of hers."

"Which is why we don't have much time," Sean said. "Bring Tiffany up. Let's see if we can sort out this mess."

"It's been a while," Sean said to Tiffany.

She nodded slowly.

"Libby tells me you're in trouble."

Tiffany nodded again.

"Why don't you tell me about it," Sean said gently.

His wife had never liked Tiffany, he reflected as he waited for Tiffany to say something. But he always had. Maybe she wasn't the brightest pebble on the beach, as Rose used to say, but Tiffany had been a good friend to Libby and in his book that counted for a lot. Not, he thought as he watched Tiffany blinking in the sunlight, that that meant that she couldn't have killed Lionel.

Tiffany swallowed a couple of times. No one said anything. Finally she began to speak.

"I didn't do it. I swear. I loved Lionel. Even if he was getting married. That was just for publicity. I was the person he cared about."

"Why do the police suspect you?" Sean asked.

"I already told Libby."

"Tell me . . ."

"We had a fight at the Dairy Queen before he died," she whispered in a voice so low that Sean had to strain to hear it.

"About?"

"About Lionel getting married."

"Go on."

"He told me and . . . and I got mad and yelled that I was going to kill him and walked off."

"You didn't tell me that," Libby said.

"I was embarrassed," Tiffany replied.

Sean shifted around in his chair. Sitting for so long made the muscles in his back hurt.

"People heard you?" he asked.

Tiffany nodded.

"But I didn't mean it! I'd never hurt him. You have to believe me," she said to Sean.

"I do."

Or at least he believed that she believed what she was telling him. Years of interviewing suspects had left him with a built-in lie detector.

"And you were at the dinner the night Lionel died?"

Tiffany swallowed and nodded again.

Which, Sean thought, meant that unfortunately for her, she had the motive and the opportunity. Whether she had the means was something else. But, as they say, two out of three ain't bad.

Sean could see why Lucy liked her for this. Even if the case was circumstantial. He could also see why Lucy would want to get this cleaned up as quickly as possible.

Famous author killed in Longely.

No. Not the kind of publicity the town fathers and mothers wanted. This was the kind of thing that made real estate values go down. This was the kind of thing that made police chiefs lose their jobs. If Sean knew anything, the press was camped around the police station's door. They'd already been at the store looking for a statement. Vultures. Every single one of them. It almost made him feel sorry for Lucy.

He looked at his daughters.

"You are to listen to me," he said. "For once in your lives you will do exactly what I say. No more and no less."

"Does this mean you'll help?" Libby asked.

When Sean nodded, Libby and Tiffany ran over and hugged him.

"Thank you. Thank you," they cried.

Sean blushed.

"Stop it," he ordered.

Suddenly there was a knock on the side door. Everyone froze.

"See who it is," Sean ordered.

Bernie sidled up to the window and peered out.

"Told you," she said to Libby, unable to keep the satisfaction out of her voice. "It's the chief of police."

Tiffany started to cry.

"That didn't take long," Sean muttered.

"What are we going to do?" Libby cried.

There was another knock.

"We're all going to remain calm," Sean said. He turned to Bernie. "Go down and bring Lucy up," he told her. "Just take your time doing it."

Chapter 18

By the time Chief Lucas Broad had climbed the stairs to Sean Simmons' room, Libby had stowed Tiffany in the steamer trunk in her closet, piled her shoes and clothes on top of it, and run downstairs to get tea and cookies.

Five minutes later Libby took a deep breath and re-entered her father's room. *I have to go back to exercising,* she thought as she carried in a tray on which rested three cups and saucers, a teapot, cream and sugar, and a platter full of cookies. *Otherwise running up and down these steps is going to kill me.*

"Cookie? Tea?" she said, offering the tray to the chief, who was standing by the dresser.

He shook his head.

"You should try a cookie," Bernie urged. "The chocolate chip and the nut bars are particularly good. Libby is known for them. She sends them to Texas and California."

Lucas Broad reached out and took one reluctantly.

"Tea?" Libby asked brightly as he bit into a chocolate chip bar.

"No, thanks."

"Gained a little weight in the gut, have you, Lucy?" Sean said as Libby put the tray down on the table next to him and began pouring a cup of tea for her father. "Must be sitting behind the desk. It'll do it to you every time."

Lucy colored and shoved the rest of the cookie into his mouth.

It's lucky that I cut the bars small, Libby thought, watching the chief as she surreptitiously paused to wipe her palms on the sides of her khaki shorts. *Otherwise we'd be performing the Heimlich maneuver now.*

"So what brings you here?" Sean asked as Libby put the cup full of tea by her father's side and began pouring one for Bernie.

"Chief, are you sure I can't get you something?" Libby asked speaking at the same time her father was. "This tea is Oolong. Organic."

"No doubt handpicked by happy natives," Lucas snapped.

"All tea is handpicked," Bernie said, donning her schoolmarm voice. "However, I can't attest to the happy native part. Actually, that's what makes good tea so expensive. It's labor-intensive. Of course the really good stuff, the tea made from whole leaves, goes to Germany. It sells there for twenty-five to forty dollars a pound. But I'm sure you're not interested in that, are you?"

"No. I'm not."

Suddenly Lucy came to attention. Like a hound scenting his prey, Libby thought watching him.

"What was that?" he asked.

"What?" Libby asked even though she'd heard it too.

"That thud. Don't you hear it?"

"Oh," Libby said. The noise was faint but unmistakable. "That."

"We're baby-sitting my cousin's eight-week-old chocolate lab puppy," Sean said, marveling at the way the lie tripped off his tongue. "We have him locked in Libby's bedroom. He must be trying to get out."

"He might have gotten stuck in the closet," Libby said. "You know how he likes to climb into that trunk of mine and then he can't get out."

"Maybe I'd better see if he's all right," Bernie suggested.

"Good idea," her father told her.

Bernie smiled at Lucy. "I'll be right back."

Lucy watched her go. Then he turned back to Sean.

"I didn't know you had cousins."

"Twice removed. On my mother's side."

"How's your lovely wife these days?" Sean asked, happily sticking another metaphorical dagger into his nemesis' side, it being a well-known fact that Lucy's wife was an embarrassment to him. Rich and politically well connected—which, it was said, was why he married her—she had all the charm of a buffalo in heat.

"She's fine," Lucy growled.

As Libby beamed at the chief, she couldn't help but remember what her mother, an avid reader of Henry James, used to say about good manners being an inviolable weapon.

"Are you sure I can't interest you in a cookie?" she asked, once again holding the plate filled with chocolate chip and nut bars out to Lucy.

"I'm positive."

"I hope you don't mind if I do." And Libby picked out a nut bar and put the plate down on the table near her father.

She was taking a nibble when Bernie reentered the room.

"You were right," she said to Libby. "He just got stuck in the trunk. But I put him somewhere else and everything is okay."

"So," Sean said, turning to face Lucy. "Would it be fair to assume that you're not here on a social call?"

"It would."

"Oh, dear," Libby said as Lucy folded his arms over his chest, which had the unfortunate effect of making his belly bulge out even more.

"We're all ears, Chief," Bernie said, which brought another scowl to Lucas's face.

"I'm here," he intoned, "strictly as a courtesy. I want to warn you that any help given to Miss Tiffany Doddy in her flight from the law, or any attempt to interfere with the execution of the warrant for her arrest will be viewed in an extremely dire light."

"I must say, it's very generous of you to take time out of your busy day and come down here in person to tell us this, but may I ask why you are?" Sean said.

"Obviously, I'm here because your daughter, Libby, is known to be a friend of hers."

"On TV they always use the word associate," Bernie said. "Actually, I believe the phrase is known associate."

"It seems to me you're making unwarranted assumptions," Sean told Lucas as he glowered at Bernie.

"I don't think so," Lucas replied, reluctantly turning back to Sean.

"Why are you picking on Tiffany?" Libby suddenly demanded.

"We have witnesses that saw the suspect arguing with the decedent . . ."

"That's circumstantial evidence," Libby protested, years of listening to her father discuss cases at the dinner table having given her a fairly good grasp of criminal law.

"There's other evidence as well which I'm not at liberty to reveal," Lucy finished.

"Maybe that's because you don't have any."

Lucy narrowed his eyes.

"Don't expect that just because you're the ex-police chief's daughter, I'm going to cut you any slack. Because I'm not."

"I wouldn't dream of it," Libby told him. "In fact, I think the opposite is true."

Before the chief could reply Sean moved forward slightly in his wheelchair and asked, "I take it this means you've lost Tiffany?"

Lucas Broad's face colored again.

"We'll find her soon enough."

There was another thud. *What the hell is Tiffany doing?* Libby thought as she said, "Boy, that puppy really wants to get out."

"He certainly does," her father observed.

"Are you sure I can't interest you in a cup of tea or perhaps another cookie?" Libby chirped.

Lucas glared at her and shook a finger in her face.

"You've been warned," he said to her.

"There's no need to be rude," Bernie told him.

"I'm being nice." And he turned, stomped down the stairs, and slammed the door behind him.

"He's not in a good mood," Bernie observed a few seconds after he'd left.

Libby smoothed down her T-shirt.

"Probably because his diet is bad. I think Mrs. Lucy feeds him prepackaged food."

"Well, that would explain it," Bernie said.

"He's embarrassed," Sean said, ignoring Bernie's sarcasm. "I know I would be if I were him."

"Do you think he knows Tiffany is here?" Bernie asked her father.

Sean snorted.

"Absolutely not. He just came over for a look-see. If he even suspected she was on the premises, he'd be here with a team and a search warrant," Sean replied as Bernie watched the chief of police walk to his car. "But you can be sure the patrols will be driving by here from now on. Nothing would please him more than nailing you guys to the wall."

"Wonderful." Bernie put her hand to her heart. "I nearly had a coronary when I heard that thump. Well, one thing I'll say about Lucy. He has good hearing."

"What the hell was Tiffany doing?" Sean demanded.

"Lifting the lid of the trunk. It hit the back of the closet wall."

"What was the second thump?"

"She fell getting out of the trunk."

"Fell?" Libby repeated.

Bernie grimaced. "Well, it was pitch black in there and she doesn't really have the best sense of balance. She was in the middle of a major anxiety attack when I came in."

"Great. So where'd you put her?"

"Under your bed."

"I see." Libby absentmindedly reached over for a cookie and took a bite, then wiped the crumbs off her mouth. "Before we get her, do you think we should come up with a game plan?"

Sean held one hand under the other to steady it and took a sip of tea.

"I've already thought about that. We call Paul Pine and ask him to come over here."

Paul Pine was Sean's friend and a top-line criminal lawyer.

"What do we need him for?"

"We need him to call Lucy and negotiate terms for Tiffany's surrender."

"You mean you're sending her to jail?" Libby cried.

"I'm afraid so," her father replied. "Right now, with a warrant out for her arrest, it's the safest place for her to be."

"But—"

"She doesn't have a choice," Sean snapped.

Libby hung her head.

"Why don't you go get her?" her father suggested in a softer voice.

Chapter 19

Sean took another sip of tea and wondered if Tiffany really believed what she was saying as he listened to her talk. According to her, Lionel Wrenkoski would be joining the saints in heaven.

"He was such a dear man," she said. "Really sweet down inside. He sent me roses before he came up from the city."

"I'm sorry," Sean said, remembering his encounters with Lionel, "but that's not the way he impressed me. I didn't find him to be very nice at all."

Tiffany flushed.

"That's because everyone picked on him in high school, so he thought he had to be tough."

Sean persisted. "But people are still saying bad things about him."

"That was his image. He sold more books that way," Tiffany retorted. "And when you're a famous author like he is . . ." She gulped down air. ". . . was . . . everyone takes advantage of you. Everyone wants a little piece of you. He never knew who to trust. That was what he liked about me. I was there for him one hundred percent."

"Even though he was marrying someone else?" Sean asked.

Tiffany dug the toe of her shoe into the carpet.

"I explained about that. That was Lydia's idea. It made good copy."

"He didn't have to go along."

Tiffany's mouth began to quiver.

"He loved me," she protested. "He said he did. He said he'd always be there for me no matter what happened. He said that ours was a union of two souls."

Union of two souls. Right, Bernie thought as she rolled her eyes. She was about to say, "Give me a break," when she caught her father's look and decided against it.

"He even gave me a necklace," Tiffany said and lifted up the chain around her neck to show off the silver heart dangling from it. "See, it's from Tiffany's, just like my name."

Yes, Bernie thought, recognizing the piece instantly. *It's from Tiffany's, all right, but honey, Lionel spent a hell of a lot less money on you than you did on those cufflinks that you bought him.*

Sean didn't know how much the silver heart cost, but he did know that this line of questioning was getting him nowhere. It was time to try a different approach.

"Tiffany, who was trying to take something from him?" Sean asked softly as Libby offered her a cookie.

She nibbled on the corner of the nut bar, then put it on the side table next to the tray.

"Well." Tiffany inscribed a circle in the rug with her toe. "You know. People."

"Any specific people?"

"Lydia."

"What was Lydia doing?" Sean asked encouragingly.

"Lionel told me she took money from one of his accounts."

Bernie, Libby, and Sean leaned forward. This was more promising.

"Do you know how much?"

Tiffany shook her head.

"Lionel didn't like to talk business with me. He said our time together was too special for that."

"Did he report the theft?" Sean asked while he threw another warning glance at Bernie, who gave all the indications of going into an eye-rolling paroxysm.

Tiffany shook her head.

"No. He said he'd take care of it privately."

"Wonderful," Sean muttered. "Do you know why?"

Tiffany twisted the edge of her shirttail around her hand. "They'd been together for a long time. Maybe he felt he owed her, although I told him he ought to get rid of her. A great artist like him. He shouldn't have had to be saddled with something like that. He had to be free to create."

"So what did he do?"

"I don't know," Tiffany said. "He never told me."

"Obviously he didn't fire her," Libby observed.

"No. But they were fighting all the time."

Sean nodded encouragingly.

"Anyone else?"

Tiffany tapped her nails on the front of her thigh.

"Well, there was Geoffrey Holder. He was in some business deal with him, something about building a theme park, but Lionel said Geoffrey was an incompetent idiot and he wasn't going to work with him."

Sean remembered hearing the deal had gone belly-up.

"Do you know why he said that?" Sean asked as he thought about Holder. An entrepreneur who'd made his money exporting plastic lawn furniture to Japan, then gone on to open a string of body shops, he had a bugaboo about skateboarders and had carried on an annoying—not to mention ceaseless—campaign to have them banned from everywhere in town. Dealing with people like Geoffrey Holder was one of the things he didn't miss about being chief of police, Sean reflected as he watched Tiffany hem and haw.

Finally she said, "Well, Lionel wanted to name the park Lord Ravenroot after one of the characters in his book, but Geoffrey wanted to call it Dracula Land."

"Kind of like a Disneyland for good little Goths, Gothettes, and vampire wannabees," Bernie observed.

Tiffany gave her a puzzled look.

"Ignore my daughter," Sean commanded.

Tiffany turned back towards him.

"Tell me where this park was supposed to be."

"I'm not sure. Somewhere north of here."

"Anyone else Lionel was angry with?"

"I'm . . . I'm not sure."

You're not sure about much, are you, Bernie wanted to say, but for once she managed to bite the words back before they emerged.

"Try to remember," Sean urged.

"It's just hard to think now."

Tiffany's voice started to quaver. Libby moved towards her.

"Would you like to lie down?" she asked solicitously.

Tiffany nodded.

"I think she needs a break," she told her father.

Sean nodded and Libby escorted Tiffany to her bedroom. Tiffany stretched out on the bed, while Libby lowered the blinds.

"Just try and rest," she told Tiffany.

Tiffany nodded and closed her eyes.

"Thanks," she murmured. "I don't know what I would have done without you."

"So what do you think?" Libby asked her father when she came back into his bedroom.

"I think the D.A. is going to nail her to the wall," Sean said.

Paul Pine walked into the bedroom of Sean Simmons half an hour later. He was wearing khaki shorts, a light blue polo shirt, and Docksiders, and even though he was sixty-three, Bernie still thought he looked like a movie star.

Maybe his neck and chin were getting a little soft, but he still had piercing blue eyes and a kissable cleft chin. He also had all his hair, which was now a gorgeous shade of white, a killer tan, and a great grin as well as being smart, funny, and genuinely nice.

When she was younger, Bernie had had a major crush on him. Even though she usually didn't have a thing for older men, Bernie would have been prepared to make an exception in his case. Unfortunately, Paul Pine was also her father's best friend, and not to mention a happily married man of thirty years with five children. Too bad. But her fantasies were great.

"So what have we got?" Paul asked Sean in the booming voice that worked so well in court.

He whistled when Sean told him.

"Anyone see Tiffany come into the shop?" he asked Libby.

"I don't think so."

"Good. I'll see what I can do with Lucy." He gazed at the wall above Sean's head and thought out loud. "Okay. As luck would have it, Tiffany came in twenty minutes after Lucy left and, mindful of what he told you"—Paul pointed to Libby—"you immediately called me for advice and I rushed right over here and, doing my civic duty, called him to arrange the surrender. Right?"

"Right," Libby repeated. "But couldn't we—"

"No." Paul cut Libby off, anticipating her request. "Under no circumstances."

"But—"

Paul waved his hands in the air. "I'm sorry, but it's not possible."

"How about representation?" Sean asked.

"There's a woman in my firm who's interested in doing some pro-bono work. I'll see if she wants to take this on."

"Good. Good." Sean watched a black squirrel running

up the drainpipe attached to the side of the building across the way. "She can get the crime scene report and the witness statements, although I don't think either of those are going to yield a lot of helpful information."

"Anyone could have put the poison in Lionel's water," Bernie said. "The water was sitting on top of the carton by the back door."

"And I put a Post-it note on the bottle with Laird's name written on it because Lydia was making such a big deal about it," Libby said.

"Do we know what was in the water, officially?" Paul asked.

Sean tore his gaze from the window.

"Lucy didn't tell me, but Clyde mentioned the tox screen will come back positive for cyanide, and I'm betting he's right."

"Then wouldn't the water smell of almonds?" Bernie asked.

"Only twenty-five percent of the population have the ability to smell that," Sean said. "I'm surprised you don't know that," he told Bernie.

"Why cyanide?" Bernie said.

"It fits the criteria. It's colorless, fast acting, and relatively easy to acquire." Sean tapped the armrest of his wheelchair with his fingers. "Tiffany's defense lawyer will need to do two things. Find people who had a motive for killing Lionel and see if anyone has any connections with any businesses that use cyanide."

"That's going to be tough," Bernie said.

"Tedious," Sean said. "Investigating is always tedious. Now, why don't you get Tiffany out here," he told her. "I'll introduce her to Paul and explain what's going to happen."

"Cookie?" Libby asked Paul as Bernie left the room.

He took a chocolate chip bar and bit down.

"These are so good," he said. "I don't know how you guys keep from weighing two hundred pounds with things like this around."

"It's a struggle," Sean was saying when Bernie came back in the room. The fact that his daughter was alone did not make him feel happy.

"Where's Tiffany?" he asked.

Unwilling to be the bearer of bad news, Bernie hesitated for a moment before speaking. Then she said, "She's gone."

"That's not possible," Libby cried.

"Au contraire, mon ami," Bernie told her as she watched Libby's shoulders slump.

Paul interrupted. "What do you mean, gone?"

Bernie turned to the lawyer.

"Just what I said. Gone. Left. As in out of here. On to other things. Hitting the road. Scrammed." *Shut up, Bernie,* she told herself. *He gets it.*

"How did she get out?"

"She defenestrated."

Paul wrinkled his brow. "Defenestrated?"

"Climbed out the window," Sean explained grimly. "My daughter has a liking for ten-dollar words." He turned to Libby. "You'd better find your friend ASAP."

Chapter 20

"Why isn't anything ever simple?" Libby lamented as she wiped off the counters in the store kitchen before turning out the lights. The heat had built up over the course of the day, and even though it was a little after ten at night, it was still hot inside.

"Because it isn't," Bernie replied. "Law of Nature Number three eighty."

"What's three eighty-one?"

"Give me a minute and I'll come up with it."

Libby rinsed out the rag and draped it over the side of the sink to dry.

"Dad was really pissed, wasn't he?" she asked as she considered the heaps of vegetables next to the refrigerator that she was going to use to make ratatouille the next day.

The colors—red from the tomatoes, gold from the peppers, the green of the zucchini, the white onions, and the purple of the eggplant—helped soothe her, as did the smell of the freshly cut basil. And boy, given the day, she needed some soothing.

"He'll get over it," Bernie told her.

"I don't like when people are mad at me."

"Except for me."

"Well, you don't count." Libby waved her hand. "That

didn't come out right. I mean, with you I know it's just temporary."

Bernie walked over and gave her sister's arm a squeeze.

"It's okay. Listen, you did the right thing, even if Tiffany didn't."

"You really think so?"

"She's your friend. What else could you have done?"

Libby bit her lip.

"Maybe you were right about my not getting involved."

"No," Bernie said. "I wasn't."

Libby gave her a quizzical look.

"Well," Bernie explained, "I guess I was feeling a little bit jealous that you wanted to help her and you wouldn't let me help you."

Maybe, Libby thought, as she pointed to the vegetables, *there is something to this therapy business after all.* "Do you think we need anything else for the ratatouille?"

Bernie looked at the pile. "Garlic and maybe some thyme."

Libby slapped her forehead with the palm of her hand.

"How could I have forgotten the garlic?"

Bernie put her arm around her sister and gave her another squeeze.

"You're on overload."

"I'm over the edge."

"How about I mix us up a batch of Cosmopolitans and we take them to the field and drink them."

Libby nodded. She'd never had a Cosmopolitan, but it sounded like something that would help in this type of situation.

"I'd like that." She started to grin. "I've got to admit Paul's expression was pretty funny when you told him Tiffany was gone."

Bernie giggled. "It was, wasn't it? Don't worry, you'll find her."

"Why do you think she ran?"

"I think she overheard Paul talking about bringing her in and she got scared."

"He does have a loud voice, doesn't he?"

"The loudest."

"Stentorian."

"Stentorian?"

"Stentor was a Greek herald who had a voice as loud as fifty men."

"Not now," Libby said. "Please."

"I'm sorry. It just slipped out."

Libby hugged herself.

"I feel so bad. I just wish I could have explained things to Tiffany."

"You will when you find her."

"You think I will find her?"

"Definitely. I wouldn't be surprised if she calls you in the next day or so and meanwhile, while we're searching, we can still talk to the people Tiffany mentioned. Kind of get a jump start on things."

Libby studied her sister's face.

"Are you suggesting this because you want to or because you figure this will take my mind off things?"

"The former," Bernie lied. *After all,* Bernie thought, *white lies are the lubricant that makes social interactions possible.*

Libby nodded her head doubtfully.

Bernie put her hand up.

"I swear."

"Really?"

"Really."

Libby scratched at a cuticle with one of her fingers. "Dad isn't going to like this."

"We don't have to tell him."

Libby considered that for a moment and then said, "So how are we going to get started?"

Bernie grinned.

"I thought you'd never ask."

Libby cocked her head and waited.

"When I was paging through your receipts and messages earlier, I noticed a note in there about talking to Mary Beth about doing a graduation picnic."

Libby yawned and stretched. The day was finally beginning to catch up with her.

"Ah, yes. Greg Holder's high school graduation. It's supposed to be the last weekend in June. For thirty-five people. They wanted it outside. The usual elegant but informal thing. I spent a couple of hours with her, but she must have decided to go with someone else, because she never called me back."

"Maybe it's time to give her a new menu to look at," Bernie suggested.

"Good idea."

"That's what I thought. I mean, it couldn't hurt. Who knows? Maybe Mary Beth will say something interesting to me about what Geoffrey has been up to these days. After all, we were in summer stock together, and if I remember correctly she never could keep her mouth shut."

"And I could fix up a basket for Lydia," Libby suggested, getting into the spirit of the enterprise. "Everyone needs food, especially in times of trauma."

"Something like gall and jimsonweed?"

"I was thinking more along the lines of muffins, fruit, cheese, and scones myself." Libby looked at her sister and smiled. "Thanks."

"No problem. This will be fun. Kinda like when we were kids and we used to play spy." Bernie looked around the kitchen. "Now where do you keep the vodka and cranberry juice?"

Chapter 21

Libby and Bernie were sprawled on one of the bleachers that lined the high school playing field, ignoring the *No Trespassing* sign prominently posted on the chain-link fence across from them. A plastic jug filled with Cosmopolitans sat between them. At eleven o'clock at night the town was silent except for the occasional barking dog.

"I like these drinks," Libby said to Bernie as she slapped at a mosquito that was biting her arm.

"A little vodka, a little lime juice, triple sec, and a dash of cranberry juice for color and there you have it. They're even nicer served in martini glasses. Of course," Bernie reflected, "everything is nicer served in martini glasses."

"They're not bad in plastic," Libby said.

"Next time I'll make us some Bellinis." Bernie leaned back on the bleachers and sighed. "I used to make out with Johnnie Ward under these. Of course then we were drinking Millers. Boy, that seems like a long time ago."

"Whatever happened to him?"

"I think he's some sort of investment lawyer down in New York City now."

Libby took another sip of her drink, then put it down on the bench next to her, leaned forward, dangled her hands between her legs, and studied the view. She could see houses lit up off in the distance. Orion had pointed his out to her when they'd come up here way too many years ago. He'd called just before she and Bernie had walked out the door. They were meeting tomorrow night after the store closed. Just thinking about it made Libby's heart race.

She wondered if the new T-shirt that Bernie had made her buy would go with her jeans skirt. She looked at Bernie, who was rolling the cup around between the palms of her hands, and considered asking her opinion, but that might mean getting into another Orion discussion. She'd just decided she'd be willing to chance it when Bernie spoke.

"Libby. Refresh my memory. What's Geoffrey Holder doing these days?" she asked her sister.

"He owns a string of body shops."

"For some reason I thought he'd sold those and was going to buy into a car franchise."

"He was talking about it . . . but that's as far as it went."

Bernie tapped her fingers on the side of her glass. "You know two readily available sources of cyanide?"

Libby topped off her glass.

"Not offhand. No."

Bernie held out her glass and Libby poured some more into it.

"Jewelry making and chrome-plating kits for car accessories. You can get them on the Internet."

Libby stared at Bernie. Her heart began to beat faster. "Do you use cyanide when you make glass?"

"No. Why are you asking?"

"Because Orion is making glass beads."

"You're sure about the cyanide?"

"I'm positive." Libby took a gulp of her drink. "How do you know about this stuff anyway?" she asked.

"Because I read. Some guy in L.A. poisoned his wife. The newspaper said that's how he got the stuff."

Libby pushed her hair off her face. "Do you ever forget anything you read?"

"Not much."

Bernie and Libby both took another couple of sips of their drinks and watched a car on the road below drive by.

"You know what else we should do?" Libby said.

"What?" Bernie asked.

"We should get on the Internet and see what we can find out about Geoff."

"Too bad we can't ask Dad."

Libby picked up her cup and drained it.

"I don't think that's an option right now."

Bernie stood up. "Let's go."

"And here I was hoping we could get picked up for trespassing."

"It would be like old times," Bernie reflected. "Except this time I don't think Dad would bail me out."

Bernie yawned and then yawned again as she motored towards Mary Beth and Geoffrey Holder's house on the outskirts of town. She was driving her father's old Caddy. Normally, she loved bouncing around on the leather seats blasting Elvis on the tape deck, but today she missed the MGB she'd left back in L.A.

Poor little thing, she thought. *I wonder who's driving you now?* The Caddy was so big, she felt as if she was driving a city bus. But, she reminded herself, it could be worse. She could be driving Libby's van. In which case she'd have to shoot herself.

Libby had been right about the Internet stuff, Bernie reflected as she concentrated on keeping the Caddy on Lilac Lane. She had to give her that. There had been lots of info on Señor G. Holder and his business holdings. Reading the stuff while she and Libby finished off the pitcher of Cosmos might not have been the wisest idea, however.

As Bernie drove between two large fieldstone pillars that marked the development the Holders lived in, she thought about how much money Geoff must be pulling in to be able to live in a place like this.

Ten minutes later, she arrived at the Holders' residence. As Bernie parked in the driveway and got out of the car, she decided that the place looked large enough to house a small army unit plus their equipment. The last time she'd visited Geoff and Mary Beth, they'd been living in a small two-bedroom ranch.

Walking up to the door, Bernie couldn't help noticing that the property looked unkempt. The foundation plantings needed trimming, shoots of bindweed were cropping up in the mulch of the flowerbed near the front wall, and there were small patches of speedwell in the lawn. It seemed as if the landscapers weren't stopping here any-more—a definite no-no in a community like this.

I'm not surprised, Bernie thought as she rang the bell. It fit in with the article she'd downloaded from *Money Talks*. According to that, Holder Enterprises was on the verge of going belly-up. Geoffrey Holder had overextended himself to partner with Laird Wrenn on the amusement park deal. Then Wrenn had pulled out and the market had tanked and it was adios Holder Enterprises.

"Mary Beth," Bernie said when she answered the door a few moments later.

Mary Beth's eyes widened.

"Bernie? Geoff told me he heard you were back work-ing at the store."

"At least for a while."

"L.A. too much for you?"

"Nope. Just needed a little down time."

"You look great," Mary Beth told her.

"So do you," Bernie replied, hoping she didn't look shocked at how thin Mary Beth had become. "I know I should have called," Bernie continued. "But Libby and I have come up with some new ideas for your son's graduation." She shook her head. "God, I can't believe time has just slipped away like that . . ."

"It's scary," Mary Beth agreed.

"Absolutely. So I just decided to throw together a few things for you and run over." Bernie extended the package she was carrying. She'd always found it was harder for people to refuse you when you bring them something to eat. "Stuff from the store."

"Why, thank you."

"This is an amazing house," Bernie said as Mary Beth took the box.

"It is, isn't it?" Mary Beth agreed. "Quite a change from our old place."

"I'd love to see it."

"And I'd love to show it to you," Mary Beth told Bernie, though it was obvious to Bernie from Mary Beth's expression that that was the last thing she wanted to do. "But the place is such a mess."

"Oh, I don't care." Bernie stepped inside. "I hope I'm not interrupting anything."

"Not at all," Mary Beth assured her.

"Wow." Bernie took in the cathedral entranceway and the pink marble floor tile. "I'm impressed."

"I designed it myself." And with that Mary Beth preceded to give Bernie a whirl-wind tour of the house.

"Very nice," Bernie kept saying. She'd seen houses like this in L.A., and for the life of her she couldn't figure out why people needed a music room, a sewing room, a weight room, and a library when it was clear that no one ever used them. Finally they got to the kitchen.

"You have an Aga," Bernie exclaimed. "I love them."

Mary Beth nodded absentmindedly. "The kitchen designer said they were a must-have piece, so Geoff insisted I get one, but I've never quite got the hang of it."

At around thirteen thousand dollars, that was too bad, Bernie thought as she watched Mary Beth put the box she'd given her on one of the counters and take off the top. Inside was an array of muffins and brownies, two things Bernie had found most people couldn't resist.

"Well, they are different from other stoves."

Bernie had had one on a shoot that she'd done. You didn't turn them on. They ran all the time, and they had a top that was very hot in some places and warm in others. Designed to function in English country cottages where it was cold and damp, they put out a lot of heat because they ran all the time. Of course, in this country, you had to shut them off in the summer or have your air-conditioning on.

"I don't remember you liking cooking," Bernie said as Mary Beth lifted out a brownie and took a nibble.

"I don't. But Geoff likes to cook on Sundays." Mary Beth took another nibble. "These are so good, Bernie."

"It's the coffee in them." Bernie handed Mary Beth the menu she and Libby had prepared. "That's why you should let Libby and me take care of your son's party for you."

"I don't know." Mary Beth brushed a nonexistent speck of dirt off her turquoise clam-diggers.

"See." Bernie pointed to the menu Mary Beth was holding. "The top one is a barbecue. We can do hamburgers, hot dogs, ribs, chicken, cole slaw, potato salad, cornbread made with fresh corn and cheddar cheese, a big watermelon full of fruit salad, cookies, and a sheet cake. The kids love it.

"Or," Bernie continued, chattering on, "you could go slightly more upscale. Kebobs. Lamb and chicken. Possibly shrimp, although that would run you more money. A big tossed salad with glazed walnuts and feta cheese. An orzo salad made with scallions and oil and balsamic vinegar. Little cherry tomatoes filled with goat cheese. Spankoita. Brownies. A two-layer, coconut-frosted graduation cake."

"It all looks wonderful," Mary Beth said dubiously.

"Why don't you discuss it with Geoff and get back to me?"

Mary Beth nodded. "I'll do that. Maybe we can have lunch some day when I have a little more time."

"Great," Bernie said, ignoring the hint to leave and changing the subject. "Wasn't that awful, Lionel dying like that?"

Mary Beth shuddered.

"I can't get the image of his hand going to his throat out of my mind. You know Lionel and his people were all supposed to come here before the dinner for a drink, but Lydia called and canceled. Something about Lionel having a headache."

"Really?"

Mary Beth grimaced. "I'd bought this very expensive port that Lydia said Lionel was fond of. A hundred and fifty dollars a bottle. I don't know what the hell I'm going to do with it now. I mean, who drinks port?"

"So he was a friend of yours?" Bernie asked.

"Lionel?" Mary Beth furrowed her brow. "Lionel never had any friends. You know that. No. He was one of my husband's business associates. Him and Nigel Herron." She gave the sentence an unpleasant twist.

Bernie leaned forward.

"I didn't know Nigel was involved in the amusement park deal."

"He is—excuse me, was—Geoff's financial adviser. What a pair those two are."

"They never did have much common sense," Bernie reflected.

The irises of Mary Beth's brown eyes turned darker.

"Right. And why listen to someone like me? Why put

some of your money aside in a savings account? After all, I'm just the little dumb housewife. Unlike my husband, the financial genius." Mary Beth waved her hand dismissively. "And now, if you don't mind, I don't mean to be rude, but . . ."

"Oh, you're not," Bernie assured her. "I understand totally." Then, instead of going left, she went right and found herself in front of the family room. It was filled with packing cartons, stacks of clothes, and computer equipment. She turned to Mary Beth and said, "Boy. Talk about getting rid of stuff."

Mary Beth hesitated for a moment, then said, "Don't tell anyone, but we're getting ready to put our house on the market."

"That's a lot of work."

Mary Beth sucked her cheeks in, then blew air out between her lips.

"So where are you moving to?" Bernie prompted.

Mary Beth put on a smile that, Bernie reflected, looked as if it had been dipped in shellac; then her lips began to tremble and she started to cry.

"Oh Bernie," she sobbed. "Everything is coming apart."

Bernie called Libby once she was on the road again.

"The Holders are separating," she told her. "They didn't hire you for the graduation party because I don't think there's going to be one."

"How do you know?"

Libby's voice sounded staticky. Bernie adjusted her headset.

"She told me." And Bernie reported the rest of the conversation.

"I wonder why Lionel was going over there for a drink?" Libby asked.

"Maybe Holder was making one last appeal to get things back on track."

"And then Lionel doesn't show up after the wife goes out and buys an expensive bottle of port. That would piss me off. Could be the straw that broke the camel's back," Libby mused.

"Could be," Bernie agreed, following Libby's lead. "I'm kinda liking Holder for this myself in a hypothetical kind of way. The thing that I don't like is that this is the type of homicide you have to prepare for. So Lionel cancels him out at the last minute and Holder does what? Runs back and gets the cyanide that he conveniently has on hand and dumps it into Lionel's water? Sounds pretty sketchy to me."

"Well, you said he had access to it."

"No. I said he could have had access to it."

"I stand corrected." Libby paused for a moment. "Maybe Holder was planning to do it anyway. He was just giving Lionel a last chance to come around."

Bernie stopped at a light. "Well, he's definitely three for three. He's got motive, means, and opportunity, which means, folks, he wins the Trifecta."

"We should tell Dad."

"Not yet."

"When?" Libby demanded.

"We'll tell him when we have something a little less circumstantial."

"And what would constitute that?"

"Evidence. A witness."

"And how are we going to get those?" Libby asked.

"I'm not sure," Bernie admitted.

Libby was quiet for a moment; then she said, "Are you still going to talk to Geoffrey?"

Bernie looked down at her second basket of treats.

"You betcha. I'm on my way there even as we speak."

"What if he won't see you?"

"Of course he'll see me. Everyone always sees me. I'm too charming to refuse. Anyway, why would he say no? I'm just going to talk to him about the menu. By the way, have you heard from Tiffany yet?"

"Unfortunately, no."

"Well, call me if you do."

"You'll be the first. And Bernie, be careful. Geoff could have killed someone."

"I'll be Cautious Connie."

And Bernie clicked off.

Chapter 22

Libby stared at Lydia's face peeking out of the doorway of her mother's house. Lydia looked even more bloated than she had when Libby had first seen her in the high school cafeteria. Maybe she'd been drinking. Either that or eating a lot of salty things. Or it was her time of the month? How many days ago had she first seen her? It seemed like eons, even though it was more like a week.

"What do you want?" Lydia snapped.

Libby hoisted the basket she was carrying as if it were a white flag.

"I thought you might like something in your time of grief."

"How kind," Lydia said, and her hand shot out, grabbed the basket, and slammed the door in Libby's face.

The whole thing was over in three seconds.

"Great," Libby said, pressing her finger on the bell and keeping it there. "Just great."

At other times, she might have—no make that *would* have—walked away, but that was not an option now. She was damned if she'd tell Bernie she couldn't get Lydia to open the door.

Finally, Lydia answered.

"Have you gone crazy?" she demanded, throwing the

door open so hard that it banged against the outside wall. "Can't you see I'm in mourning?"

"Good," Libby said. "You have time to talk."

"I'm going to call the police if you don't go away."

"Then I can tell them about the money you stole from Lionel's accounts," Libby surprised herself by saying.

Lydia's mouth dropped open for a second. Then she recovered and said, "I don't know what you're talking about. Now get the hell out of here."

But it was too late. Libby had already scooted inside.

"Sure you don't," she said, closing the door behind her.

"What the hell do you want?" Lydia barked in Libby's face, but Libby folded her arms across her chest and stood her ground.

"I don't think Tiffany killed Lionel," Libby told Lydia.

Lydia laughed.

"Which means you want to give them another suspect. Like me. Boy, that really makes me want to talk to you. You know, you need to work on your people skills."

"Never mind me. You have a motive."

"So what?" Lydia sneered. "Big deal. If it comes down to that, so do half the people in this town. And even if I do, which I'm not admitting, why would I want to chose a public place to kill Lionel when I have access to him 24/7? Why didn't I just slip something into one of his jars of Marshmallow Fluff if I wanted to off him and let the housekeeper take the blame? No. Face it. Tiffany killed Lionel. After seventeen years of stringing her along, he finally told her to get lost and she flipped out and did him in."

"Well, I don't believe that," Libby argued back.

"You never could deal with life the way it is."

"Can it. For one thing, where would Tiffany get the cyanide?" Libby demanded.

"If that's what it was. Anyway, that's the police's problem."

"It's mine too."

Lydia looked at Libby and rolled her eyes.

"So now you're a private detective? Please. Do us all a favor and go back to cooking."

"I can't."

Libby watched Lydia take a deep breath. After she'd exhaled, she said, "This is your sister's doing, isn't it?"

"Actually, it happens to be mine. You can talk to me or you can talk to the police. The choice is yours."

"And why haven't you told the police already?"

Maybe because they don't care, Libby thought. But that was definitely not what she was going to say now. She thought about what her father would do in a situation like this.

"The reason is no concern of yours," she told Lydia, bulling her way through. "But rest assured, I will if I have to."

Libby watched Lydia study her face for a few moments. Whatever she found there must have made Lydia believe her because for a second she saw Lydia's shoulders sag. Lydia rubbed her hand over her face.

"So are you going to tell me?" Libby asked.

Lydia chuckled.

"Tell you what? That Lionel was a cheap son of a bitch? Tell you that I made him what he was? Tell you that without me he was nothing? So I took a little money from him. So what? In the scheme of things, it was nothing. He owed me. He owed me way more than I ever took from him, I can tell you that.

"He was a user. He stole ideas from everyone. Hell, he practically plagiarized his first book. The funny thing was that he was actually starting to believe his own press. He really thought he was a good writer, God help us all.

"He even thought he was a vampire. I mean, how weird is that? Sleeping in a coffin. Wearing a cape. Those fangs of his. All my ideas. He didn't even know what a vampire was until he was a senior in high school. Up until then, all he read was *Sports Illustrated* and *Popular Mechanics*.

"He was nuts and I was crazier for staying with him. Once he found out I'd taken the money, he made me into his slave. I should have turned myself in to the police. It would have been better. I mean, look at me." Lydia pointed to herself. "I'm a mess. My eating is out of control. I can't stop. At least in jail I'd lose weight."

Jail as a weight-losing strategy. *That's a new one,* Libby thought as she asked, "If you felt that way about him, why didn't you leave?"

"And go where? He was the top. I thought if I stayed, somehow I'd be able to work things out. I'd be able to have it all. But you can't. You never can. All I've done is make myself into . . . well . . . I don't know what." Lydia straightened up. "But I'll tell you one thing. There was a list of people who would have liked to see Lionel Wrenkoski dead. Some people spread joy. He spread misery wherever he went. But I didn't kill him. I didn't hate him enough to sacrifice my life for that."

"So who did?"

Lydia crossed her arms over her chest and glowered at Libby.

"Why the hell should I tell you? Whoever did it should be rewarded, not punished."

Libby thought about mentioning Tiffany, but said instead, "Because I brought you cranberry scones and a jar of homemade strawberry jam and because a long time ago I used to look up to you."

Lydia cocked her head.

"You did?"

Libby nodded.

"Really and truly?" Lydia asked.

"Yes. I thought you were the most sophisticated person I knew. I wanted to be just like you."

Maybe Bernie was right, Libby thought as Lydia turned

and said, "My mother has some nice Kona beans that my cousin sent me from Maui. How about if I make us a cup of coffee."

Maybe truth was an overrated commodity.

Libby was mulling over her conversation with Lydia as she drove back to the store. She hadn't told her anything she didn't know, and after a few minutes Libby found herself thinking about Tiffany again. In truth, she hadn't stopped thinking about her since she'd climbed out the bedroom window of their house.

Libby had called everyone she could think of, as well as checked out every place Tiffany might be holed up in without any results. It didn't help that her father was holding her personally responsible for the fiasco, and what was worse was that she couldn't help agreeing with him.

Poor Tiffany.

Some people just didn't have any luck.

Libby rubbed her forehead and made a mental note to herself to drink only one Cosmo in the future. Her head felt as if someone were drumming on her skull. The Advil hadn't helped, and this line of thought was not making her headache feel any better. Libby tapped her fingers on the van's steering wheel as she slowed down for a stop sign.

She should get back to the shop. She had to phone her order in to the wholesaler and get going on the lemon chicken she was planning on serving tomorrow. Only she couldn't seem to concentrate on anything.

She took a deep breath.

"The hell with it," she said to herself as she turned onto Townsend instead of making a right onto Green. Everyone would survive without her for half an hour. She needed some time out.

Ten minutes later she pulled into the parking lot of Elm Wood Park. The lot was empty, but that wasn't unusual. Since Longely had metamorphosed from a middle- to an upper-income place, few people came here anymore. Which was fine with Libby. For all practical purposes, she had thirty acres of woods all to herself.

She sat in the van for a few minutes and gazed at the Hudson River while she munched on one of the chocolate chip cookies she always carried in her backpack along with a Swiss army knife, a needle-nose pliers, a can of mace, Band-Aids, a fifty-dollar bill, and a bottle of water. Bernie always teased her about her emergency pack.

"So when's the world ending?" she always asked.

But it made Libby feel better to know she was prepared for whatever came along. As Libby wiped the crumbs off her hands, she wondered how fresh pineapple chunks would taste in the cookies. They'd probably put out too much moisture. But dried pineapple might not be bad. Better yet, dried apricots or mango slivers. Maybe even candied ginger. *I'll try that first,* Libby thought as she got out of the van and sat on one of the benches that faced the river. *I have half a pound of candied ginger in the pantry. Might as well use it up.* Then she thought about how nice it would be to be out on the water. No one could bother you there.

For a while Libby watched a tug going upstream and remembered how she, her mother, and Bernie used to picnic on the grass overlooking the river. Then she got to thinking about how she and Tiff used to come here when they were seniors in high school and spent hours watching the river and talking and eating M&Ms.

And then Libby remembered something else. She remembered the house Tiff had found in the middle of the woods.

"You've got to come and see it," Tiff had told her, dragging her along. "It's really scary. It would be a great place to have a party."

The hut.

I haven't looked in the hut.

God, what an idiot she was.

I just hope I remember where it is, Libby thought as she jumped up and headed for the trees.

This is ridiculous, Libby said to herself as she slapped at a gnat. Tiffany probably didn't remember this place at all. In fact, she was probably in Southern California by now. Why the hell would she be here in the woods? She hated bugs. But Libby kept walking. This was the last place in town she hadn't checked, and she was damned if she wasn't going to dot every *i* and cross every *t* as her mother used to say.

"Blasted roots," Libby muttered as she stubbed her toe on one.

The town should maintain this place, she thought, pushing a branch away from her face. What the hell was she paying taxes for? And that plant she'd just brushed against. Was that poison ivy? Libby could never remember whether poison ivy had three or four leaves.

Then Libby realized it was getting darker. She glanced up through the branches. The sky was filled with rain clouds. Even better. Now she could get wet on top of everything else. If she were smart, she'd turn back, but instead she took a bite of the cookie she'd forgotten she was holding and tucked the rest of the bag in her T-shirt pocket and kept trudging on.

Even she had to admit these were good. No, they were better than good. They were great.

Most people used a half pound of butter in their batter, but Libby used an extra quarter stick and that, in her humble opinion, made all the difference. What people who didn't cook didn't understand was that recipes were living things. They evolved over time. She was thinking about whether she should add a little more butter to her lemon snaps when she spotted the hut through the trees.

Underbrush interspersed with high grass jostled up against the hut on three sides and part of the roof had fallen in, but then, after all this time, what had she expected? But obviously people still came here because someone had cleared a patch of ground in front of the hut. In addition, someone had hung a black plastic garbage bag from the opening. To serve as a door, Libby presumed, which meant someone had been living there. Or still was.

Whether it was Tiffany or not remained to be seen. Libby stopped. Now that she was here, she wasn't sure what to do. Maybe it would be better if she got her phone and called Bernie. In situations like this, two people were always better than one. Especially if the person in the hut was someone who would object to having their privacy intruded on, which, considering that they were living in the middle of the woods, was probably the case.

And Libby had to admit the hut creeped her out. The place looked like something out of a Grimm's fairy tale. She'd just decided to head back to the van when she heard a crack behind her. The hairs on Libby's arm stood up. She started to turn, but before she could, something hit her in the back and she fell to the ground. When Libby looked up, Tiffany was standing over her pointing a gun at her head.

"You shouldn't have come," she said.

"I can leave," Libby offered.

Tiffany shook her head.

"It's too late for that."

And then, on top of everything, it started to rain.

Chapter 23

Geoffrey Holder's place of business was located five and one-quarter miles away from Elm Wood Park and ten miles from his house. A large, square concrete building surrounded by a fenced-in blacktopped parking lot, it was well positioned between the outskirts of the town and a Thruway exit. A big sign proclaiming, *You want it fixed right the first time? Come to us,* was bolted onto the roof.

Unfortunately, it looked as if people weren't getting the message because the lot was mostly empty. In fact, Bernie observed as she pulled up in front of the entrance, there were only four other cars in a lot that could have held fifty—easy.

Bernie squared her shoulders, grabbed the basket, and got out of the Caddy. She didn't know what she'd get out of Holder, but hopefully it would be worth the time. One thing she did know, though. Whatever happened, Libby was going to owe her big for this.

"Things not going so well?" Bernie said to the receptionist, a jowly older woman with blond teased hair that Bernie decided had to be a wig.

She gave Bernie a baleful look.

"We're going Chapter Eleven."

"Everyone seems to be doing it these days. Maybe it'll help."

The receptionist snorted at the idea.

"My Timmy says it never helps. Just postpones the inevitable. My Timmy says that this is what happens when you get ideas above your station. He says Mr. Holder shoulda stuck with what he knows—fixing cars instead of fancying himself the next . . ." The woman paused for a moment. "I don't know what . . .

"Who would go to someplace like Dracula Land anyway? Freaks. And I'll tell you one thing about them. Freaks don't got much money. The thing never made sense to me. Didn't make sense to a lot of people. Everyone tried to tell him, but he wouldn't listen. It was like he was under a spell or something. They did good work here too."

The woman shook her head and Bernie was fascinated to see that while her head moved, her hair didn't.

"Good thing I got me grandchildren to occupy my time when this place goes under." She pointed to a picture sitting on her desk. "Three of them. Two girls and a boy. So, dearie, what brings you here?" she finally asked Bernie. "If your car needs work, take it down the road to Lloyd's. They do a clean, fast job. Use dealer-specified parts too."

Bernie lifted the gift basket. "Actually, I want to give Mr. Holder this."

"Nice present."

"It's muffins from A Little Taste of Heaven. His wife wants me to talk to him about the graduation party for his child. I thought this might help sway his mind."

"Muffins?" The receptionist snickered. "A couple six-packs a beer woulda done ya better." The phone rang and the receptionist picked it up. "No. We ain't accepting any new vehicles." She hung up and got back to Bernie. "And I gotta warn you," she told her. "The boss ain't the easiest person to talk to these days. But you wanna try, go ahead." And the receptionist waved her arm towards a door to the left.

"His car was here when I came this morning, but he wasn't in his office. I'm not sure exactly where he is. Maybe you should try the paint room. That's out in the back away from the main building."

"Could you page him?" Bernie asked.

"Sure I could," the woman agreed, "if the system worked. But it don't so I can't. It's been down for about a month now, and we ain't had the money to fix it. Or," the woman went on, "you could leave the basket here and I'll give it to him when he comes out."

"If you don't mind, I think I'll go find him."

"Whatever you say. I'll buzz you in." As the door clicked open, the woman said to Bernie, "When you find him, tell him his wife left a message for him."

Bernie nodded her agreement and walked through. She found herself in a narrow corridor. The sign on the first door said, *Geoffrey Holder.* She knocked. No one answered. She had her hand on the doorknob and was just about to turn it when a voice behind her said, "Can I help you?"

Bernie jumped and spun around.

"Sorry if I startled you." The man extended his hand. "I'm Robert Sullivan, but you can call me Rob. Everyone does."

But Bernie wasn't listening. She was staring at his intensely green eyes. Finally she tore her gaze away and shook his hand.

"Bernadette Simmons."

"That's a pretty name."

"It comes from the French."

Now that was an unnecessary bit of information, Bernie thought as Rob rocked back on his heels.

"So tell me, Bernadette . . ."

"Bernie . . ."

He grinned and Bernie could feel her knees turning to jelly. *You are taking a vacation from men,* Bernie reminded herself as she watched Rob's grin grow wider. *As if he knows what he's doing to me,* she thought angrily.

"I had an uncle named Bernie. So, Bernie, what can I do for you?"

She repeated the explanation she'd given the receptionist. Rob gave a mock bow and extended his hand with a flourish.

"Let's go find the lucky gent. I've been looking for him myself."

Get a grip, Bernie told herself as she followed him down the corridor. Then, before she could stop herself, she'd offered him a ginger muffin with lemon icing from her basket.

"God, these are good," he said as he devoured it. "You make them?"

Bernie lied and said yes. Well, she had chopped the ginger, hadn't she?

She and Rob continued down the hall while Rob peeked into the other four offices.

"Aren't too many of us left," he observed as they came to the end of the corridor. He held open the last door, which had a sign on it that read, *Work Area. Authorized Personnel Only,* and said, "After you."

"I don't think I've seen you around," he said as Bernie stepped inside.

She scanned the area. It had spaces for four cars, but the room was empty.

"That's because I've just moved back to town."

"Lucky for Longely."

Bernie started to fiddle with her ring and stopped herself.

"I'm not sure my sister would agree with that."

Rob chuckled.

"Maybe she's afraid of the competition. Would you be interested in meeting for a drink later?"

"Are you always this quick?"

"Only when I see something I like."

Bernie could feel herself flush.

"Possibly," she said, furious with herself for acting as if she were fourteen.

"That's good enough for me."

Bernie took a deep breath and tried to concentrate on what she'd come here for.

"Your boss doesn't seem to be here," she observed, looking around the room.

"No, he doesn't," Rob agreed. "Come on. Let's take a peek in the paint room," he suggested, beckoning for her to follow him. "It's sad really," Rob said to Bernie as they walked out the side door into the yard. "This used to be a good business."

"So what are you going to do?" Bernie asked him.

Rob shrugged. "Do computer stuff. Train dogs. Something will turn up. It always does."

"You really train dogs?"

"I did out in Venice. Venice Beach," he added. "That's out in L.A."

"I know where it is. I was living in Brentwood."

"Fancy that. So what brought you back here?" he asked as he opened the door to the paint room.

Bernie stepped inside.

"Family stuff." Time enough to get into the real reason later. "And you?"

"Same thing."

Bernie glanced around. The paint room was divided into three compartments by clear hanging plastic panels that partially obscured the view. So they could do three cars at a time, she supposed.

"He doesn't seem to be here," Rob said.

"Where else could he be?"

Rob gave a quick shake of his head.

"You got me."

"Have you seen him today?"

Rob rocked back and forth on his heels. "His car was in the lot when I got here, but in answer to your question, no, I haven't seen him since I got in."

"Isn't that a little unusual?"

"Not these days. He probably went off to play golf with one of his buddies. He's been doing that a lot lately."

"But," Bernie objected, "his car is still here."

"Someone came and picked him up."

Bernie folded her arms across her chest.

"I don't know," she said doubtfully.

A little kernel of unease was growing in her chest. In her experience, Type-A guys like Holder usually drove their own cars to wherever they were going, but maybe she was generalizing.

"Are you always this suspicious?" Rob asked.

"I think the word you want is skeptical," Bernie replied absentmindedly, "and the answer to that question is yes."

"Must make relationships hard."

Bernie didn't answer. Her attention was focused on the room. She scanned the area again, looking more carefully this time.

"What's that?" she asked, pointing to a small black shape by the far wall near one of the big barrels. Actually, it looked like the bottom half of one of A Little Taste of Heaven's take-out containers, she told herself. Nevertheless.

"What?" Rob asked. "I don't see anything."

"Over there. At two o'clock."

"I still don't see it."

"That," Bernie said, immediately sorry that she sounded so impatient with him.

But Rob didn't seem to notice.

"Oh." He laughed. "That's what you're pointing at. It looks like a piece of trash to me."

"Maybe, but I'd still like to check it out."

Rob bowed.

"Be my guest."

Bernie put the basket she was carrying down on the floor, pushed the first panel aside and started walking. Then she pushed the second panel aside and the third. A moment later she was staring at a black shoe.

"This is bad," Rob said as he moved up next to her.

"Definitely," Bernie agreed, tentatively taking another couple of steps forward.

Despite knowing what was coming, she gasped when she saw what was lying on the floor behind the metal drums.

One thing was for sure, Bernie thought. Geoffrey Holder wasn't going anywhere now, not with a hole the size of a walnut in the middle of his skull.

Chapter 24

As Libby stared at the gun in Tiffany's shaking hands, she surprised herself. She knew she should be feeling scared, but instead she was pissed off.

All the time she'd spent worrying about Tiffany, all the calls she'd made, the places she'd looked. Not to mention the fact that her father was angry with her and their store was being watched by the cops and this was the thanks she got. Getting pushed down and sitting here in the rain and getting wet and muddy while Tiffany threatened her. No. She didn't think so.

"What the hell is the matter with you?" Libby barked.

Tiffany's eyes filled with tears. Her lips quivered. "Don't talk to me that way."

"I'll talk to you any way I want." Libby got up and wiped her hands off on her jeans before straightening up. "I ought to slap you. Now give me that gun," she ordered.

"No." Tiffany took a step back.

"Yes." And before Libby realized what she was doing, she'd reached over and grabbed the damned thing out of Tiffany's hand. "Is it loaded?" Libby asked as she tried not to think about what her father would have said to her if he could see what she was doing.

"I don't know," Tiffany confessed. "I've never held a gun before."

"Me either," Libby admitted as she realized she was pointing the thing at herself.

She carefully turned it around and placed it on the stump of a tree near her. Even though she'd seen her father clean his service revolver on the kitchen table hundreds of times, she didn't know anything about guns. He'd never explained anything about them to her, and she'd never asked because they'd scared her, maybe because her mother had hated having them in the house so much.

"Where'd you get the weapon?" Libby asked Tiffany, who promptly broke down in tears.

"It was so horrible," she sobbed.

"What?"

"Geoffrey Holder."

Libby began to get a bad feeling.

"What about him?"

"He's dead."

And Tiffany began to cry in earnest.

Libby wiped the raindrops out of her eyes and sneezed.

"I didn't even know I'd taken the thing till I got back here, honest." Tiffany nodded towards the gun. "You believe me, don't you?" she asked.

"Of course."

Libby desperately wanted to. She told herself she did as she extracted the small bag with the two cookies in it out of her T-shirt pocket, took one for herself, and offered the other one to Tiffany.

"Thanks," Tiffany said.

"Don't mention it," Libby replied.

Eating cookies at a time like this was a strange thing to do, she thought, but the feel of chocolate chips on her tongue did make her feel better. She supposed it was her version of downing a shot of Scotch.

"I'm such an idiot," Tiffany wailed, taking Libby back to the present.

"Yes, you are," Libby agreed, then felt immediately guilty for saying that even if it was true.

"I should never have run away. I'm sorry for everything." Tiffany sniffled. She took a bite of a cookie and asked, "What are we going to do?"

"We're going to walk back to my van and call my father."

And hope he doesn't bite my head off, Libby added silently as she rubbed her forehead. This was definitely going to be an eight-aspirin day. But come what may, Libby decided, she *was* having that drink with Orion. And she *was* going to wear her new T-shirt. Then she immediately felt bad for thinking about things like that at a time like this.

Libby looked at Orion. They were sitting on the sofa in his parents' living room. He seemed so quiet—no, the word was contained—and she was having a hard time keeping still.

"Just like old times," he remarked as Libby folded her hands in her lap so she wouldn't pick at her nails.

"The sofa's new."

"That's not what I meant."

"I know."

"I like your T-shirt."

"Thanks."

Libby took a deep breath and tried to look casual as Orion moved closer and put his arm around her shoulder. This was like being back in high school, she told herself as she felt her pulse race. They should have stayed at the bar and had another beer. She wasn't ready for this. Not yet. Especially not after today.

"Where are your parents?"

"At Lake George visiting friends." Then Orion bent over and gently kissed Libby on the lips.

"I never stopped thinking about you."

Libby moved back a little.

"I don't know . . ."

"What's to know?" Orion asked.

"This . . ." Libby stood up. "It feels weird."

"You're still mad at me, aren't you?" Orion asked. "I wouldn't blame you if you were."

"Well . . . it is hard to trust someone who did what you did," Libby conceded.

"What can I do to change your mind?"

Libby couldn't think of an answer. She'd blanked out. Orion reached over, took Libby's hand, and patted it when she didn't reply.

"Considering the day you've had, maybe this isn't the time to talk about things like this."

"It has been horrible," Libby said.

"Little Tiffany killing two people." Orion shook his head. "Hard to fathom."

Libby removed her hand from his and stood up. "She didn't do it."

Orion got up too and faced Libby. "I really hope she didn't. But then it'll be someone else we know. It's not as if it's a stranger doing this."

"Maybe it is," Libby countered.

"Do you really believe that?" Orion asked her.

"I'd like to," Libby said softly. "But no. I don't."

She watched Orion straighten and smooth back his hair with the palm of his hand.

"I was speaking to Geoff the other day," he mused. "And now I'm going to be going to his funeral." He paused for a moment. "And I thought things were going to be quiet when I moved back."

Suddenly Libby felt as if she couldn't breathe.

"I have to go," she told him.

"Can I see you again?" he asked.

"Definitely," Libby said.

He leaned over and kissed her.

"You taste sweet," he told her as he escorted her to the door.

Something is wrong with me, Libby said to herself as she got into her van. She'd fantasized about being with Orion for the past ten years and now, when she had the opportunity, what had she said? *I have to go. Bernie is right,* she thought as put the key in the ignition. *I need professional help.*

Sean sat in his wheelchair, sipping Wild Turkey from a jam jar. He knew the jam jar annoyed Libby. They had, as she kept reminding him, perfectly good glasses downstairs, but for mysterious reasons he preferred using this one, maybe because it reminded him of when he was a kid and it was all they'd had.

As he gazed at his two daughters, he wondered what his dear departed wife would have said about what happened today. Nothing good. Of that he was sure.

It was a little before twelve o'clock at night—past his bedtime, but neither of his children gave the slightest indication that they were ready to go to bed. Neither was he, for that matter. They were all too wound up from the day's events.

First there had been the call from Bernie and then the call from Libby, not to mention the call he'd made to Paul. He hated asking anyone for favors. Once was bad. Twice was insupportable. No matter what the problem was, he would never have called Paul for himself, but he was the first to admit he'd always been a sucker for his girls.

"You're sure she's not going to run this time," Paul had asked him.

Sean had looked at the quivering, sodden mess that was Tiffany standing before him and said, "I'm sure."

"You're positive? Because I don't want . . ."

"Trust me on this."

"Be there in ten," Paul had told him before hanging up.

As Sean had studied Tiffany, he doubted that she'd even have the energy to climb back down the stairs to the street again, let alone jump out of another window.

"You want to tell me what happened?" he'd asked her. But she'd just cried harder.

"Try pulling yourself together," he'd urged, but that had only led to a fresh bout of sobbing. She'd still been at it when the patrol car arrived to take her into custody.

Sean sighed and turned his attention back to his daughters.

Libby was sitting in the armchair, her legs slung over the side of the chair, methodically eating her way through the plate of lemon bars that she'd brought up from downstairs, while Bernie was perched on the end of his bed alternately eating olives and making serious inroads into the pitcher of vodka martinis she'd mixed herself.

"So." Libby broke a lemon bar in half. "Paul will represent Tiffany."

"Someone in his firm will," Sean corrected.

"And isn't that person lucky," Bernie observed. "Now he or she can defend Tiffany for two homicides instead of one."

Libby put the first half of the cookie in her mouth, chewed, and swallowed, leaving a faint dusting of powdered sugar on her lower lip.

"She said she didn't kill Holder and I believe her," she told Bernie while she cleaned the sugar off her face with the back of her hand. Then she put the plate on the table next to her and swung her legs down.

"So you keep saying," Bernie observed. "And I'd love to believe you, but she had the weapon that Holder was shot with in her possession."

"She explained that. She found it near Holder's body and reached down and took it with her."

"Why? Because she thought it looked nice? The color appealed to her?" Bernie said.

Which was, Sean noted, what he'd been thinking as well, though he wouldn't have phrased it in quite that way.

Libby leaned forward.

"Tiffany was scared," she shot back. "She grabbed it on impulse and ran away. Haven't you ever done anything like that?"

"No," Bernie said. "I can't say I have. But then, I've never been in her situation either. Here's another question though. Why was Tiffany in Holder's place of business?"

"I already told you. She said she got a call to come over."

"From this mysterious woman who she can't identify? Now let me get this straight. Here she is being looked for by the police and she hitches a ride out to Holder's business and walks in the back way? It's something I would definitely not do."

"She's not you," Libby snapped.

"Thank God. And how did she get this alleged phone call considering she's in the middle of the woods?"

"On her cell. Everyone has her number. She uses it to book her hair appointments."

"The call shouldn't be hard to verify," Sean pointed out. "Paul can get a court order for the phone records."

"Maybe we should hire a private detective to help with the defense," Libby suggested to her father.

"I don't think your friend has the money for that," Sean replied gently.

He started to raise his glass to take another sip of his drink, but it began to slide out of his hand. He hurriedly put it back down on the tray before Bernie and Libby could see what was happening.

God, he hated this. He could feel one of his black

moods descending on him when he saw tears rolling down Libby's cheeks.

"What is it?" Sean asked, his problems suddenly forgotten.

"I shouldn't have called you," she said to her father. "If I hadn't called you, Tiffany wouldn't be in jail now."

Sean made a soothing noise. "You did the right thing."

"Not for Tiffany I didn't," Libby said.

"Bernie and I will do the best we can," Sean told her. What else could he say in the circumstances? "Right, Bernie?"

"Right, Dad."

Libby wiped her eyes with the back of her hand.

"You think there's a chance?" she asked.

"There's always a chance," Sean answered. He closed his eyes. Suddenly he felt exhausted.

"We should go," he heard Libby say.

"No." He couldn't bear the thought of his daughter going off like this. "Just give me a second." A moment later, he opened his eyes to see Libby and Bernie staring at him in concern. "I'm fine," he snapped.

"Like hell you are," Bernie shot back.

He'd never been able to get the last word in with her, he thought. Not even when she was six years old.

He made a supreme effort to clear away the fuzziness in his mind and focus.

"I was thinking," he said to Libby. "Most killers, unless they're professionals, use one M.O., *modus operandi*. So the fact that Tiffany supposedly poisoned one person and shot another might work in our favor."

"I hope you're right," Libby said. "I really do."

"So do I," Sean said. "So do I."

Chapter 25

Libby was in the bathroom brushing her teeth, when her sister came through the door.

"Don't I get any privacy?" Libby asked with her mouth full of toothpaste.

"If you want privacy, close the door. So how was your date with Orion?"

Libby spat and rinsed.

"It wasn't a date," she said when she was done. "We had a drink together."

"And?" Bernie asked as she folded her arms and leaned against the door frame.

"And nothing."

"Don't nothing me. What happened?"

"We had a beer at R.J.'s and split an order of wings."

"And . . ." Bernie made a come-on motion with her hands.

"We went back to his house."

"And?"

"He said, 'This is like old times.' "

Bernie groaned.

"He actually said that?"

Libby nodded.

"And then?"

"We were sitting in the living room and he put his arm around me and kissed me."

"And?"

"And nothing."

"Why not?"

"Oh, Bernie," Libby found herself saying. "I don't know what's wrong with me. I got the worst anxiety attack. Suddenly I had to get out of there."

Bernie patted Libby's shoulder.

"You were right. My advice, for what it's worth, is—don't go to bed with him. At least not for a while."

"I'm not planning on it," Libby said.

"Stay with that thought. Listen, Orion is in the middle of separating from his wife. For all you know, he could go back to Sukie—guys do that kind of thing all the time—and then how would you feel?"

"He doesn't sound as if he's going to."

"You didn't know he was seeing Sukie when he broke off your engagement either," Bernie reminded Libby. "Just tell yourself, the goalie is in place."

Libby crinkled up her face.

"The *what* is in place?"

"The goalie." And Bernie pointed to between her legs. "Get it?"

Libby giggled.

"Don't laugh. I don't want to see you getting hurt twice by the same person. You should be like me and make the same mistake with different people."

Libby grinned.

"You know Dad offered to have him beaten up."

"That's comforting in a peculiar kind of way." Bernie went over to the sink and removed her makeup. Then she reached in the medicine cabinet and took out a jar of moisturizer. "Try this on your face," she said to Libby. "It's got grape seeds and green tea in it."

"Nice," Libby said as she began patting it on her cheeks.

"It should be for what it cost." Bernie took a dab and began working it into her skin. "By the way, have you ever heard of a Rob Sullivan?"

"Tall? Green eyes?"

"That's the one."

"He comes in the store about once a month and buys fried chicken, cole slaw, and chocolate chip cookies."

"What else do you know about him besides his culinary preferences?"

Libby clicked her tongue against the roof of her mouth while she searched her memory.

"Okay," she said when she'd come up with the requisite facts. "He's some kind of writer. He was working on a TV pilot out in L.A., but it got canceled and then his sister got killed in a car crash and he came back to be with his mom. She lives over on Edgemont and sells dolls out of her house. Why do you want to know?"

"Just curious."

"You're never just curious."

Bernie grinned as she put the top back on the jar.

"We're just going to have a drink. I met him today at Geoffrey Holder's place."

Libby rolled her eyes.

"Trust you to discover a corpse and meet a man at the same time."

"It's a talent. By the way, he liked the ginger muffins."

"What's not to like?" Libby observed, but her mind was on something else.

"What are you thinking about?" Bernie asked.

"Well, remember when I told you that Rob was a writer . . ."

"Yes . . ."

"That got me thinking about something Lydia said to me at her house."

Libby stopped and busied herself cleaning out the soap scum in the sink basin. Bernie waited for her sister to continue. A moment later she did.

"Lydia said something about Lionel stealing his idea for his first book—or words to that effect—and I was thinking about what you told me about the book you found at Nigel Herron's house and about him always wanting to be a writer."

"Yes." Bernie leaned forward.

"Well, what if Lionel stole Nigel's idea. What if he stole his character? Think about it," Libby said, warming to her theme. "All that money. All that fame. And it could have been yours. Wouldn't that make you crazy with envy?"

"Envious enough to kill?"

"People have killed for less."

"Granting that, why now? Why after all this time?"

Libby bit on her nail.

"Maybe something happened."

"Like what?"

"I don't know," Libby said. "But I'm going to find out."

"How?"

"You're going to talk to Nigel and I'm going to have another conversation with Lydia."

Bernie began brushing her hair.

"I told you that Nigel was Geoff's stockbroker, right?"

"Right."

"And even though Mary Beth didn't say so, I gathered that things weren't going well."

"What are you saying?"

"I'm saying that Nigel has a connection to the two dead people."

"I don't know. It's hard to see Nigel killing anyone. Maybe boring them to death . . ." Libby looked down at her feet.

Bernie studied her sister.

"What's the matter?" she asked.

Libby began pleating the towel lying on the edge of the sink. A minute later she blurted out, "I keep thinking that this whole thing is my fault."

"Cut it out."

"It is," Libby insisted. "Maybe if I'd talked to Tiffany the first time . . ."

"Stop being like Mom," Bernie told her. "You're not responsible for the ills of the world."

"I never said I was."

"You're right. You didn't. You just act as if you are. And for God's sake, not to mention for the sake of your hips, stop eating all those cookies."

"I know. I know," Libby moaned. "I can't help myself."

"Sure you can," Bernie replied.

"Every time I get upset, I eat."

"Drink martinis instead," Bernie advised. "They have fewer calories."

"No, they don't."

"Oh, yes, they do. I've compared calorie counts. Besides," Bernie continued, "you'll drink fewer martinis than you will eat lemon bars."

"That's because I like lemon bars better than I like martinis."

"My point exactly," Bernie said, stifling a yawn. "Two martinis or a pan of lemon bars. You do the math."

Chapter 26

Okay, Libby. Where are you? Bernie wondered as she reached into the display case and re-centered the sign for the almond croissants. It was a little after eleven, and her sister still wasn't back yet. She hoped Libby had just gone to the Studmeyer farm to get the goat cheese like she'd said she would and hadn't stopped off to talk to Lydia, which she'd promised she wouldn't.

The lunch crowd would be coming in soon, and Bernie didn't feel like dealing with them by herself, although she supposed if worse came to worst, she could drag Amber away from skinning tomatoes out in the kitchen and put her to work waiting on people out front.

Bernie planted her elbows on the top of the display case, never mind that Libby would have a fit if she saw her do it, and watched a woman across the street trying to get a full-grown Newfoundland to heel. Maybe she should get a dog, Bernie mused. A small dog, a very small dog.

Something like a Yorkie maybe, something she could put in a tote bag and carry around with her. She was wondering what her father would say—he hated small dogs. Rats, he called them—when Rob Sullivan walked through the door.

As Bernie straightened up, she cursed herself for not putting on mascara this morning. Without it, she looked as if she had no lashes.

"What are you doing here?" she asked, cringing inwardly when she heard herself.

Wonderful, Bernie. Could you sound any stupider? As Rob smiled, she noticed that in the daylight his eyes were an even deeper green.

It's axiomatic that no one with eyes that color is nice, Bernie warned herself.

And if I'm attracted to him, then he definitely isn't nice even if he seems to be on the surface.

I just haven't discovered what's wrong with him yet, is all.

"I came to get another ginger muffin," Rob told her.

"Really?"

"Yes. Well, not really. I'll take one and some coffee, but I really came to see how you were doing after yesterday."

"And how'd you know I'd be here?"

Rob grinned.

"I'm brilliant."

"Besides that."

"My mom told me."

"That I believe."

"Would you believe that I came around to ask you out for that drink and also to tell you something you might be interested in."

"Such as?"

"Patience. Are you really okay?"

Bernie nodded.

"Because the cops gave you a pretty rough time."

"I'm tough."

"No, you're not. You just like people to think that."

Bernie flushed because what Rob said was true.

"Tell me what you came to say," she told him trying to get the conversation back on track.

"Well, this might be nothing, but I was going through Geoff's desk after the police left and I found a note scribbled on the top page of one of those legal tablets. It said 'Janet? Eight-fifteen?' I called and told the detective in charge of the case, but he didn't seem too interested. He's probably right—it's probably just a random scribble—but I thought you should know. Anyway it gives me another reason to come and see you."

"Do you still have the paper?"

Rob leaned on the counter.

"I sure do."

"Good. I'll relay the information to Tiffany's defense lawyer," Bernie told him, aware of the smell of his aftershave.

"My muffin?" Rob said.

"Oh, yes." Bernie realized she'd been staring at him. "I don't know what's the matter with me this morning." She handed him his ginger muffin and his coffee. "The milk and sugar are over there."

"Did you really bake this?"

"With my own little hands," Bernie said making a mental note to get the recipe from Libby.

"Tonight around eight at R.J.'s?" Rob said.

Bernie nodded. *Remember,* she told herself. *The goalie is in place goes for you too.*

"Eight it is."

She was still staring at him walking down the street and telling herself that meeting him would only lead to the kind of trouble she didn't need when Bree Nottingham breezed into the store.

"Where's Libby?" she demanded.

Bernie pulled herself together.

"She's out doing errands. Can I help you?"

Bree put her lips together in an O of disapproval.

"How inconvenient. When will she be back?"

"Soon, I hope."

Bree indicated the display case.

"Are these cookies all made with butter?"

"Straight from the dairy farm."

"Which one has the fewest calories?"

Bernie thought for a moment. Fortunately, this was knowledge she had at her fingertips.

"The lemon cookies. They have the least amount of shortening in them."

"How many calories would you say they had?"

Bernie pulled a number out of the air.

"Fifty."

"Are you sure?"

"Well, we haven't sent them to the lab for testing, if that's what you mean."

Bernie watched Bree click her tongue against the inside of her cheek while she thought. *Make up your mind,* Bernie wanted to tell her.

"Fine," Bree finally said after agonizing a little longer. "Give me one and don't bother to put it in a bag. I want it for here."

Bernie gave Bree the lemon wafer wrapped in a small sheet of wax paper and watched as she took little bites. A vision of a mouse nibbling on a piece of cheese had jumped into Bernie mind when Bree's cell phone rang. She dug it out of her bag.

"No. No. No," she said into the receiver. "What's the matter with you? I distinctly remember saying ten, not fifteen. You should listen more carefully." And she clicked off. "Honestly," she told Bernie. "Some of the people I have working for me are brain dead." She took another nibble of her cookie. "Nothing is going right these days, and when I'm upset I eat."

What? Bernie wondered. Lettuce leaves and the occasional tomato slice?

"This past week and a half, with everything that's been happening, I must have put on five pounds." Bree took another nibble. "I can't even imagine how much weight Libby's put on, poor dear."

"Actually, she's lost weight," Bernie lied.

"How wonderful! Maybe she'll share her secret with me. It's nice to see that she's doing well."

"Why shouldn't she be?"

"Well, with all that's occurred. She's never been able to handle stress well."

"That's not true."

Bree waved her hand in the air. "It's just that I can't get that vision of Libby being carried from Phys Ed class sobbing and screaming out of my mind. It was so traumatic for me. I can't imagine what it must have been like for her."

"For the last time, she'd taken some of my mother's medicine by mistake and had a bad reaction to it. And she wasn't sobbing and screaming."

Bree smiled sweetly.

"I love the way you defend your sister."

A vision of punching Bree in the mouth flashed through Bernie's mind. *Deep breath,* she told herself. *Deep breath.*

"You know . . ." she began when Bree interrupted.

"Whatever her problems are, I have to say she did a marvelous job at the reunion."

"I'm glad you think so."

Bree took another bite of her cookie.

"And what happened wasn't her fault. I mean how could she know that someone would poison Laird's drinking water? Although in retrospect, perhaps labeling those bottles with his name wasn't the smartest thing she could have done."

Bernie could feel her temper rising again.

"What are you suggesting?"

"Me?" Bree looked amused. "Absolutely nothing. I'm making an observation. It's just that she's just been so invested in Tiffany. Protecting her and everything."

"I hardly think trying to get her legal counsel comes under the heading of protecting. And since when is that a crime?"

As Bree took another nibble of her cookie, Bernie wondered if anyone could eat slower.

"It's not. But I think you ought to know that's not what some people are saying."

"Well, those people are wrong."

"Whatever you say, dear." Bree checked her watch. "Here." She handed the uneaten half of the lemon cookie back to Bernie. "Can you throw this out? It was delicious, but I'm full." Bree shook her head and adjusted an errant lock of hair. "I'm just glad we can put this thing behind us and begin to heal."

"What do you mean?"

Bree flicked an invisible crumb off her yellow silk blouse.

"Well, now that we know who the murderer is. I don't mean to be crass, but it's hard to sell real estate when you've got a murderer running loose, especially a murderer who's killed two of Longely's most upstanding citizens.

"Something like this plays hell with property values. People don't want to buy, and I can't say I blame them, when they can purchase in the next town and not be afraid for their lives."

"Haven't you heard of the old saying about being innocent until proven guilty? The case against Tiffany is circumstantial."

Bernie watched Bree reach into her black microfiber Prada tote and come out with a tube of lip gloss and a mirror.

"I'm sorry. I thought you heard. Tiffany confessed."

"What?" Bernie cried.

"Early this morning. Call Paul Pine and check if you want to," Bree said. "He'll tell you."

"I'm going to." And Bernie reached for the phone.

Chapter 27

"Just a minute." Libby pulled the van over to the side of the road and put it in park. She was too upset by what her sister was telling her to drive and talk. "Bree Nottingham is lying," she said into her cell.

"Unfortunately, she isn't," Bernie told her.

"But Tiffany couldn't have confessed. I don't believe you."

"I didn't believe it either, but she did."

"Then Lucy forced her to."

"I don't think so."

"You don't know for sure."

"Paul said she looked okay—well, as okay as she was going to look given the circumstances. He got a call from Tiffany around nine-thirty this morning asking him to come down to the jail. When he got there, she told him she wanted him to negotiate a deal."

"There has to be some kind of mistake," Libby cried.

"Mistake or not, I just thought you should know before you hear it on the news."

"The news?" Libby repeated stupidly.

"It was on the radio already. By tomorrow it'll be every-where. This is a big story."

Libby could hear the impatience in Bernie's voice. She

lowered the phone and clutched it to her chest. She could hear her sister saying, "Libby, Libby. Are you okay?"

"I'm fine," she said, and she pressed the off button and dropped the phone into her bag.

She knew that would make Bernie mad, but she didn't want to talk to her right now. She didn't want to talk to anyone—anyone except Tiffany, that is.

"Why did she do it?" she asked out loud. She rubbed the corners of her mouth with two of her fingers and shook her head. "Great. Now I'm talking to myself."

Without thinking she reached over and took one of the brown sugar snaps she was bringing to Lydia and ate it. The taste of brown sugar melting on her tongue helped clear the fog in her head, and after a second cookie she knew what she had to do. Libby drove over to the police station with her foot on the gas pedal, ignoring the van's shimmying.

"Tough," she said to the vehicle. "It won't hurt you to go over fifty miles an hour for once."

Libby wanted an explanation for Tiffany's action and she wanted one now. Ten minutes later, she was at the police station. She parked in front of the *Do Not Park. Offical Business Only* sign and ran inside the building. The place had been an old feed store that the town had converted to a police station fifty years ago. Normally, Libby liked its rustic air, but today she didn't notice. She charged through the doors and went straight over to Clyde.

"I want to speak to Tiffany," she demanded.

Clyde looked up from the paper lying on his desk.

"Now, Libby," he said. "I'm sorry, but you know I can't do that. She can only see her lawyer or members of her family."

"She doesn't have any family members here. They're down in Arkansas someplace."

"Then she needs to have a delegate appointed."

"Come on, Clyde," Libby pleaded. "You've known me all my life."

"If it were just me, I would. You know that." Clyde grinned apologetically and fiddled with his shoestring tie. "But the boss . . ."

"Screw the boss."

"Libby, I have to follow my orders. You of all people should realize that. Please don't make a scene."

At which point Libby became aware that an officer, someone she didn't know, had magically appeared and taken up residence by the door that led to the cells.

"But she didn't do it."

"She says she did, and even if she didn't, I still can't let you see her. This one is going by the numbers."

"I need to talk to her. Please."

Clyde put his elbows on the table and rested his chin on his hands.

"If I were you, I'd go talk to her lawyer and see if he can arrange something for you 'cause that's the only way you're getting in the back."

"So you're not going to let me speak to her."

"I think that's safe to assume," Clyde replied as the other officer moved forward. "You're a smart girl. Why don't you leave and let us go on with our business."

"Fine."

Libby turned on heels and marched towards the door.

"Give my regards to your dad," Clyde called after her.

"Give them to him yourself," Libby tossed over her shoulder as she went out the door.

She shouldn't have gone charging in there like that, she told herself as she got in the van and slammed the door. If she were Bernie, she would have charmed her way in and could be talking to Tiffany right now. But not her. Oh, no. She always had to do things the hard way. And on that note, Libby picked up the phone, dialed Paul Pine's office, and asked for his secretary.

*   *   *

Libby paused at the entrance to the lounge of the Longely Country Club and studied the interior. It looked the same as it had the last time she'd been there seven years ago, all knotty pine and colonial furniture. Even though it was sunny outside, it was dark in the lounge, so it took Libby a minute to spot Paul Pine. He was sitting at the far end of the room looking out the window.

Okay, Libby said to herself as she strode towards him. *Channel Bernie. Be nice. Be charming. Bat your eyelashes and say something like, Oh Paul, I'm so upset. Can you help me? I don't know what to do.*

"How could you?" Libby blurted out instead when she reached him.

What is wrong with me? Why can't I ever say the right thing? Libby wondered as Paul looked up. He took a sip of beer from the stein he was holding and put it down on the table.

"I take it you're talking about Tiffany?" he asked.

"Why else would I be here?"

Paul gestured to the seat next to him.

"Sit down. Can I get you something to drink?"

Libby took a deep breath and let it out.

"Thank you, but I prefer to stand."

"Please," Paul said, indicating the chair on his right.

Libby reluctantly sat in it.

"Soda?" Paul asked. "A beer? Tea? Coffee?"

Libby balled her hands into fists to keep herself from saying something awful.

"I just want to know what happened."

She watched Paul take another sip of his beer and grab a handful of peanuts from the dish on the table and pop them in his mouth one at a time.

"I can see that you're very upset."

"That doesn't even begin to cover it," Libby replied.

Paul sighed and rubbed his chin with his knuckle.

"Tiffany called me up this morning and asked me to come down, so I did, even though technically someone else in my firm has been assigned to her case. When I walked into her cell, she told me she wanted to confess to both murders." He held up his hand before Libby could speak. "Let me finish before you say anything.

"Naturally, I asked her if she'd been coerced into doing this, and she stated that she hadn't been, that she was doing it of her own free will. And, I'm going to add, that I didn't see any bruises on her. We discussed it for a while, but she was pretty resolute." Paul took another sip of his beer. "And, frankly, I have to say, in my professional opinion, she would be better pleading out. The evidence against her is largely circumstantial, but there's a lot of it and it's pretty damning."

He ticked it off on his fingers. "Tiffany's fight with Laird Wrenn in front of the Dairy Queen, her showing up in the cafeteria kitchen the night of the reunion dinner, her running away from the police. None of that looks good, and I'm not even mentioning her possession of the gun that killed Geoffrey Holder, let alone her lack of an alibi for that event."

"But all of that can be explained," Libby cried.

Paul folded his arms over his chest.

"Maybe it can be. But personally I wouldn't want to have to face the jury with her case." Paul looked at his watch. "Anyway, I called up the prosecutor at home and asked him what he could do for her if she pled out and he said he'd talk to his people and let me know. He came back with twenty- to life, which is pretty good considering that she's up for murder one on two homicides. I relayed the offer to Tiffany. She asked me what I thought, and I told her she should take it and she agreed."

"But she didn't do it."

Paul leaned over, took another peanut out of the bowl, and ate it.

"I'm sure I don't need to remind you of the old chestnut of not confusing justice with the law. What I do want to ask you is, if she's innocent, why did she confess? She wasn't beaten. She wasn't questioned for twenty-four hours straight. What motive would she have?"

"I don't know. That's why I want to talk to her."

Paul leaned back. Libby watched him study her face. "Would you feel better if you could?" he finally asked.

"Yes. Absolutely."

"All right then."

Paul took out his cell.

"Who you going to call?"

"Your father's arch enemy."

"He'll never let me in."

"Trust me. He will." Paul popped another peanut in his mouth and punched in the numbers.

"Why would he do that?"

"Quid pro quo, dear. Quid pro quo." Then he gestured to Libby to be quiet. "I'm doing this as a favor to your dad," he said after he clicked off. "Lucy will let you have ten minutes with her."

Libby got out of the chair and impulsively went over and hugged Paul.

"Thanks so much."

Paul waved his hand in the air.

"Forget it. It's nothing. But now you can do me a favor. I'm having a surprise birthday for my wife next month. Could you cater it? I really love those little crab cakes of yours."

Libby nodded distractedly.

"Just give me a call and we'll discuss the menu."

"Thanks." Paul took another sip of his beer. "You know," he told her, "it's none of my business, but you'd be a lot happier if you'd stop taking everything to heart."

"Tell me how to do that and I will," Libby shot back. Then she got up and left.

The parking lot had filled up in the twenty minutes Libby had been talking to Paul, but she didn't have any trouble spotting her van. It stood out like a poor relation in the sea of Beamers, Saabs, Ford Explorers, and Range Rovers.

"I love you anyway," she told it, patting the dashboard, "even if you are old and rusty and dented." She was turning the key in the ignition when she realized she'd better call Bernie and fill her in on what was happening.

"Nice of you to let me know," Bernie commented after Libby was done.

"Well, I'm sorry, but you're not the only one who gets upset."

"We need you back at the store."

"I'll be there as soon as I can."

"You'd better be."

"I said I *will*. Don't you care about Tiffany?" Libby demanded.

"Of course I do. But she's not going anywhere, and I have people lining up five deep in front of the counter. I hope you got the goat cheese because I'm running out."

"Don't worry," Libby said looking at the package on the front seat of her van and wondering how long the cheese could stay there without being refrigerated. "I picked it up."

"Can you at least come by and drop it off?"

"No. I can't. I have to go see Tiffany. They're transferring her to the county lockup. This is going to be my last chance."

"Libby," Bernie said. "It'll take you five minutes. I need it."

"Use the mozzarella or the cheddar."

"How can you say that? They're not at all alike."

"The hallmark of a great cook is making do."

"Screw that. Bring the cheese by."

"Sorry. No can do," Libby responded and she clicked her cell off before Bernie could say anything else. All she wanted to do was talk to Tiffany.

Chapter 28

It had taken Libby thirty minutes to get to the Longely Country Club from the town jail. It took her fifteen minutes to get back.

Cyde jerked his head towards the back when Libby came in.

"She's in there. Go on through. You've got ten minutes. Tops."

Libby opened the door leading to the jail cells and stepped inside. The space had been added on when the town council had decided to use the feed store for the police station. The three cells looked the way they had when her father had brought her here when he used to baby-sit her before her mother found out and put a stop to it.

Actually, she'd rather enjoyed playing in the cells with her dolls, although she'd never told her horrified mother that. She'd pretend she was locked away in a tower waiting for her prince to come rescue her. Anyway, it wasn't as if she was playing next to murderers and robbers. The cells were usually empty except for the occasional drunk or speeder and even that was pretty rare. As she walked towards Tiffany, she couldn't help thinking about what her father used to say to her mother from time to time over dinner.

"I'll tell you one thing, Rose," he'd say as he cut himself a piece of pot roast. "Justice may be blind, but it can tell who has money and who doesn't. At least it can in this town."

Libby wondered if that was what had happened here as she took Tiffany's hands through the bars of the cell. They felt cold, even though it was as warm in the building as it was outside. Libby noticed that Tiffany had washed and combed her hair and was wearing a fresh pair of jeans and a clean T-shirt, but she had deep circles under her eyes and blotches of red around her nose and on her cheeks. It looked as if her roseacea was acting up.

"I'm sorry," Tiffany told her. "You shouldn't have come."

"Of course I should come," Libby protested. "I'm your friend."

"Maybe it would be better if you weren't. All I've done is cause you trouble."

"That's not true."

Tiffany freed her hands from Libby's grasp and hugged herself. Her eyes misted over.

"Yes, it is," she said as tears trickled down her cheeks.

Libby could feel tears welling up in her eyes as well.

"Don't be silly," she said, brushing them away with the back of her hand. "Tell me why you're doing this."

"Doing what?"

"Confessing."

Tiffany sniffed.

"Because I did it."

"I don't believe you."

"I'm telling you the truth."

"No, you're not," Libby said. "You know you're a lousy liar. I can always tell when you're lying. You waffle, and you're waffling now."

"Why would I confess to something like this if I didn't do it?"

"I don't know. That's what I'm asking you."

"Libby, leave it alone," Tiffany cried. "Everyone has spent too much time on me already."

"That's really a stupid thing to say."

Tiffany shook her head.

"No, it's not. You know everything I've done in my life has ended badly. I'm barely making a living out of the shop. I owe money. I can't deal with the calls anymore. I've let Laird make a fool out of me. Who would want to marry me now? No one. I'll never have any children. Geez, I can't even keep a plant alive. I buy them and then forget to water them." The tears fell faster. Tiffany dabbed at them with a Kleenex. "I'm tired of struggling. I'm tired of everything."

"Okay," Libby said. "Let me get this straight. You're confessing because you want a rest? How about going to a spa?"

Tiffany smiled through her tears.

"Now you're sounding like Bernie."

"Yeah, I guess I am," Libby agreed. "But I'm right."

Tiffany patted Libby's hand.

"Will you come visit me in prison?"

"No. Because you're not going to be there."

"Libby, drop it," Tiffany warned.

"No."

"This is my decision."

"Well it's a rotten one."

"I don't care if you agree with it or not. It's done."

"Not if I have anything to say about it," Libby replied grimly.

"It's too late."

"We'll see about that."

"I want you to stay out of my life," Tiffany cried.

"I don't think so. You can't invite me in and then kick me out."

"Let me alone."

"No."

"I'm going to tell Mr. Pine I don't want to see you anymore."

"You do that." And Libby turned and headed for the door.

Clyde looked up as she walked by him.

"Didn't go well, did it?" he asked.

Libby shook her head.

"Didn't think it would."

Clyde reached out and offered her a stick of gum. "Here. Take it. It'll make you feel better."

Libby doubted it, but she accepted anyway, grateful for the kind gesture.

"How's your dad doing?" Clyde asked.

Libby shrugged. "I think he'd do better if he went out once in a while."

Clyde nodded. "Expect he would. Well, tell him I said hello. You know the best thing about your daddy?" Clyde asked.

Libby shook her head.

"He always fought for what he believed in."

Libby smiled at Clyde. "Thanks," she said. "I really appreciate that."

Chapter 29

By the time Libby got back to the store, the lunch crowd had abated.

"Nice of you to drop in," Bernie told her sister. She was about to say something more about Libby's manifest lack of consideration for other people but when she looked at the expression on Libby's face as she marched into the kitchen, Bernie's anger vanished. "Is that the goat cheese?" she asked as Libby put a white package into the fridge.

Libby nodded. "I hope it's all right. It's been sitting out in the van all this time."

"It'll be fine," Bernie reassured her. "Cheese is just curdled milk. So it'll be a little more curdled, that's all. Big deal. It'll taste a little tangier. Besides if it's really bad, I'll run out and get more.

"You know," she mused. "It's interesting. Up until fifteen years ago, I don't think anyone knew what goat cheese was. Or if they did, they turned up their noses at it. Now it's one of the biggest sellers on the market. What do you think accounted for the change? California Cuisine? Marketing?"

"Oh, Bernie," Libby said, turning and flinging herself into her sister's arms. "This is so awful. I just can't stand it."

"I know," Bernie said as she stroked her hair. "I know."

"It's like Tiffany just decided to give up."

"Maybe you should too," Bernie said gently.

"I can't." Libby pushed herself away from her sister. "She's my friend. I have to do something."

Bernie slid her silver and onyx ring up and down her finger while she thought. Should she tell Libby what Rob had told her or not? That was the question. The note he'd found on Geoff Holder's pad probably meant nothing. And the case was closed.

If she told Libby, it would just give her something else to hang on to when she should be letting go. On the other hand, if the note did mean something, Bernie would never forgive herself. She tapped her ring on her teeth.

"What are you thinking?" Libby asked.

"I'm thinking Amber can mind the store for a minute while we go up and talk to Dad."

"Why?"

"Because we could use some advice."

Sean listened to what Bernie had to say without comment.

"That note Holder wrote to himself probably doesn't mean anything," he said when she was done. "It just gives the time, not the date. The date could refer to last April for all we know."

"But what if it refers to the day Geoff Holder was killed?" Libby asked. "What if Janet was there?"

Sean turned to Libby.

"So what if she was? Last I heard, being around someone isn't a crime. Maybe she wanted an opinion on detailing her car. Maybe Janet and Geoff were discussing funds for the new playground."

"Janet doesn't have children."

"You know what I mean," Sean snapped. "Not to mention the fact that it could be a different Janet. I wouldn't even want to speculate on how many are in the phone book."

"Yes. But Janet is Nigel's girlfriend, and Nigel is linked to both victims."

"Circumstantially."

"Circumstantial was enough for Lucy to take Tiffany into custody."

"Granted," Sean said. "But before we get into that," he told his elder daughter, "there are some fundamental questions that have to be addressed."

"Like what?"

"Like whether or not you have a right to interfere in your friend's life, for openers. She has specifically asked you to leave this alone."

"Would *you* let someone commit suicide?" Libby demanded.

"This isn't quite the same thing."

"If throwing twenty years of your life away isn't suicide, I don't know what is."

Sean wheeled his chair over to the window and looked out. He could see the pansies in his neighbor's window box. His wife had always had a big basket of them sitting on the bench in front of the store. He wondered why Libby had switched to geraniums.

"Let me ask you another question, Libby," he said after a moment had gone by. "Why is Tiffany doing this if she isn't guilty?"

"Because she's depressed. She's overwhelmed. She needs psychiatric care, not jail."

"Even if what you say is true, she's legally sane. Her decision holds in a court of law."

"I'm aware of that," Libby replied. "That's why we have to find the real murderer or at least some piece of evidence that points in a different direction that we can give to Paul."

Sean continued looking out the window.

"What do you say, Bernie?" he asked.

"We did promise."

"The situation has changed."

"I still think I should go down to Janet's shop and see if she's got anything new in."

"And she needs more clothes anyway," Libby added.

"She always needs clothes," Sean said. "What are you going to say when you get there?"

"Well, I'm not going to charge in and ask her if she was at Holder's place the day he was killed, if that's what you mean," Bernie said. "I just figured I'd go in and chat and see what develops. I'm always amazed at what people will tell you."

"I'm always amazed at what they won't," Sean shot back.

"That's because you come across as scary and I come across as nice," Bernie replied sweetly.

"And I could go collect the pot I left at Nigel's," Libby added.

"You're going to go into the home of someone you're telling me might be the prime suspect in two murders?" her father asked.

"He's not home," Libby reminded Sean. "He's at work in the city."

"How are you going to get in?" Bernie asked her.

"He gave me his key for the party," Libby said. "And with everything that's going on, he forgot to ask for it back and I forget to return it."

"This doesn't sound like a good idea to me," Sean said.

"You'd do it too if you were me," Libby insisted.

"Nothing you find is going to be admissible in court," Sean warned her.

"I know that," Libby said. "But at least this will give us a direction to focus on."

Sean tried again.

"Technically, what you're doing is illegal."

"Don't tell me you've never bent the rules in an investigation," Libby retorted.

"That's not the point," Sean argued.

"Dad. I'm an adult. Let me make my own decisions. Please."

Sean sighed. Much as he hated to admit it, what Libby said was true.

"Just don't get caught."

"I won't," Libby told him. "I promise."

"I'm glad that's settled," Bernie said as she lifted her right leg, bent it at the knee, grabbed her ankle with her right hand and pulled it toward the back of her thigh. Then she balanced on her left leg and raised her right arm.

Libby pointed to her sister's leg.

"Can I ask why are you doing that?"

"It's one of my Yoga exercises," Bernie said, switching to the other leg as their father wheeled his chair around. "It helps the flow of Chi."

"Chi?" Libby repeated.

"Energy."

"It also stretches out the hamstrings," Sean informed her. Then he said to Bernie, "Do you have any of that rhubarb-strawberry pie Libby made this morning left?"

She gave him a puzzled look.

"Last time I looked we had four pieces. Why?"

"What about some ice cream?"

"We have a couple of quarts of vanilla left. I made it yesterday," Libby volunteered. "It's got real specks of vanilla in it."

"Good," Sean said. "Run down and pull the pie out of the display case and put aside a pint or so of the ice cream."

"Am I missing something here?" Bernie demanded.

"You'll see," Sean told her. "Hand me the phone."

A mystified Libby did.

"I'm going to call Clyde Schiller and invite him over. He's a sucker for your pie."

"He'd come without the pie," Libby said. "You know he wants to see you."

"Well, I'd feel better if I had something to offer him." Sean coughed. "The deal is this: I gave my word and I intend to keep it. So we'll poke around a little more, and if we find anything that's germane to Tiffany's case—and yes, Bernie," Sean said before his daughter could, "I know the word germane comes from the Latin and means akin. That's one of the positives about going to parochial school and having to take Latin."

He cleared his throat.

"Anyway, as I was saying before I got sidetracked, we'll proceed as far as we can and if we don't find anything, Libby, you have to promise me that you'll put this thing to bed."

"I will," Libby said. "I swear I won't say anything about Tiffany ever again."

"I'm going to hold you to your word," Sean warned her.

"I know."

"Scout's honor?"

"Scout's honor," Libby replied gravely even though she'd never been a Brownie much less a Girl Scout.

"Good. It's settled," Sean said.

Besides, he thought, looking at his daughter, who was beaming at him, if anything comes of this, which he doubted, it would be fun seeing Lucy and the current prosecutor look like fools.

"Here," Bernie told Janet as she handed her a raspberry scone. "I brought this for you."

She looked tired, Bernie thought as Janet thanked her. As if she hadn't been sleeping well. Guilty conscience or indigestion? Hopefully, she'd find out soon enough.

"Thanks," Janet replied and she took a bite. "These are so good."

"It's the cream," Bernie said. "It makes them tender."

"How can something that tastes so good be so bad for you?"

Bernie laughed.

"You're behind the times. Fat is good for you again. Someone I worked for out in L.A. used to say, 'If it's not fat, it's not food.' "

"Amen to that," Janet said. "Although I'm not sure my hips and ass would agree."

Bernie patted her rump.

"Mine either," she said as she began walking through the store. She stopped in front of a pale blue leather jacket and whistled appreciatively. "Nice," she said to Janet.

"Nice? It's great. It's summer weight. Really light. Feel the leather. I've sold three of them since they came in last week. This is the last one left."

"Lucky for me you're out of my size," Bernie said. "Not that I could afford it anyway. Eight hundred dollars is a little more than I can lay out at the moment."

Janet walked over to a row of skirts and picked one out. "How about this?" And she held up a silvery colored wrap skirt. "Seventy-five bucks. Wear it with a black or white T-shirt for the day or put on a tank top for the evening and you're good to go."

"I'll try it on." Bernie said thinking of her date with Rob tonight. "So," she continued as she walked into the dressing room and slipped off her jeans and put on the skirt. "What do you think about Tiffany?"

"I think it's awful. Come out and let me see how it looks. Not bad," Janet said when Bernie walked out onto the floor. "Not bad at all."

Bernie studied her reflection in the mirror.

"No, it isn't, is it?"

"It's great. Here. Put this on." And Janet handed her a light green and blue scooped-neck sweater.

Bernie slipped it over her T-shirt.

"How's Nigel?"

Janet shook her head.

"I'd like to kill him."

Bernie raised an eyebrow.

Janet tittered and put her hand to her mouth.

"That was an unfortunate phrase, wasn't it? But I'm just so frustrated."

"Why?" Bernie prompted, striving to look casually interested.

"I probably shouldn't say anything, but what the hell. Nigel's been drinking ever since Lionel was killed, and now that this thing happened with Geoff . . . he's gone over the edge."

"I didn't think they were friends."

"Not good friends. But when you know people since high school and two of them get killed . . . well . . . it makes you feel kinda vulnerable. Especially in a place like this. I mean half the time I forget to lock my door at night. The whole thing is weird."

"Very."

Janet started chewing on one of her cuticles.

"I don't know what to think anymore. All I do know is that Nigel's going through half a bottle of Scotch a night. He wasn't this upset when his father died. Well, he wasn't upset at all about that as far as I can tell, but that's a different matter."

Janet worried her cuticle some more.

"Frankly, I don't know what to do. He just drinks and sits at his computer and stares at the blank screen. I suggested he go see someone, since he obviously needs counseling, and he told me to fuck off."

"Charming," Bernie said, thinking of Joe.

"Isn't it, though? He won't let me help him. He bites my head off whenever I say anything. If I ask him if he wants to eat in or go out, he tells me not to bother him. He's borderline abusive. I hate to do this but I'm about ready to tell him that I'll see him when he's gotten himself back under control.

"And that's another thing about Nigel. He's got these trust issues. He never talks to me about his day or what he's been doing or anything like that. I know he's been having a problem at work, but I don't have the slightest idea what it is. I thought I could deal with it, but now I'm not so sure."

Janet sighed.

"At least he was smart enough to stay out of that amusement park deal, unlike some other people around here. But if he keeps going this way, he's going to lose his job, and given the way the stock market is performing I don't think he'll get another one anytime soon."

"What do you mean?" Bernie asked.

"I mean keep not showing up at the office and you're going to get fired."

"He's home now?"

"Yes. Probably sleeping, the creep."

"Sleeping?" Bernie repeated, sure that Janet had noticed the note of alarm in her voice, but then realizing that she didn't as she kept on talking.

"Yeah. Last night, he called me at two in the morning drunk as hell wanting to read some of the new book he's been working on to me. So he could get my opinion. He's been doing that for the last four nights. Then, of course, I can't get back to sleep, so I've been going downstairs and clicking on the Home Shopping Network.

"The day before yesterday I almost bought a jade bracelet," Janet exclaimed. "I'm so tired I don't even hear my alarm when it goes off in the morning." She pointed to her face. "I mean look at these circles under my eyes. I look like crap and don't bother to tell me that I don't. I can't go around getting four hours of sleep a night. I need to come in every morning and open up the store."

"I hear you," Bernie said as she slipped off the sweater. "Here," she said handing it to Janet.

"You don't want it?"

"No. I do." Bernie hurried towards the changing room.

A moment later she re-emerged, skirt in hand. She gave it to Janet as well.

"I'll come by and pay for the sweater and the skirt later."

"Anything the matter?" Janet asked.

"Nothing. I just forgot to turn the water under the potatoes off," Bernie told her as she headed for the door.

Libby, she prayed as she hit the street, *for once have your cell on.*

Chapter 30

"Glad you could drop by," Sean said to Clyde Schiller as Amber set a tray filled with plates, napkins, silverware, a bowl of vanilla ice cream, and almost half a rhubarb-strawberry pie on the table between them.

Clyde leaned forward and rubbed his hands together.

"You did me a favor callin' like you did. Otherwise I'd be spending the afternoon cleaning out the garage."

Amber straightened up.

"Need anything else, Mr. S?" she asked.

Sean shook his head.

"This will be fine."

"Well, ring if you do. I'm just downstairs." And she left the room.

"Nice girl," Clyde said as her footsteps sounded on the steps.

"Very," Sean agreed. "Libby's lucky to get her."

"You know I tried coming over here before, Cap," Clyde said. "A couple of times, but Libby said you weren't seeing anyone. Called too, but the woman that answered the phone said you weren't taking any calls either. Figured you'd ring me up when you were ready."

Sean shrugged. He wasn't going to explain himself to Clyde or to anyone else for that matter.

" 'Cause," Clyde continued. "I might be doing the same thing myself in your position. Want me to dish out the pie?"

"Please," Sean said and watched as Clyde put one slice on his plate and another on Sean's and added a scoop of ice cream to each.

He put one of the plates in front of Sean and the other in front of himself.

"Go ahead," Sean said, wondering if his hand would shake if he picked up the fork. "Eat."

"After you," Clyde said.

Sean took a deep breath and prayed. Then he picked up the fork and cut into his piece. It was okay.

Clyde nodded and began to eat. Sean watched him convey a piece of the pie to his mouth.

"Good stuff," Clyde said after he swallowed.

"The best," Sean agreed.

"As good as your wife's," Clyde observed.

"It's her recipe," Sean said, putting his fork down. Eating in front of people was exhausting. He couldn't stand the idea of spilling food down his shirt, so he didn't eat with people anymore if he could help it.

Clyde took another bite.

"I love my wife, but she can't cook worth shit. Must be nice to have someone around who can."

"I ain't denying it," Sean agreed.

"Where'd Libby get the rhubarb?"

"Mackenzie's market."

"The wife shops there." Clyde shook his head. "I swear I don't know what it is she does to make things taste so bad. Fortunately, she's planning to hire a cook for the bed and breakfast we're gonna open. Otherwise we'd be out of business in a month." He took a spoonful of ice cream. "Mmm," he said, savoring the taste. "Libby was pretty upset yesterday, I can tell you that."

"She still is."

"I felt bad telling her she couldn't see Tiffany."

Sean sighed. "You were just doing your job."

"Yeah. But like you used to say, Cap, that don't make it any easier." Clyde ate another three bites of pie. "Good crust," he allowed.

"Libby puts an egg in it along with the butter. I think that makes all the difference."

"Well, for sure it's not a bad thing." And Clyde polished off the rest of his slice. "You should have seen Lucy's face when he got off the phone with Paul. It was a rare treat, I don't mind telling you. You woulda loved it."

"I'm sure I would have," Sean agreed, sorry that he'd missed the sight.

Clyde shook his head and absentmindedly wiped the corners of his mouth with his thumb and pointer finger.

"Poor Libby. Must be hard seeing your friend admit to something like that. Kinda pulls the rug out from under ya."

"I imagine so," Sean said.

"Mind if I help myself to another piece of pie?" Clyde asked.

"That's what it's here for."

Clyde leaned over and carefully conveyed another slice to his plate.

"She always was the sensitive type," Clyde reflected. "Just like her mom."

"Unfortunately," Sean said. God knows he'd tried to toughen Libby up, but it had been like trying to toughen up his wife's shih tzu.

"Maybe cookin' good and being like that are related," Clyde speculated. "Though one of my uncles was a good cook, and he was one of the meanest sonofabitches that ever lived."

"If you like, I can have Libby run a pie over to your place," Sean offered.

Clyde bit his lip.

"I don't know."

"She's making four of them a day. A fifth won't be any trouble. And local strawberry season is gonna be over soon," Sean reminded him. "Make this with California berries and it ain't the same."

"I know. It's just that some people might think . . ."

Sean made a dismissive noise.

"What? Now you're not allowed to eat?"

Clyde patted his stomach. "That's never been my problem." Then he cut into his new slice of pie. " 'Cause," he reflected, "Lucy wouldn't be too happy if he found out I was visiting you either. Not that he could do anything about it. Paying a social call on my old boss ain't a crime, at least it ain't yet."

And he ate another bite. Sean watched him. When Clyde had eaten a second and a third, he looked up.

"Remember that guy Duffy we had in the cell maybe eight years ago?" Clyde said.

"How could I forget?" Sean said. "It was the highest profile case we ever handled."

"Well, I got to talking to Martin, the psychiatrist, after it came out that Duffy hadn't killed that woman and her kids after all. You know, I asked him why Duffy had come forward and confessed to the homicide and then to top it off grabbed the gun out of the deputy's holster and got himself shot if he hadn't done anything, and he told me he thought he'd just lost hope and this was a suicide by cop."

Sean rested his hands on the wheels of his chair.

"A woman who gets the wind knocked out of her 'cause she just found out the man she's been figuring on marrying for the last seventeen is going off to marry some fashion model might be inclined to do something similar. She might feel she's got nothing left in her life."

"She might," Clyde agreed. "Especially if she doesn't have too much going for her anywhere else in her life. A couple of years ago she dyed my wife's hair brown when she was supposed to turn it red."

Sean gestured with his chin. "Have a little more ice cream. It'll melt if you don't."

"And it would sure be a shame to waste."

"It sure would be. Libby gets her vanilla beans from Madagascar."

Clyde took another spoonful.

"My mother used to bury a vanilla bean in the confectioner's sugar. I used to love the way that smelled."

Sean smiled. "Mine did that too. Now, is there anything else you can't tell me?"

"Well, if I was poking around, I might want to be poking in Lydia's direction."

"And why's that?"

"My wife tells me she had a thing going with Geoffrey Holder."

Libby inserted the key in the lock of the back door of Nigel Herron's house and turned it. It clicked and she stepped into the back hall. Normally, she wouldn't have given a thought to being in someone else's house. People gave her keys to their places all the time so she could come in and get things ready.

But this was different. She wasn't here to unload supplies and do prep work. This was breaking and entering. Well, not really. It was more like unlawful entry because she did have a key. She shook her head. She'd better be careful. Bernie was rubbing off on her.

Maybe this wasn't such a good idea, after all, she decided as she walked through the kitchen. Why was she looking for that book anyway? It probably wasn't important. It was just that Nigel had made such a fuss about being a writer, and from what Bernie had said, his book sounded an awful lot like Lionel's style.

It was probably just coincidence, Libby thought. But she'd already gone online and ordered a copy of Lionel's— excuse her, Laird's—first book. She was having it overnighted too so she could compare them, and she couldn't do that if she didn't have a copy of each. If they were the same, then Nigel could have a motive for killing Lionel. Years of festering resentment? It could work as well as anything else.

One thing was clear, she decided as she headed up the stairs. She'd never make a good cat burglar. She just didn't have the nerves for it. Nothing seemed to bother Bernie, but everything always bothered her. Bernie had nerves of steel, and hers were liked overcooked linguini.

It was something she really hated about herself, she thought as she tried to remember which bedroom Bernie had said the book was in. Not that it necessarily had to be there now. Maybe she should have checked the study first.

Okay, Libby she told herself. *Let's just calm down. This whole thing was your idea. No one else's. If you can cater a sit-down dinner for thirty people with five hours' notice, you can do this. Prioritize. As long as you're up here, do the bedrooms first and then check the rest of the house. You're going to do this quickly, quietly, and efficiently. Geoffrey is at work. No one is here. If anyone sees the van, you'll just tell them you came to collect a pot you left behind from the dinner party.*

Thank God, her mother couldn't see what she was doing, Libby thought as she entered the first room. This was a woman who, all the time she'd been alive, had never gotten so much as a parking ticket and now her daughter was engaged in a bit of unlawful entry. It was for a good cause—although according to her mother, the ends never justified the means.

"It's the devil's own path," she'd always said. And she'd never liked Tiffany. "What do you see in her?" her mother had asked. "She's only going to get you into trouble." Looked like she'd been right, Libby thought, but then she could never remember a time when her mother hadn't been.

As Libby started going through the first room, she couldn't help thinking of what Amber had said when they'd been serving dinner here about a serial killer being loose. After all, if Tiffany hadn't killed two people, and she hadn't, that meant that the person who killed Lionel and Geoff Holder was still around.

And what was worse was that it obviously wasn't some stranger who had done it, it was someone Libby knew. Someone who probably came into the store every day. The thought flashed in Libby's head like a neon sign.

No. No, she told herself as she began to hear the background music to the Jason movies playing in her head. *Do not go there. This is not a productive line of thought at all.* Libby bit her lip and tried to focus on the room.

Ten minutes later she'd ascertained that the book was not there. At least, Libby thought as she walked back into the hallway, Nigel's house was neat and there didn't seem to be too much stuff in it. If he were like Bernie, it would take her five hours instead of ten minutes to look through a room.

Then Libby remembered she wasn't wearing gloves. She'd left her fingerprints all over everything. Geez. Now she'd have to go and wipe everything down. If she could remember what she'd touched. She was trying to recall exactly what her father had said about which surfaces absorb prints and which don't when she walked into the second room, took one look, and shrieked.

Nigel Herron was standing there, and he didn't have any clothes on.

He clasped his hands over his genitals and gasped, "What the hell are you doing here?"

Libby smiled weakly.

"Ah," she stammered. "Looking for a pot?"

Chapter 31

So what they say about nose size being a good indicator of other things is true, Libby thought as she tried to concentrate on the more important matters at hand.

Like how she was going to explain this.

And then something else occurred to her as she watched Nigel back up towards his bed, something she really didn't want to think about. Like maybe she wasn't going to get the opportunity to explain.

Like suppose he really had killed Lionel and Geoff. Why not kill her as well? It was the logical thing to do. Her father would never forgive her if that happened.

Libby knew she should get out of there, but for some reason her legs had lost their ability to move. This was what people must mean when they say they're paralyzed with fear, she realized.

She could only stand and watch Nigel as he reached the side of his bed and then bent down. Libby put her hands over her mouth. *Oh, my God,* she thought. *He's got a gun under the dust ruffle. He's going to kill me.*

"Don't shoot!" she screamed.

Nigel straightened up. He was holding a black sheet in front of him.

"Shoot you?" he repeated incredulously. "What are you? Crazy?" Nigel said.

Relief coursed through Libby's body.

"That's exactly what I am. Crazy. And I am so sorry about it," she said, taking a step back. She could move again. Thank God. She began backing away. "I have to go back into therapy. Immediately. It's all the cream cheese icing I just ate. Way too much sugar. It makes me nuts. Always has. Really. Some people can't drink, I can't eat sugar."

Shut up, Libby, she thought, but she kept chattering on.

"Did you know that I'm hypoglycemic—or is it hyperglycemic? I always get those two mixed up. Now, if you don't mind, I think I'll be going. I need to lie down or take a Valium or get a shock treatment or something."

"I mind your leaving very much," Nigel said as he wound the sheet around himself. "I demand an explanation for this intrusion. Were you trying to steal something?"

"Yes. That's it," Libby told him. "You should call the police and report me. In fact, I'll turn myself in. I'm going to drive straight to the police station and do that right now. You can call and tell them I'm coming."

Suddenly Nigel's eyes darkened.

"Oh, I get it. Of course. You think I killed Lionel and Geoff Holder."

Libby took another step back.

"No. No. Why would I think that? That's ridiculous," Libby told Nigel while he tucked the edge of the top portion of the sheet into the waist to form a skirt. "You were his friend."

"And Tiffany is yours."

"What does that have to do with anything?"

"It means you've decided to come up and search for evidence."

"That would be illegal. And stupid. I already told you. I came to pick up my pot."

"In my bedroom?"

"I couldn't find it downstairs," Libby stammered. "I figured maybe you'd brought it upstairs . . ."

"To use as a chamber pot? What exactly did you hope to find?"

"Nothing," Libby said.

"You were obviously looking for something. What was it?"

"I already told you . . ."

Nigel waved a hand at her.

"Don't be absurd. I'm not that credulous. What the hell ever gave you the idea that I'm a murderer?"

"Well . . ." Libby began.

"So you admit it," Nigel finished triumphantly at the exact moment that Bernie crashed into the room brandishing one of Nigel's carving knives.

"Are you all right?" she asked Libby as she moved in front of her.

"I'm fine," Libby assured her. "A little shaken up. How did you know . . ."

"Janet," Bernie said. "Next time keep your damned cell phone on."

"Oops," Libby said.

"Oops is right."

"Another crazed Simmons girl," Nigel observed. "How charming. Do you think you could put my knife down?" he asked Bernie. "It's making me nervous."

Bernie lowered it a couple of inches.

"So, what's *your* excuse for barging in here like a maniac?" Nigel asked her. "Twinkies?"

Bernie shot him a puzzled look.

"Forget it," Libby said. "I'll explain later."

"You two really are a pair, you know that?" Nigel said as he wrapped the sheet more tightly around his waist.

"And proud of it," Bernie said.

"If you want to know the truth," Libby said to Nigel,

emboldened now that Bernie was here. "I was looking for your book."

"Libby!" Bernie exclaimed.

"Well, what's the difference now," Libby said.

"This is true," Bernie granted after a minute of reflection.

"My book?" Nigel said. "All this is about my book?"

Libby took a deep breath and let it out.

"Among other things. I mean, Lionel did steal it from you, didn't he?"

"Plagiarize," Bernie corrected.

Libby snorted. "Whatever."

"Well, they are different."

"Excuse me, ladies," Nigel said. "Sorry to interrupt, but are you talking about the one I wrote in high school?"

"Are there others?" Bernie asked.

"Several."

"But Janet said . . ."

"Janet doesn't know everything," Nigel said, cutting her off. "And yes. You're perfectly correct. He did plagiarize that book from me, and I never did anything about it, not even when it was evident that it would be a success."

"Why didn't you?" Libby asked, genuinely curious.

Nigel pulled the sheet tighter and sat down on the edge of his bed.

"Well," he replied. "I suppose I thought no one would believe me. I was never very good in school, you see. It was only later that I found myself."

"So you must have resented Lionel," Libby continued, thinking that if anything happened, Bernie could protect her. "He was successful and you weren't. All these years of watching him succeed . . ."

"And I couldn't take it anymore?" Nigel said.

"Exactly."

"Well, you're partially correct," he conceded. "I did re-sent him. I resented him for years. Resentment can corrode your soul if you let it."

Libby and Bernie exchanged looks.

"But then, at a friend's urging, I took a two-day seminar at the Institute for Change and learned that the universe is infinitely bountiful. I went home and began writing again, and when I had gotten something I liked I called up Lionel and he agreed to publish it."

"Out of the goodness of his heart, no doubt," Libby said.

"No doubt," Nigel said.

"You were blackmailing him into publishing it."

"Not at all. My stuff is good."

Bernie thought about what she'd read of his and decided silence was called for.

"He just decided to do the right thing," Nigel continued.

"Lionel? After all these years?"

Nigel shrugged.

"Far be it from me to question the ways of men. I prefer to think that he thought I would sell, but maybe he felt guilty. Who knows? In any case his house was giving him an imprint . . ."

"Which you just happened to know about," Bernie interjected.

"It wasn't a secret. I read about it in *Publishers Weekly*. I was to be his first pick. So as you can see, killing him would be the last thing I would do. No Lionel. No imprint. No book for me. And as for Geoff—what did I have against him? Tell me that?"

"It's what he had against you."

Nigel raised both eyebrows. "Would you care to elucidate?"

"I certainly would," Bernie replied. "You were his stockbroker."

"His financial advisor."

"Whatever. You still lost a lot of his money," Bernie hypothesized.

Nigel inclined his head. "I did indeed. But that hardly makes me unique. Everyone is in the toilet these days. The bubble's burst, or haven't you heard?"

"And he got mad," Bernie continued.

"No one likes losing money—not, I might add, that there was much money left to lose after Lionel got through with him."

Bernie wondered where to go next. There was only one thing she could think of.

"He wrote a letter of complaint to your firm."

Nigel took a step towards Bernie.

"Did Janet tell you that?"

Bernie raised the knife she was holding.

Nigel looked at it and said, "Don't be ridiculous."

"Then back up."

"Fine." Nigel stepped back. "Satisfied?"

Bernie nodded.

"Now will you answer my question?"

"I don't know why I'm bothering." And Nigel whirled around and strode over to his night table. Libby and Bernie watched apprehensively as he rummaged through the drawer.

"What are you doing?" Bernie asked nervously as Libby mouthed the word gun at her.

"Looking for something."

Bernie had just nodded her head towards the door and said, "Now?" to Libby when Nigel turned around. Bernie was relieved to see he was holding a piece of paper in his hand. He took a couple of steps forward and flung it at Libby's feet.

"Read this."

Libby picked it up and scanned it.

"He's cleared," she told Bernie.

"Of any misconduct," Nigel told them. "I was just doing what Geoff wanted me to. He authorized every single one of those trades. I told him not to do options, but he wouldn't listen. He thought he could get back the money he'd lost with Lionel. It was a case of very bad timing."

"Then why are you drinking?" Bernie asked.

Nigel glared at her.

"Since when do I have to answer to you?"

"You don't. It's just that Lionel dies and you start hitting the bottle. You have to admit the coincidence is . . . tantalizing."

"Tantalizing?" Nigel scoffed. "Hardly. Minorly interesting perhaps. I assume you heard this from Janet."

"She's concerned about you."

"If that's what she says."

"She is, you know."

"Then you can tell her I'm drinking to mark the end of my fledgling literary career."

Bernie sighed. The last thing she wanted was to be a go-between for these two.

"I think you should tell her yourself."

"I can't since I'm no longer speaking to her."

And with that Nigel walked over to the night table, took the bottle of Wild Turkey that had been sitting on it, and poured some into the glass sitting next to the bottle. He lifted the glass in a toast. "Bottoms up, ladies." Then he gulped it down and poured himself another.

"Maybe you should join AA," Libby suggested.

Nigel looked at her and sneered.

"That did Tiffany a lot of good, didn't it?"

Chapter 32

Libby took a step towards Nigel. "What are you implying?"

"Implying? I'm just stating the obvious. Now get lost and leave me to my drinking."

"Come on Libby. Let's go," Bernie said before her sister could say anything else. Then she took Libby's hand and dragged her out of Nigel's bedroom, down the stairs, and out the door. "Well, that went well, don't you think?" Bernie said when they were standing by her father's Caddy.

"This is why I never took to crime." Libby looked back at Nigel's house. "Somehow I don't think he'll be asking me to cater any more of his dinner parties."

"Somehow I think you're right."

"Are you going to tell Janet what Nigel said?"

"Hum." Bernie thought for a moment. "No. In my experience being the messenger never works out well."

Libby brushed a bee off her arm.

"He was always so polite too."

"Maybe that's because you weren't walking in on him with his clothes off."

Libby started to giggle. "Oh, my God," she said. "You should have seen the expression on his face."

Bernie grinned. "I can only imagine."

Suddenly Libby stopped laughing as a thought occurred to her.

"You're not going to tell Dad about this, are you?"

"Good heavens, no!" Bernie exclaimed. "We'd never hear the end of it. He'd probably have one of his old buddies following us around for the rest of our lives."

"For sure."

Libby and Bernie watched a cardinal alighting on the fir tree in front of Nigel's house. Then Bernie sighed and straightened out her tank-top strap.

"I have to admit," she said, "I am disappointed. I really liked Nigel for this."

"It would have been nice," Libby said wistfully. "He could still be guilty."

"Yes, he could," Bernie agreed. "But his explanations make sense."

"If they're true."

"Well, there is that," Bernie conceded. "But they're easy enough to check. One of us should call up Lionel's publisher and find out."

Libby went over to her van and got her sunglasses and put them on.

"Maybe there's something else going on that we don't know about. I mean, why didn't he call the police on me if he doesn't have anything to hide? I know I would have in his situation."

"I don't know." Bernie swatted at a flying ant. "Just be glad he didn't."

"I think it's because he does have something to hide," Libby said.

"Everyone has something to hide," Bernie pointed out as she looked down at the knife she was still holding. "It might be a good idea if I returned this to him."

"Did I say thanks?" Libby said when Bernie got back from putting the knife in Nigel's mailbox.

Bernie waved her hand in the air. "You can do the same for me sometime." And she changed the subject back to Nigel. "I'll tell you what I think. I think Nigel didn't call the police because he was embarrassed. The story he told us makes him and Lionel look bad."

"So you believe him?"

"Yes, I do. Why else would he say something that makes him look like an idiot?"

Libby sighed.

"And after all this we still don't know why Geoff had Janet's name scribbled on his pad. Maybe Dad's right. Maybe it isn't important. Maybe we're just fixating on it because it's all we've got."

"Maybe." Bernie twirled her silver and onyx ring around her finger.

"I should get back to the store," Libby said.

"Wait up," Bernie said. "Didn't Geoff have a . . ."

Libby snapped her fingers.

"A cousin. Janet Grady."

"I thought she was out in Marina del Rey or someplace like that."

"Maybe she's visiting her parents."

"Well, there's one way to find out."

And Bernie reached in her bag for her cell. Libby watched her while she dialed Directory Assistance. Bernie shook her head a couple of minutes later.

"Right house, but I'm getting the answering machine," she mouthed. She left a message and hung up. She tapped her phone against the palm of her hand. "Wouldn't it be nice if Bree Nottingham was the killer," Bernie said.

Libby startled.

"Where did that come from?"

"Wishful thinking. Of course *she* would have committed the perfect murders."

"She is annoying, isn't she?"

"Annoying is hardly the word I'd pick. By the way, she wants to talk about the whatever-it-is she's holding for Lionel at Susan Andrews' house."

"She's already talked to me about it at least a dozen times." Libby stifled a yawn. Suddenly she felt exhausted. "I really do have to get back to the store. I have all that potato salad to make."

"Meet you there," Bernie said and got into her car and drove off.

Libby sat in the van for a few minutes and ate a couple of the cookies that she had stashed in her bag and reflected on what could have happened. Then she put the van in gear and started towards the shop.

She was thinking that she should offer filled picnic baskets for the summer in three different price ranges when she spotted a white panel truck with the name *Janet's Automotive Parts* painted on the side.

"Janet," she said to herself as the truck turned left. Of course. She hung a left too. The potato salad could wait. The truck drove down Ash Street, took a right onto Beech, and crossed Lotus with Libby right behind it. Halfway down it pulled into the parking lot of Roy's Body Shop and came to a halt.

Libby pulled in after it, put the van in park, and jumped out.

"Excuse me," she called as the driver got out of his truck.

He turned around.

"I know this is going to seem weird to you, but were you slated for a delivery at Geoffrey Holder's Body Shop yesterday morning?"

"A pickup, but no one was there. Then I heard why on the radio." The driver picked up his gimme cap and scratched his head. "It's kind of creepy thinking that I was knocking on the door and Geoff was just lying there."

"Eight-fifteen. That's pretty early for a pickup, isn't it?"
The driver put his hat back on and hitched up his jeans.

"Not in this job. I start my rounds at seven in the morning." The driver looked at her more carefully. "Hey. I know you. You're the woman that runs the food shop A Little Taste of Heaven. My wife buys stuff from you all the time."

"Tell her to come by and I'll give her a couple of free scones," Libby said.

Generosity never hurts, Libby thought as the man smiled. Then she turned and hurried towards the van.

"Bernie," she said when her sister picked up her cell. "You're not going to believe this, but I know who Janet is—or rather what Janet is."

"That's okay. Wait till I tell you what Dad told me," Bernie countered.

Chapter 33

Bernie looked at her watch as she walked into R.J.'s. It was a little after nine. She was on time but not too on time. Too on time would mean she was anxious, which was something she didn't want to give the appearance of being. Especially considering who—or, if she was being grammatical correct, whom—she was meeting.

The place hadn't changed much since she'd left, she reflected as she spotted Rob nursing a beer at the bar. Same paneling on the walls, same dartboard on the far wall, same pool table in the back, same sign in front of the bar proclaiming, *The Hell with Apples. Two Pills a Day Keeps the Doctor Away.*

Since it was a weekday night, the place wasn't crowded. As Bernie made her way towards Rob, she estimated she knew maybe five people here. In days past she would have known everyone. She couldn't decide how she felt about that. Bittersweet would be a good word. That or conflicted.

"Not like L.A.," Rob noted as Bernie sat down on the bar stool next to his.

At least he was on time, she thought. Joe had always been a half hour late. Usually more.

"That's for sure." She surveyed the crowd. The people

who frequented R.J.'s tended to be teachers and contractors and small shop owners. Unlike the bars she'd gone to in L.A., where everyone was in "The Industry" or wanted to be. "I like this better. It's more relaxed."

"Me too."

Bernie took a deep breath.

"There's something I should tell you before we proceed."

Rob cocked his head.

"I'm listening."

"I've sworn off men."

"Really?" Rob said.

"Yes. Really."

"What a coincidence," Rob replied. "I have too. See. We have a lot in common already."

Bernie laughed.

"Bad time out in L.A.?" Rob asked.

"You could say that."

"Me too. See. There's another connection."

Bernie could feel herself relaxing and she didn't want to. *This guy is way too charming,* she thought as the bartender came up.

"Hey, Brandon," Bernie said to him. "I thought you'd be in Maui by now."

"I was and now I'm here again. All that sun and surf began to get to me." He smiled at Bernie. "I'd heard you were in town."

Bernie spread her arms.

"And here I am back at the old place."

"And looking really good too, I might add."

Bernie grinned and made a mental note to thank Janet for selling her the skirt and top.

"I also heard," Brandon continued, "that Libby wasn't too pleased about paying your cab fare."

"You could say that. She's deducting it from my salary."

"Harsh." Brandon put his elbows on the bar and leaned on his hands. "Very harsh. You back for good?"

"For the summer at least."

"Cool. It'll make life around here more interesting. Be careful of her," Brandon confided to Rob. "She stirs thing up."

"So I've noticed."

Rob grimaced and Bernie wondered if he was thinking of Geoff Holder's body as she indicated the bottle of Brooklyn Brown in front of him.

"I'll have what he's having," she told Brandon.

"Another similarity," Rob noted. Then he said to Brandon, "I'll have another one and some of those peanuts."

Brandon nodded. A moment later he was back with their order. He set the beers, glasses, and peanuts down in front of them.

"How's Libby doing?" he asked Bernie.

"Okay," Bernie said. "Considering . . ."

"She must be feeling bad about Tiffany."

"Well, she's not feeling good."

"The police were in here asking me and Mary about her before they arrested her."

Bernie furrowed her brow.

"Asking what?"

"If she'd ever said anything bad about Lionel. Stuff like that. I told them no."

"And had she?"

Brandon laughed. "Shit. Who hasn't?" And he moved away.

Rob watched him go. "That's helpful."

"But true. Actually, no one but Tiffany has ever said anything nice about Lionel. At least not that I remember."

Rob nodded absentmindedly. "I didn't know your sister was Tiffany's friend."

"Best friend," corrected Bernie.

"And that's why you were out at the place?"

"You got it." Bernie poured her beer into her glass. "Did you know that an iced glass makes beer foam up more, not to mention kills the taste?"

"Why am I not surprised you know this?"

"I know lots of things."

Rob raised both his eyebrows, then lowered them.

"I bet you do," he agreed.

Bernie could feel herself flush. *Red alert. Red alert,* she told herself. *Change course.* She smoothed down her skirt, suddenly conscious that it was riding up around her thighs.

"So," she said. "Where did you grow up?"

Rob popped a peanut in his mouth and poured his beer into his glass.

"Changing the subject, huh? That's okay. I'm a military brat so I grew up everywhere. How about you?"

"I've always lived here, and I've wanted to leave for as long as I can remember."

"And now you're back again."

Bernie nodded.

"Would that have something to do with why you've sworn off guys?"

Bernie took another sip of her beer. "It would."

"Are you going to make me drag the story out of you?"

"It's banal."

"I want to hear it anyway."

Bernie shrugged and told him.

"There's a good side to this," Rob said when she was done.

Bernie looked at him incredulously. "Like what?"

Rob took another sip of his beer.

"You're here for your sister. It sounds as if she could use some support."

"I hadn't thought of it that way," Bernie conceded.

"Besides, if you weren't here, we couldn't have met."

"Kismet," Bernie said.

"Synchronicity," Rob offered. "Although, on reflection, Karma might be a more applicable word."

"I agree," Bernie said.

"After all, I used to be a writer."

"Are you working on anything now?"

How sweet. *He's actually blushing,* Bernie thought as he replied.

"A murder mystery."

"Can I read it?"

"You really want to?"

"I really do."

"When I'm done." Rob studied the two men throwing darts for a moment, then turned back to Bernie. "I have some procedure questions."

"You want to talk to my dad?"

"That's where I was going."

Bernie made a circle of peanuts on the counter and started eating them. "I'll ask, but he doesn't like talking to people he doesn't know since he's gotten sick."

"That's what my mom said."

"She's right." Bernie finished her beer and signaled Brandon for another one. "Speaking of mysteries," she said. "My sister found out who Janet was."

"Who?"

"It's not a who, it's a what. Janet's Automotive Parts."

Rob groaned. "Do I feel like an idiot? It isn't as if I haven't seen that truck before. Obviously I should turn my hand to something other than a mystery."

"Me too," Bernie said. "I'm certainly not getting very far on this Tiffany thing."

"Maybe because there's no place to get."

"Maybe," Bernie conceded. "But I told Libby I'd help her until we've exhausted every possibility, so that's what I'm going to do."

Rob took another sip of his beer.

"I don't know if I should tell you this or not."

"And why is that?"

"Because your sister isn't going to like this."

"You're not telling her, you're telling me."

"You're not going to like this either."

"I'm a big girl . . ."

"So I noticed," Rob cracked.

Bernie punched his arm. "Just tell me, goddamnit."

Rob rubbed his bicep. "That was pretty good."

"I used to do Boxercize." *He's so adorable,* Bernie thought as she leaned towards Rob and whispered in his ear, "Tell me now or I'll kill you."

"Why didn't you say that in the first place?" Rob put his glass down and faced her. "About four weeks ago I came into Geoff's office, and there were Geoff and Tiffany going at it full tilt on top of Geoff's desk."

"Geez."

"But that's not the worst part." Rob finished off his beer. "The worst part is I was showing Geoff's wife, Mary Beth, in at the time. It was their anniversary, and she was dropping by to take him out to a surprise lunch."

"Well, that would certainly explain some things," Bernie said, thinking back to her conversation with Mary Beth.

Chapter 34

Bernie leaned against one of the kitchen cabinets and watched Libby rolling out the dough for tomorrow's pies. *I should never have told her what Rob said when I walked in the door,* she thought.

She should have waited until tomorrow morning. At least then she could have gone to sleep. Of course, she reflected, she *could* go up now if she wanted to. Nothing was stopping her. She just hated to leave Libby alone when she was this upset.

"Libby, you should go to bed," Bernie said for the third time. "It's almost twelve, and you have to get up at six."

"What's the point?" Libby replied, her eyes fixed on what she was doing. "I couldn't sleep."

"How do you know until you try?"

"Believe me. I know." And Libby gave the dough another half turn. "Anyway, it's easier to do this at night when it's cooler. It's supposed to be in the eighties tomorrow, which will mean I'll have to contend with softened butter."

"I thought that's why you had the marble slab and the fan."

"They only go so far."

"I could never get the dough to form a circle," Bernie observed, trying to jolly Libby up.

"I couldn't either when I started."

Libby gave the dough another half turn.

"Actually, what Rob told me about Tiffany is a good thing," Bernie told her. "You should be happy."

Libby kept her eyes fixed on the dough.

"And how do you get that?" she demanded. "It gives Tiffany a motive for killing Geoff."

"It also gives Geoff's wife a motive for killing him. I mean, first he loses all their money and then she catches him in flagrante delicto with Tiffany."

Libby finally looked up.

"Flagrante delicto?"

"From the Latin," Bernie explained. "It means caught in the middle of the act."

"Why can't you talk the way other people do?" Libby complained.

"Like I should have used the good old Anglo-Saxon word, fuck? As in Mary Beth caught her husband and Tiffany fucking on top of his desk? Probably because I like a little variety in my vocabulary, not to mention other things." Bernie hoisted herself up on the counter and sat there with her feet dangling. "No," she continued. "Seeing something like that would be enough to drive anyone over the edge." And who, she thought, would know better than her?

"And where does Lionel fit in all this?" Libby demanded. "Why would Mary Beth kill him?"

Libby pried a piece of peanut from between her back teeth with her fingernail.

"Sorry about that," she said when she was done. "Maybe Mary Beth blames Lionel for the family's financial woes. From what Nigel said, the amusement park fiasco was what made Geoff start speculating in the market. Mary Beth might be thinking that if Lionel hadn't pulled out of the deal, Geoff wouldn't have lost the rest of his money in the market and Mary Beth would still have her house.

"Losing your house, now that would be a biggie. So is the other thing. I can testify to that." Bernie clasped her hands together and cracked her knuckles. "Of course, there is a question of timing," she mused. "Why kill Lionel first and then wait on her husband? I mean, I nearly went in the kitchen and got a knife and stabbed Joe when I saw him in bed with that . . . person. That's why I left. Because otherwise I would have.

"But now that I think of it, Mary Beth is a brooder, and I'm not talking about the hen variety."

"I didn't think you were."

Bernie cracked her knuckles again.

"Remember when she found out that Brandon had taken her bike and dumped it in the bushes? She spent a month planning her revenge. I would have just walked up and popped him one in the jaw."

"You did when he took yours," Libby reminded her.

"So I did." Bernie smiled in remembrance. "He had a nice black-and-blue mark."

"Mother was not pleased."

"No, she wasn't, was she? But Dad thought it was great." Bernie tapped her fingers on the kitchen counter. "So maybe Mary Beth saw them and went numb and then the more she thought about what she'd seen, the angrier she got. But it was easier to kill Lionel first because she had some distance from him. Or maybe he was like a dress rehearsal for her hubby. And there is the fact that Mary Beth could have gotten the cyanide she killed Lionel with from her hubby's shop."

Libby shook her head.

"No matter what you say, I can't see Mary Beth killing two people. She's so . . . so buttoned down. She never raises her voice."

Bernie cracked her knuckles again.

"And when people like that go, they go big time."

"I'm sorry. I still don't see her for this." Libby picked up the piecrust, put it in the pie tin and began to crimp the edges. "Mary Beth strikes me as the kind of person that implodes, not explodes."

"Well, we also have Lydia tied to the two murder victims," Bernie added. "If Clyde knows what he's talking about."

"Of course he knows what he's talking about." Libby picked up a fork and began pricking holes in the dough. "Now, her I can see killing Lionel. Without him around, she doesn't have to worry about being accused of stealing, plus I heard from Paul that she's been named executor of his estate. So she definitely benefits from his death. But what does she get out of Geoff dying?"

"Maybe she was jealous."

"He was married when she took up with him. How could she be jealous?"

"Yeah. But that's different. That relationship was already in place when Lydia started seeing him. I'll bet you anything he started sleeping with Tiffany after he started sleeping with Lydia."

"So it's okay for him to be unfaithful to his wife but not unfaithful to Lydia?"

Bernie picked a fleck of flour off her new skirt.

"In essence, yes. This thing with Tiffany and Lydia reminds me of a woman I knew out in L.A. She was going out with this married guy, and that was okay with her because she wasn't interested in the whole family/kid/dog thing. But then he brought someone else on board and she flipped out. She claimed it was disloyal."

Libby rolled her eyes.

"It's true," Bernie insisted.

"People are so weird." Libby swept the loose flour and

rice-sized pieces of dough into the trash bin with the side of her hand. "There is another possibility," she said.

"Which is?"

"Geoff was blackmailing Lydia. Maybe she got the cyanide out of his place and he found out and confronted her and asked for money. After all, he really needed it."

"That would work," Bernie said as she watched a moth flutter around the kitchen light.

"But the bottom line is this," Libby said.

Bernie turned and looked at her sister, who was drumming her fingers on the rolling pin.

"Tiffany should have told me."

"Would it have made a difference in what you did?"

"No," Libby conceded. "But she should have told me anyway."

"Maybe Tiffany was embarrassed to tell you," Bernie suggested.

Libby snorted. "Lying never helps."

Bernie didn't say anything as Libby put the pie tin in the refrigerator and took out a second piece of dough, put it in the center of the marble slab, and picked up the rolling pin again. *In this light she looks just like Mom,* Bernie thought as Libby lightly scattered flour on the slab.

"Maybe she feels you wouldn't have approved," Bernie finally suggested.

"Well, she's right about one thing at least. I don't." Libby started working. "Do you?"

"I don't think it was the smartest thing to do," Bernie replied carefully, not wanting to get into a discussion with Libby at this time of night.

"And that's the difference between us," Libby retorted.

"I suppose it is."

Bernie watched her sister work. Her movements were precise and economical. In five minutes she'd rolled the dough out and had it in the pan.

"And even if what you say is true about Mary Beth and Lydia," Libby said as she put the second crust in the refrigerator and started in on the third. "How does this help us?"

Bernie slid down off the counter, went over to the kitchen cabinet, got out the cocktail shaker and began mixing up a batch of Cosmopolitans. Libby looked as if she could use one, and she wouldn't mind a good-night drink herself.

"Well, for one thing," she informed Libby as she measured out the cranberry juice, "it gives us two new suspects."

"There's no way we can prove or disprove anything," Libby said.

"I'm not so sure about that," Bernie replied, handing her a drink. "I think we should talk to Dad."

Sean heard Libby and Bernie coming up the stairs. Light and delicate they were not, he thought as he clicked off the infomercial he'd been watching on the television.

"Hey, girls, come and say good night to your old man," he called out.

"We were just about to," Bernie said as she and Libby trooped into his room. "When do you sleep?"

"Usually between three and six," Sean conceded.

And that was if he was lucky.

Bernie handed him a Cosmopolitan.

"For you," she said.

Sean took a sip and nodded his head appreciatively.

"Not bad," he allowed.

"Better than Wild Turkey on a night like this," Bernie observed.

"Your mom made a mean Manhattan."

Bernie smiled.

"I used to like the maraschino cherries."

Libby took a step forward. *She worries too much,* Sean thought as he noticed Libby tapping her foot on the floor.

"What's going on?" he asked her, even though he had a pretty good idea what she was about to say.

"I thought we agreed that you'd get into bed by twelve."

Right again, Sean, he told himself. *Give yourself a pat on the back.*

"No. We discussed it. I never agreed to anything," Sean clarified. "Given what this wheelchair costs, I want to get the most out of it that I can."

"The doctor said sleeping in it is bad for your circulation."

Sean decided he wasn't going to tell Libby he knew and didn't care.

"So," he said instead. "Tell me about life in the outside world."

"If you don't want to take care of yourself, it's your business," Libby huffed at him.

Sean held on to his temper.

"That's right," he said softly. "It is."

"Drop it," Bernie said as Libby started to reply.

Sean watched as Libby folded her arms across her chest and got that disapproving look on her face.

"So," he said into the deepening silence, "are you girls going to tell me what's happening or not?"

Bernie and Libby looked at each other.

Then Libby said to Bernie, "It's your story. You tell him."

Bernie sat down on the edge of the bed near him and tossed her hair off her forehead.

"Fine. I will."

"You have to concentrate on Geoff Holder's homicide," he told them when Bernie was through with her recital.

"Why's that?" Bernie asked.

"Because anyone could have had access to Lionel's

water from the time you labeled the bottles till the time he died, meaning it would be extremely difficult to establish a reliable table documenting everyone's whereabouts given that there are only two of you. For that you'd need more manpower than we have in the entire Longely police force.

"And working backward from the cyanide to the murderer would also be difficult given our limited resources and unofficial status." Sean moved his wheelchair slightly closer to the window fan. Funny, but now he liked the breeze on his face. He never had before. "The Holder homicide is the simpler of the two, and since they're connected, solve one and you'll solve the other."

Libby leaned forward. She was standing, Sean noted. Which meant she was still annoyed with him, but not as annoyed as she had been because she was asking him a question.

"Why is the Holder homicide simpler?"

"For openers, it's got a smaller cast of characters to work with." He took another sip of his Cosmopolitan. This thing packed more of a wallop than he thought it would. He wondered what the hell Bernie had put in it. "Okay." Sean rested his glass on the table next to him. "What do we know about Geoff?"

"We know he was two-timing his wife," Libby replied. "And that he was a bad businessman."

"Besides that."

"We know he had an appointment with Janet Automotive Parts at eight-fifteen in the morning and he never answered the door," Bernie replied.

Sean smiled.

"And what time does the place usually open for business?"

Bernie fiddled with her ring.

"I don't know exactly, but don't places like that usually open between seven and eight a.m.?"

Sean nodded.

"Which means . . ."

"Which means," Bernie continued. "He was dead before eight-fifteen."

"Exactly."

"Which also means," Bernie continued, "we should find out what Mary Beth and Lydia were doing between . . ."

"Let's say, for argument's sake, between six and eight in the morning," Sean found himself interjecting.

"Why not before?" Bernie objected.

"It could be," Sean conceded. "I'm just going with the most likely scenario."

Libby peeled a piece of dough off the tip of her finger.

"It would make life easier if we knew exactly," Libby said.

"I guess I could call Clyde and find out," Sean said reluctantly.

Libby smiled at him.

"Thank you, Daddy."

Sean smiled back.

"And then we could talk to the neighbors and see if anyone noticed anything," Bernie suggested.

"Yes, you could," Sean agreed.

Bernie thought for a moment.

"Do we know them?" she asked Libby. "Because that would make it easier."

"I know the people who live on either side of Lydia's mom," Libby volunteered. "I catered dinners last year for both of them."

"Well, that's a start," Bernie said. "We could also talk to Lydia and Mary Beth."

"And say what?" Sean watched his daughter take a sip of her drink and consider the answer.

"Here's what we can't say." She pantomimed tapping someone on the shoulder. "Mary Beth. Excuse me. Did you leave the house early so you could shoot your husband? Inquiring minds want to know."

"Exactly," Sean said.

"There is another possibility," Libby said suddenly.

Sean waited.

"Garbage pickup and newspaper delivery."

"Excellent," Sean said as he reached for his drink.

Maybe, Sean reflected, Libby did have some of him in her after all.

Chapter 35

Bernie wiped a drop of sweat off her cheek as she laid the phone down. She couldn't remember it being this hot in June before. Or humid. This was August weather. And it certainly wasn't doing her hair any good.

"How do you stand being in the kitchen in the summer?" Bernie asked her sister.

"You get used to it. So," Libby asked her, "what did you find out?"

Bernie pushed her hair back behind her ears. Maybe, she reflected, she should get it all cut off.

"Well?" Libby said.

Bernie took a drink of water and told her what she'd been able to ascertain.

"Garbage pickup on Lydia's street is scheduled for nine-thirty A.M. give or take twenty minutes—which doesn't help us—and the development the Holders live in uses a private service called Enterprise Carting. I haven't been able to get them on the phone yet."

Libby put the chicken she was frying on brown paper to drain.

"Well, that's a start."

"They're located in Ashford on Clinton Street."

Libby thought. "Clinton Street is near Sam's Club. I could swing by there when I go and get some more chicken."

"Since when do you go to Sam's Club?" Bernie asked her sister, who had once called the super-sized chain stores a blot upon the American landscape.

"I've been going for the last couple of years," Libby replied a tad defensively.

"What made you change your mind?"

Libby mentioned the name of a prominent caterer down in New York City.

"And he's right. It's all a matter of being selective." Libby wiped her forehead with her forearm. "Anyway, my vendor was out of chickens and I need to get some for tonight. We're doing a small dinner for eight at the Sharp residence."

Bernie groaned. Great, she thought. She'd been planning on getting a hamburger with Rob.

"It'll be easy," Libby told her. "We're doing Indonesian chicken, which everyone always likes and is so simple that Amber can make it by herself, as well as the cucumber salad." Libby looked at the clock on the wall. "When she gets here. Which had better be soon. The jasmine rice with cashews and stir-fried spinach with a hint of balsamic vinegar we're doing there. And Edna Sharp wants something light for dessert, so we're giving her the cassis sorbet, which I made last week." Bernie could see Libby studying her face. "Unless you're busy."

"No. Heaven forbid," Bernie retorted. "Why would I want to do something else when I can be slaving in the kitchen with you? Cook by day, detective by night. What could be better?"

Libby indicated the calendar hanging on the wall.

"It *is* written down."

"Is that new?"

Libby blotted the cooked chicken, then slid two more pieces into the pan.

"I've been doing it for the last two years."

"Oh."

Bernie found herself gazing at the fried chicken. She should have had breakfast, she decided. Her mouth started to water. She herself hated making fried chicken. It splattered fat everywhere, but she loved eating it. Especially when it was perfectly done. Which Libby's always was.

"Don't touch it," Libby warned as she went to pick off a little bit of crust on the piece of chicken that was draining on the paper.

"I wasn't going to do anything," Bernie replied with as much dignity as she could muster.

"Yes, you were. You always do. You want a piece, buy it," Libby told her before continuing, "We should be at the Sharps' at six o'clock . . ."

". . . Sharp," Bernie said. "Not to put too fine a point on it."

Libby didn't even groan, much less look up from the chicken. "What about the newspaper deliveries?"

"Lydia gets the local paper, Mary Beth doesn't get anything."

Libby pursed her lips. "Do we know who the local paper guy is?"

"Sam Hanlon."

"That's Googie's older brother."

Bernie watched Libby adjust the heat under the pan. "How about I talk to him and the Enterprise people and you talk to the neighbors," she said.

Libby nodded.

"And," she continued. "Just so you know, Dad talked to Clyde and Clyde said the postmortem put Geoff's death somewhere between seven and eight o'clock in the morning, which tells us nothing we didn't already know. Of course," Bernie reflected, "time of death isn't as precise as people like to think. It's really an estimation. There are all sorts of factors involved—like heat. Actually liver temperature . . ."

"Enough," Libby told her sister.

"Okay." Bernie watched Libby turn the chicken. "I can respect that. What if nothing comes of this?"

Libby finally looked up.

"What do you mean?"

Bernie crossed her arms over her chest.

"Talking to these people. What if it doesn't lead anywhere? Then what?"

"If nothing comes of this," Libby replied slowly, returning her gaze to the pan, "I guess that'll be that. I can't see any other avenues to explore. Can you?"

Bernie ducked her head.

"No," she replied. "I can't."

"And Tiffany will get her wish," Libby reflected.

"It appears so," Bernie agreed. Then she walked out into the front of the store. It was a quarter to twelve, and the lunchtime crowd was beginning to trickle in.

Chapter 36

Libby studied Enterprise Carting for a minute before she went inside. The building was small and undistinguished and set back on the street. Add two spindly cedars by the door and a raggedy lawn, and you had the sum and substance of the place.

She couldn't remember going by it before, but then, she reflected, Ashford wasn't her town either. Even though it was only a ten-minute drive from Longely, she tended to go through it on her way to other locales.

Its major claim to fame as far as she could tell was that it was home to several large discount chains, stores that people like Bree Nottingham had fought successfully against allowing within Longely's boundaries claiming they'd ruin the atmosphere and hence lower the property values. And for once Libby had to agree with Bree, even if she did go to Sam's Club and Wal-Mart on occasion.

"Yes?" the girl sitting in front of the desk said to Libby.

Except for a small statue of the Venus de Milo sitting on the reception desk, the inside of the building was just as plain as the outside, Libby observed. There weren't even any chairs to sit on in the waiting area.

Then, as she studied the girl, Libby realized that she'd

been so busy frying chicken and waiting on people at the store that she hadn't thought about what she was going to say when she got in here. *Good going, Libby,* she told herself. Stellar. The girl cocked her head, and Libby found herself staring at the turquoise stud in the side of her nose.

"Well, I was hoping you could help me," Libby began.

The girl waited.

"It's like this." Libby tried to think of a good story and failed. *I am so bad at this,* she told herself. "I need to know . . ." And she stopped again. "Oh, the hell with it," she said, finally telling the girl the truth.

The girl's eyes widened.

"This is about those murder cases?" she said.

Libby nodded.

"And you wanna help your friend?"

Libby nodded again.

"Way cool." The girl swiveled in her seat. "Hey, Stan," she yelled into the back. "Come out here for a second. I got someone who needs to talk to you."

Stan turned out to be Libby's age.

"So what can I do for you?" he asked as he brushed back the reddest hair Libby had ever seen with the palm of his hand.

But before Libby could answer, the girl behind the counter said, "She's investigating those two murders in Longely, unofficial-like because she doesn't think her friend, Tiffany whatever her name is, did them."

"Okay, Sis." Stan held up his hand, and the girl stopped talking. "That right?" he asked Libby.

"That's right."

"Well, I don't know if I can help you much."

"I was hoping I could speak to the person who was picking up the trash at Paradise Estates."

"That would be me," Stan said.

Libby looked around.

"Maybe we could go somewhere and talk."

"Here'll be fine." He nodded out back. "I'm about to start workin' on one of the trucks."

"Well. Okay. Stan," Libby began. "I was wondering if you would have noticed if there was a car in the driveway or if it was gone at . . ." and Libby fished in her pocket and read off Geoff Holder's house address.

Stan smoothed his hair down again.

"Doubtful."

"Wait," Libby said. "I haven't given you the date."

"Wouldn't matter," Stan said. "Those people that live there. They keep their cars in the garage. So I mostly don't know if they're there or not, and frankly, I just come by and pick up the trash. I don't notice much unless someone's left something interesting like a TV or something like that on the side of the road. You'd be surprised what the people up there throw out. Sorry, but I don't think I can help you much."

Great, Libby thought as she thanked him and told him to call her if he thought of anything. Maybe this wasn't such a good idea after all. It wasn't until she pulled into the parking lot at Sam's Club that she realized she hadn't even gotten Stan's last name.

Things didn't go much better when she spoke to Googie's brother, Sam. She caught up with him on her way back to the store as he was fixing the fence on his parents' house.

He was shorter than Googie, she reflected, but he had more piercings. Looking at the rings through his nipples made Libby want to cringe.

"I've been thinking since you called," he told her, "and honestly, I can't remember whether Ms. Kissoff's car was there or not when I delivered the paper."

Libby tried to keep her eyes on Sam's face and off his chest.

"Does Lydia park it in the garage or in the driveway?"

Googie's brother pulled up his shorts and shifted the hammer he was holding from one hand to the other and back again.

"You know, I just get out the car, stuff the papers in the mailboxes and run back as fast as I can. I'm not really looking at anything that time of the morning. Sorry," he said.

"It's okay." Libby managed a smile. This was turning into a repeat of her conversation at Enterprise Carting. "I really wasn't expecting you to remember anyway. Hoping but not expecting."

Sam gave her a blank look.

Libby waved her hand. "Never mind." And she got back into her van. Well, that was that. So much for playing amateur detective. She had to get the chickens back to the store anyway and put them in the marinade Amber had hopefully prepared. But before she did that, she got her cell phone out of her bag to call Bernie and see what was going on at her end. At which point Libby realized she'd forgotten to charge the phone the night before.

Damn, she thought, throwing the cell on the seat beside her. *What good are these things anyway? They never work when you want them to.*

Well, this is great. She was batting two-nothing, as her father would have said. As she put the car in gear and pulled out of the driveway, she hoped that Bernie was having better luck than she was, but somehow, the way things were going, Libby doubted it.

Bernie knocked on the house to the right of Lydia's mom. No one was home. The same thing was true at the house on the left. Bernie reflected that she'd forgotten no one was home during the day anymore. Except, of course, for Lydia, who was coming towards her. The one person she didn't want to talk to. Wasn't that always the way?

"Can I help you?" Lydia asked Bernie.

Bernie looked at what Lydia was wearing—a pair of too-short shorts and a tight T-shirt that did nothing for her figure—and decided that even if you were just mopping the floor or digging in the garden it wouldn't hurt to wear clothes that fit.

"No. No." Bernie waved her hands around. "I was just letting the neighbors know about our new delivery service."

"Really?"

"Really," Bernie said, hoping that Libby wouldn't slay her on the spot if this ever got back to her—although she really had to say, on reflection, she thought it was a good idea.

"Too bad I wouldn't be around to take advantage of it," Lydia told her.

"You're leaving?"

Lydia brushed some dirt off her hands.

"Well, I'll be back for the memorial service and the dinner, but I've got to go into the city. I have too much to do."

"When are you going?"

"Right after I put the rest of the tomato plants in for Mom."

Libby would not be pleased to hear this, Bernie thought as she headed back to the Caddy. But of course it was to be expected. Really, why the hell should Lydia stick around? If Bernie were her, she wouldn't. Think about it. If she were the killer, there'd be the guilt factor, and if she weren't, there'd be too many bad memories.

And then it occurred to Bernie that Mary Beth would be leaving soon too. After all, she had said something about joining her parents in Maine. Bernie tapped her fingers on the car's steering wheel. There didn't seem much point in going over to Paradise Estates now. Probably no one was home. On the other hand, she'd be busy tonight with that damned dinner party and then she was meeting Rob for a drink after she was done and at least this way she could honestly say to Libby that she'd covered all the bases.

Guess I'm wrong about people not being home these days, Bernie thought when the woman to the left of Mary Beth Holder's house opened the door.

Bernie didn't recognize her. Not that it mattered, Bernie decided. In some ways it even made things easier.

"Hi," she said starting in on the spiel she'd settled on. "I'm with A Little Taste of Heaven."

The older woman nodded. "Good food."

"We think so." Bernie indicated the mop and yellow rubber gloves in the woman's hands. "If this is a bad time, I can come back later."

"This is fine. I could use a break from cleaning out the basement anyway."

Bernie put on her best smile.

"My sister and I are trying to decide whether or not to expand our breakfast business."

The woman waited.

"We're trying to gear it specifically to the early crowd. You know, mothers with children. Commuters. Things like that. In fact we're thinking of setting up a little coffee kiosk outside the store. So we're taking a survey to see if it would be worthwhile."

"Sorry, but I'm the wrong person to talk to. I don't drink coffee."

Bernie couldn't imagine life without coffee.

"Tea?" she asked.

"Hot water with lemon."

Bernie managed to keep from wrinkling her nose.

"How about her?" Bernie indicated Mary Beth's house. "Do you think she'd take advantage of our new service?"

"Well." The woman thought. "Mary Beth's usually out of here by seven-thirty so she can take her kids to school. So maybe she'd like something like that. She does drive by your store. Except in the summer," she added.

Bernie waited.

"Then she drives her kids to summer camp, and she's gone even earlier. Around seven o'clock."

Bernie made a face.

"I know. It's terrible isn't it? Camp starts at eight and it's a forty-five minute ride," the woman said.

"That sounds dreadful," Bernie agreed, thinking what the woman had told her pretty much let Mary Beth out of the picture as far as she was concerned.

Somehow she couldn't see Mary Beth waking up, running out to her husband's body shop, shooting him, calling Tiffany on the phone and luring her out there, then coming back home, waking up her children, getting them dressed, fed, and off to camp. Just thinking about doing all that before eight o'clock in the morning made Bernie feel exhausted.

On the other hand, maybe Mary Beth was one of those obnoxious people who got up at four-thirty in the morning and started mopping the floors. And maybe the kids hadn't gone to camp the day Geoff had been shot. Maybe they'd been sleeping over at someone else's house.

Bernie would have to find out, but the more she thought about the scenario, the more ludicrous it became and the more she was convinced that Tiffany had shot Geoff Holder. Bernie was thinking that, unfortunately, Libby wouldn't want to hear that, when she became aware that the woman in front of her was talking.

"What can you do?" she was saying. "When my kids

were younger, they'd sleep in late and then I'd take them to the beach. That was the nice thing about summer, but now everyone is programmed to within an inch of their lives. Lessons. Sports. Especially sports. My God, all that traveling. Eating dinner in your car. I'm glad I'm not raising my kids anymore, I can tell you that." The woman gave her a dubious look. "I'm sorry I can't be of more help."

"No. No. You've been wonderful," Bernie assured her. "Really." And she handed her a jar of Libby's homemade strawberry-rhubarb jam. "For your trouble," she told her. Then she got in the car and drove back to the shop. There was no need to talk to the woman on the other side of Mary Beth. She'd found out what she needed to know.

When Libby looked up from the potatoes she was slicing, Bernie could tell from the scowl on her face that she was not pleased.

"We're running a delivery service now?" she said before Bernie had time to tell her what she'd found out. "Lydia's mom called up and wanted dinner delivered to her home tonight. I didn't know what the hell she was talking about."

"I'm sorry," Bernie told her.

"You might want to check with me before you make changes in the business."

"It just came out. I didn't think anyone would take it seriously."

"Lydia's mother has."

Bernie grabbed one of the strawberries sitting in the colander by the sink and bit into it.

"Actually, when you think about it, it's a good idea."

"Fine. Then you can run the food over," Libby said and turned back to the ginger she was working on.

"Okay." Bernie wondered how her sister could mince anything so fast and not cut her fingers. "I have to go back anyway."

"How so?"

"I still have to talk to Lydia's neighbors."

Chapter 37

Libby moved her hand as the waitress grabbed her water glass and refilled it. Ordinarily, Libby would have said something about the spots on the glass, but not here. At Julie's Diner, service might not be elegant, and the silverware and glasses weren't pristine, but the food was good and the waitstaff hustled.

Bernie thought, and for once Libby had to agree with her, that Julie's still made the best hamburger and coconut cream pie in town. Their fried onions weren't shabby either.

As Libby looked at Orion sitting in the booth across from her, she could almost believe that time hadn't passed.

"Which is the whole point of going to that place," Libby could hear Bernie saying in her head. "He wants you to forget about the last ten years."

Libby banished Bernie's voice as she watched the waitress behind the counter deliver a BLT to a man sitting on the far end. Orion leaned forward.

"Come on," he urged. "Finish your French fries."

Libby shook her head. Ever since last night, when Bernie had come back from talking to Lydia's neighbors, her appetite had deserted her. Which only happened when she was really upset.

And that wasn't good.

Because when she wasn't hungry she didn't feel like cooking.

And if she didn't cook she'd lose her business and everyone would be out on the street.

Of course, when she'd said that to Bernie, Bernie had just rolled her eyes and told her to stop being a drama queen.

Orion lifted a French fry and tasted it.

"Let's see," he said holding it out in front of him. "The color is a little off. Probably because it was cooked at a hundred and fifty degrees for six minutes instead of six degrees for a hundred and fifty minutes. And the salt . . . the salt I believe is harvested from a beach on the south of France, where one family has been doing it for the last five hundred years."

Libby laughed despite herself.

"Stop making fun of my sister," she told Orion.

"I can't help it. She's such an easy target."

"She is, isn't she?"

"No one needs Encarta with her around. She should go on one of those quiz shows."

"That's what I told her."

Orion finished the French fry, picked up another one, and dangled it in front of Libby.

She shook her head.

"I'm supposed to be losing weight."

"Says who?" Orion demanded.

"Says everyone."

"Well, they're wrong." And Orion squeezed Libby's hand.

She was glad she'd called Orion up. People did change—no matter what Bernie said.

Orion gestured to the T-shirt Libby had bought at Janet's.

"You should get more stuff like that. You look good in it."

"You think?"

"I know."

Libby watched Orion eat another French fry off her plate.

"I think I'll have everything worked out with Sukie soon," he told her. "Bree said she could find me a nice place out here. Nothing too big. I never did like the city much," he reflected.

"That's nice."

"Just nice? Then we'll be able to see more of each other. I thought you'd be happy."

"I am," Libby hastened to reassure him.

She was, wasn't she? She had to be. She'd wanted nothing else for the past ten years.

"It's just that I feel so bad about Tiffany," she explained.

Orion wiped his fingers with the paper napkin on the table.

"You've done the best you could. After all, the police didn't come up with anything."

"The police never looked. Not really."

"Maybe they're right."

Libby shook her head.

"No, they're not. I just keep thinking there's something I'm missing."

"Like what?"

Libby started to bite her lip and made herself stop.

"If I knew, I wouldn't be asking. Maybe I should talk to Lydia's neighbors," she said to Orion. Even though Bernie already had, it wouldn't hurt to hear what they had to say again.

Orion took his hands in hers.

"Libby, Libby, Libby," he murmured.

"What?" Libby asked him, aware of the feeling of his flesh on hers.

Even though the air-conditioning was on in the diner she suddenly felt uncomfortably warm.

"One of the things I love about you is your persistence, but you have to know when to give up."

"That's what my dad said."

Orion let go of Libby's hands and sat back.

"I can't believe we're in agreement about anything."

"Amazing, isn't it?" Libby took a sip of her water. "It's just that I can't imagine Tiffany killing two people."

"But she confessed."

"I don't care. I still can't believe it."

Orion ate another French fry.

"I can."

"Why do you say that?"

"Tiffany's got quite a temper."

"Not like that."

Orion balled up his napkin and threw it on the plate.

"People always think they know people, and the trouble is they don't."

"What are you saying?" Libby demanded.

"Just what I said. You want a piece of pie?"

Libby shook her head as she studied Orion's face. The thought, *He's hiding something,* popped into her head.

"I want to know what you mean," she insisted.

Orion frowned.

"All I meant is that sometimes people do things that they're not too proud of and they don't talk to other people about them, okay?"

"What did Tiffany do? Specifically."

Orion signaled for the waitress and asked for a piece of coconut cream pie when she came over.

"You're like a pit bull," he told Libby when the waitress walked away.

"What did Tiffany do?" Libby insisted.

"She didn't do anything. I was using her as an example."

"No, you weren't."

Libby watched Orion watch the waitress as she took the pie out of the cooler and cut a slice and put it on a plate.

"This is one of your most unattractive qualities," Orion told her as the waitress started towards them.

"Really?" Libby could feel her cheeks get red.

How could she have forgotten how charming Orion could be one minute and how evasive the next? She never really knew what he was thinking.

"Yes," Orion replied. "Now let's just drop the topic."

Libby watched the waitress put the pie down in front of Orion. He lifted his fork and took a bite.

"Tiff isn't worth getting that worked up over. Face it. She's an impulsive person. Like when she got that tattoo of Bugs Bunny on her back."

"How do you know about that?"

"Tiff told me."

"Oh," Libby said. "And since when are you calling her Tiff?"

"Everyone does."

"No, they don't. Only the people closest to her do."

"Really?"

"Yes. Really."

"Interesting." Orion picked up his fork again. "This is good pie. Are you sure you don't want a taste?"

"I'm sure." And suddenly Libby knew what Orion was hiding. She didn't know how she did, but she did.

"You slept with her, didn't you?"

Orion looked up.

"Tiffany?" He snorted. "Don't be stupid. When would I have the time?"

"Not now. Before. When you and I were going together."

"That's ridiculous," Orion said, but Libby could tell that he was lying.

"No, it's not."

Orion didn't say anything.

"For how long?" Libby said. "How long?" The words came out through gritted teeth.

"Five years. But it wasn't that often. Just every now and then. It didn't mean anything."

"How could it not mean anything?"

"It just didn't."

Libby got up and walked over to Orion's side of the booth. Orion looked up at her.

"What are you going to do?" he asked.

"This."

Libby saw Orion's jaw drop as she picked up the plate with the coconut pie.

He can't believe I'm doing it, she thought as she pushed it into his face. Then she marched out the door and called Bernie on her cell phone.

Chapter 38

"You feel better?" Bernie asked Libby.

Libby nodded. "Much. Thanks for coming to get me."

"No problem," Bernie told her. "It would have been a pity to have ruined a good exit by going back into Julie's and using the phone."

Libby didn't say she hadn't because she'd been too embarrassed to. She, Bernie, and Rob were sitting by the swan pond, watching the street lights reflect off the water.

Rob handed her a beer.

"Have one."

"Really, I shouldn't."

"Really you should," Rob insisted.

Libby took it.

"I wish I had been there," Bernie said.

"It was pretty funny," Libby admitted. Despite herself she started chuckling, thinking about it. "Seeing him like that."

"I bet," Bernie said.

"I can't believe I did it," Libby mused.

"He deserved it," Rob said.

"You think so?" Libby asked.

"Absolutely."

"I second the motion," Bernie added. "Now drink up."

Libby took a sip of her beer. As the liquid slid down her throat, she found herself automatically analyzing its taste. There was a hint of bitterness followed by a taste of cinnamon and a slight sweetness she couldn't pin down.

"This isn't bad," she noted.

"Brooklyn Brown, baby. Brooklyn Brown," Rob said.

Libby watched the willow leaves swaying in the breeze.

"You know," she told Bernie and Rob after a couple of minutes had gone by, "I think at some level I've always known. I just didn't want to admit it to myself."

"I'm sorry," Bernie said.

"No need," Libby told her. "I feel fine, I really do." She paused for a moment. "I don't understand, but hearing about Tiffany . . . pushing that pie in Orion's face. It's like I'm over this long, lingering disease. I'm finally over Orion."

And when she said it, Libby knew it was true.

"I'll drink to that," Rob said.

"On to better men," Bernie added.

"I just can't believe that Tiffany would . . . did . . ."

"Sleep with Orion?" Bernie finished for her.

"Yes, and then go on as if nothing had ever happened. I mean, I used to cry on her shoulder about Orion and she was sleeping with him all that time! How could she? I don't get it."

Rob tapped his fingers on his beer bottle.

"Maybe it wasn't such a big deal to Tiffany."

Libby turned towards him.

"How could it not be? I was her best friend."

Rob shrugged.

"Some people think of sex more like recreation."

"Like she thought they were playing golf?" Libby asked as she watched Rob put his bottle down on the grass.

"Yeah." He smiled at her. "Only in this game they were using two balls instead of one."

Bernie punched Rob in the arm.

"What?" he said to Bernie. "It's true."

Libby turned what Rob had said over in her mind.

"I think you might be right," she said at last.

Rob laughed.

"I always am."

Bernie punched him in the arm again.

"Ouch," Rob cried. "That hurt."

"It was supposed to," Bernie told him.

As Rob was rubbing his bicep, something else occurred to Libby.

"You didn't know about Tiffany and Orion, did you?" she asked her sister.

"No." Bernie held up her hand. "I swear I didn't."

"Would you have told me if you had?"

"I would have tried."

"What does that mean?"

"It means," Bernie said, "that most people in your situation don't want to listen. When I look back, I realize a couple of people tried to tell me about Joe and my friend. I just didn't want to hear it."

Libby was taking another hefty gulp of her beer when Rob turned towards her.

"So tell me," he said, "do you still think Tiffany didn't do it? Inquiring minds want to know."

Libby shook her head. "Three hours ago I would have said absolutely not. Now I'm not sure."

Bernie cracked her knuckles.

"Dad always says the simplest solution is usually the right one."

Libby sighed.

"I really feel like a moron."

"Well, you know what they say about love blinds," Rob said.

Bernie cleared her throat. "I believe the line is, '*Love comes from Blindness, Friendship comes from knowledge.*' Comte de Bussy-Rabutin."

"Obviously not in this case, " Rob replied.

"You have a better quote?" Bernie asked him.

"Yes. This."

Libby watched Rob as he reached down, plucked a handful of grass, and threw it at Bernie.

She laughed and threw some back.

Suddenly, before Libby knew how it happened, the three of them were having a grass fight. As Libby giggled and tried to stuff some down Bernie's T-shirt, she realized that she felt lighthearted for the first time in a long time.

Chapter 39

As Bernie set up the coffee urn in Susan Andrews' dining room, she reflected that, in a manner of speaking, she'd helped cater Lionel's death and now, three weeks later, she was catering his official send-off.

"Bernie."

Bernie looked up to see Susan standing in front of her.

"What do you think?" Susan asked and showed her the collage she'd made in honor of Lionel's memorial.

"What do I think?" Bernie replied stalling for time.

"Yes?"

The words "aesthetically challenged" flitted through Bernie's mind. And she thought Susan's other pieces had been bad. This was in a league by itself. Had Susan become possessed by the bad art fairy? Bernie wondered as she examined the collage more closely.

Susan had taken the picture of Lionel from the back of one of his dust jackets and blown it up. Then she'd cut it into large pieces and combined them in a random fashion with bits of Lionel's capes, pieces of his fangs, pages torn from his books, the title *Damned to Death* cut from the spine of assorted dust jackets, assorted pieces of handwoven fiber, and a doll-sized glass bottle.

Bernie was thinking that the dead, stuffed dove pasted

in the center certainly provided the *pièce de résistance* when she felt something tugging at her foot. She glanced down. Bebe, Susan's fat, shaved miniature French poodle, was trying to chew through the strap on her pink sandal.

"Hey." Bernie tried to shake the dog off her shoe.

The dog hung on.

"Bad Bebe," Susan admonished.

The dog paid no attention.

Little monster, Bernie thought as she reached down to grab her, but before she could Susan had scooped her up and cradled her in her arms.

"She just loves leather," Susan explained gaily.

"That may be, but these are new."

Susan cocked an eyebrow.

"You're not a dog lover, are you?" Susan asked.

"Not an unqualified one. No."

Bernie was trying to figure out which was worse—Susan's artwork or her dog—when Susan said, "Would you like to know what the collage symbolizes?"

"Definitely," Bernie lied.

Susan raised her free hand and gestured towards the collage.

"It's about Lionel's life and death."

Now why hadn't she seen that, Bernie wondered.

"The dove symbolizes resurrection," Susan explained when Bernie didn't say anything. "The drops of water"—Susan pointed to some blue spots on the cloth—"symbolize Lionel's death. I wanted it to be abstract but representational at the same time."

Bernie cleared her throat.

"Well, you've certainly done that."

"A synthesis of his life and death."

Where was Libby when she needed her, Bernie thought as she watched Susan beam.

"I've been working on it ever since poor Lionel died."

Bernie just nodded.

"I thought we could put it in the dining room next to the buffet table."

"Uh." Bernie looked at the table she'd just set up with its yellow linen tablecloth and white china. *I'd just as soon have Lionel's body in here,* she thought. *It would be just as appetizing.* "How about putting your collage in the living room?" she suggested. "That's where most of the people will be staying."

"You think so?"

Not with that thing in the room, Bernie thought.

"Absolutely," she said. "This way it will work as a centerpiece. Something for people to meditate on."

"I was thinking of giving it to Lydia as a memento after the memorial is over," Susan said.

"I'm sure she'll appreciate it."

Susan ran her fingers down Bebe's naked back.

Bebe was not a thing of beauty, Bernie thought as Susan said, "Lydia did say she was coming."

"Then I'm sure she will."

"I hope so." Susan fiddled with her earring. "She's been so busy with Lionel's new book on top of the *New York Times* best-seller list. It's so nice everyone is coming to the memorial service."

In Bernie's humble opinion, memorial services had clergy; this was a party. But Bernie just nodded and glanced at her watch. She still had a lot to do before people started arriving. Susan followed her glance.

"Oh, my God," she cried. "Why didn't you tell me it was so late. I have to go and get the flowers."

Bree Nottingham had ordered arrangements of jonquils, sweet peas, white roses, and ferns from the local florist, but they still had to be picked up.

Susan put Bebe back on the floor and wagged her finger at her. "You be a good doggie," she told her. "I'll be back in a little while," she told Bernie. Then she left the house.

Bernie looked at the poodle. The poodle looked at Bernie.

Bebe growled. Bernie growled back. Which might not have been a good idea, Bernie reflected as Bebe lunged for her sandal.

"If you think you are eating my new Robert Clergeries, you have another think coming," Bernie told the dog as she grabbed it by the scruff of the neck.

The little dog snapped and snarled like a thing possessed.

"You're the spawn—okay, spawnette—of the devil," Bernie told Bebe as she deposited the little monster in the laundry room and quickly closed the door.

Bernie stood there for a moment listening to Bebe hurl herself against the door. When that didn't work, she started howling. Really loudly. Bernie went over and turned on the radio. Bebe continued to howl. Bernie briefly considered throttling the little beast but reminded herself that Libby and her spiritual advisor back in California would frown on that behavior.

"Deep breath, deep breath," she said out loud.

When she felt slightly calmer, she took off her sandal and examined the strap. There were a few tooth marks but nothing that couldn't be fixed. *The hazards of catering no one tells you about,* Bernie thought as she put her sandal back on and ran through her to-do list in her mind.

She and Libby had already set up the tables, both the ones inside and the ones in the backyard, and covered them with tablecloths and placed little vases filled with yellow tulips on each table. Then Libby had helped her set up the chairs before she'd taken the van and gone back to the store to finish getting ready.

The food was also under control. Or as under control as it ever got in situations like this. Bernie and Libby had already made and frozen the spanakopita and the cheese coins, which were a nice old-timey recipe made of butter and flour and sharp grated cheddar and rolled into little logs, then sliced and baked.

And of course there were the store's wontons, which Libby filled with a mixture of tofu seasoned with ginger, sesame seed oil, pepper, and soy sauce. Googie was still working on the grape leaves, and this morning she and Libby had arranged the platters of fruit and cheese as well as baskets of bread, not to mention six kinds of cookies for people who liked something sweet.

The nice thing about the spanakopita and the wantons, of course, was that they were frozen in advance so all you had to do was heat them up as you needed them, thereby reducing the wastage factor, which was especially important in an event like this where anywhere from fifty to one hundred and fifty people could show up.

So all that remained to do was set up the hot-water urn for those who preferred tea and pipe the crème fraîche into the cherry tomatoes and put dabs of crab and artichoke dip on endive leaves and plate them. But before she did that, she had to clean off the counters in Susan's kitchen and do the dishes in the sink, which would probably take her a good half an hour.

Between the art supplies, weaving supplies, random pieces of wool, stuff left over from a plumbing job, cookbooks, kitchen gadgets, mail, dog food, and heaven knows what else, there wasn't much work room left. Libby had been appalled when she'd seen the mess, and for once Bernie had agreed with her.

Most people would have had the sense to clean up before Libby and Bernie arrived, but not Susan. She'd just laughed when Libby had looked at the counters and said her collage, had taken all of her time. Of course now that Bernie had seen the collage, she thought Susan would have been way better off on her hands and knees scrubbing the floor.

"Fine," Libby had said to Bernie as Bernie walked her out to the van. "We'll just charge her extra."

So be it, Bernie thought as she rinsed off what looked

like three days worth of dishes and put them in the dishwasher. Then she scrubbed the pots and placed them on
the drying rack.

Next she stacked the cookbooks and put Susan's mail
into a neat pile. *Could you have any more gadgets?* Bernie
wondered as she threw the cherry pitter, the zester, the fat
drainer, and the kitchen-sized blowtorch in a wicker basket and put them on the counter near the door.

In Bernie's humble opinion, gadgets were the mark of a
bad cook. All you really needed were some decent pans, a
sharp set of knives, and the right ingredients. Take this
stupid mini-blowtorch that people used to brown their
créme brûlées. How many times were you ever going to
use that? Once a year? A broiler worked just as well,
Bernie thought as she started gathering the magazines into
a pile. She glanced up at the clock on the wall. She'd been
at this for twenty minutes already. Too much time.

Nevertheless, Bernie's eyes fell on a recipe as she put
Susan's papers into a pile. *Lesson One* was typed across
the page. *I bet this is from the Chinese cooking class Libby
took,* Bernie thought as she automatically scanned the
recipe for stir-fried beef with bamboo shoots.

And then it hit her.

Oh, my God.

She couldn't believe it. It was too incredible.

She put the recipe down and walked over to the phone
and dialed the shop.

Googie answered.

"A Taste of Heaven. How may I help you?"

"Get Libby," Bernie ordered.

"She's upstairs."

"Get her anyway."

"Fine," Googie said. "No need to be rude."

Bernie paced until Libby got on the line a few minutes
later.

"Yes?" she said.

"When was the Chinese cooking class you took?"

"Three or four days ago. Maybe more. With everything that's going on, I've lost track of time."

"No. The first one."

"Sometime in May. Why?" Libby asked.

"Did you make stir-fried beef and bamboo shoots?"

"It was the first thing we cooked."

"Were the bamboo shoots fresh or canned?"

"Fresh. That was the whole point. Using fresh ingredients. Only the teacher had already boiled the shoots, because otherwise we wouldn't have had time to do everything we needed to. Why?"

Bernie was just about to tell her when she felt something wet on her back and smelled something awful. She spun around. Susan Andrews was holding an open can of silicone lubricant in one hand and that goddamned kitchen torch in the other.

Susan splashed more lubricant on Bernie's T-shirt and turned the container so that Bernie could read the words, *Extremely Flammable,* which were written on the can in big red letters.

"Now do what I say," Susan mouthed.

Bernie nodded. Alcohol would burn off her skin, but the stuff she had on her would stick to it. Which meant she wasn't in a position to argue.

Chapter 40

"Bernie, are you all right?" Libby asked, retying the belt on her robe.

"I'm fine," her sister told her. "I'll talk to you later." And she hung up.

Libby stood there with the receiver in her hand for a moment, then turned towards Googie.

"Did my sister seem weird to you?" she asked him.

He looked up from the grape leaves he was filling.

"She's always weird."

"Did she seem upset?"

"She was definitely uptight." Googie wiped his hands on his apron. "I'm going to wear a white T-shirt if that's okay with you, because my brother borrowed my white shirt last night and puked all over it."

Libby nodded absentmindedly.

"Did you hear what I said?" Googie asked.

Libby made an un-hunh noise.

Bernie's call bothered her, but she couldn't explain why. It wasn't the randomness of the question about the recipe that bothered her. Bernie was always asking random questions. Libby ran her fingers through her hair. Maybe it was the tone in her sister's voice. Bernie had seemed excited. But then she was always excited.

Libby paced back and forth for a few seconds and then picked up the phone and called Bernie again. Bernie answered on the first ring. She sounded normal enough, Libby told herself when she hung up. She looked at her watch. She had half an hour to take a shower, get dressed, and get over there and help Bernie finish setting up.

"I'm going back upstairs," she told Googie.

He nodded distractedly. But when Libby had climbed the steps, instead of taking a right and going into the bathroom, she took a left and went into Bernie's room. Libby looked at Bernie's old teddy bears and the movie posters of *The Breakfast Club* and *The Lost Boys* she still had on her wall.

For some reason Libby's throat started to constrict. She could feel the tears starting to come. *This is ridiculous,* she told herself. Maybe it was, but she couldn't shake the feeling that something was very, very wrong as she went into the bathroom and turned on the shower. The feeling wouldn't go away. She tapped her fingers on the shower curtain. There had to be something behind it. She closed her eyes and concentrated.

Nothing. And then Susan Andrews' face popped into her head. She heard her talking in the store the morning after Lionel's death about Lionel asking her to put a stake through his heart. She'd thought then that it was an odd thing to say. But Susan said lots of odd things. Now she wondered if it were wishful thinking.

Another picture flashed through her brain. Lionel's picture hanging on the wall in Susan's library. The black candles under it. And now that she thought about it, Susan seemed to be deriving a lot of enjoyment from having the memorial service for Lionel in her house. Normally she hated having large groups of people over and had since her husband died.

So she had a change of heart. So what?

None of this added up to anything, certainly nothing she could call the police about.

And yet . . . Libby took a deep breath.

"Screw it," she said.

She turned off the shower and put on the shorts and T-shirt she'd just taken off. Then she slid her feet into her sandals and ran for the hall closet where her father kept the gun she wasn't supposed to know about.

So she'd lose another customer, maybe even several, and she'd look like a fool.

Big deal.

Better that than a dead . . .

No, she told herself as she ran down the steps. *Don't even think the words. Just concentrate on getting to Susan Andrews' house.*

Chapter 41

As Bernie looked at Bebe dancing around Susan's feet, she thought, *I should have realized the dog had stopped barking.* But maybe that wouldn't have made a difference. Whenever she was really intent on something, everything else dropped away and she developed tunnel vision.

"You're making a mistake," she said to Susan.

"I heard what you asked your sister."

"Then you know that Libby knows too."

Susan snorted.

"I doubt that very much."

"She'll figure it out."

"No, she wouldn't. She's too busy making scones and running her shop."

Bernie didn't want to admit that this was probably true.

"What about the party?" she said instead.

"What about it?"

"Well, how are you going to get rid of me before everyone comes?"

"I'm going to duct-tape your mouth closed and put you in the trunk of my car and dispose of you after the memorial service."

"That would work," Bernie reluctantly conceded. "Except what are you going to tell Libby?"

"That you went out for soda and never came back."

"Without a car?"

"Shut up," Susan snapped.

"You don't improvise well, do you?"

"Bree is right. You do talk too much." As Susan gestured with the torch, Bernie decided she really was crazy. "It's your fault you're in the situation you're in."

"My fault?" Bernie cried. "Where do you come up with that little bit of twisted thinking?"

"Well, if you hadn't known that bamboo shoots contain cyanide, you'd be happily filling cherry tomatoes right now."

"So being ignorant is a good thing."

"In this case, yes. Now move. I have to do my hair before my guests come."

Bernie took a step towards the door that led to the garage.

"Yes. You wouldn't want to greet them with messy hair."

"That's right. I wouldn't."

As Bernie took another step, she pondered whether she could get close enough to Susan to kick her before she pressed the trigger on that damned butane torch. Maybe she could if she were fast enough.

"Geoff was blackmailing you, wasn't he?" she asked Susan.

"You know why sex is bad for women?" Susan asked in return.

"Is this a punch line to a bad joke?"

"It makes them talk too much."

"You were sleeping with Geoff?" Bernie asked.

"Me and everyone else," Susan said grimly.

"What did he have that was so irresistible?"

"He was available," Susan said. "Now let's move."

"You know," Bernie started to say when all of a sudden there was a loud pop, and a glass by the sink shattered.

As she turned to the noise, she heard Libby say, "Drop

the torch," to Susan. "Don't even think of it," Libby said as Susan's finger tightened on the torch trigger.

Bernie gave Libby the thumbs-up sign.

"Better listen to her," she advised Susan. "She's a crack shot."

"She can't shoot," Susan said.

"What do you think I just did?" Libby asked her.

"You missed me."

"That was a warning shot," lied Libby.

"You wouldn't shoot me if you could," Susan sneered.

"She will if you hurt me," Bernie said.

Susan thought for a few seconds, then lowered her torch and began backing towards the door that led to the garage. Bebe went with her. It was the moment Bernie had been waiting for. Before Susan realized what was happening, Bernie took a couple of steps towards her and kicked the torch out of her hands. Then she tackled her. She and Susan went down in a heap.

"Kill, Bebe," Susan commanded as Bernie tried to pin her arms to the floor.

Bebe moved in and nipped at Bernie's leg.

"Goddamn it," she cried and shook the dog off as Susan kicked at her and tried to wiggle free.

"Help me!" Bernie yelled to Libby as Susan tried to scratch her face.

The next thing she knew Libby was on the floor too and everything was a thrashing mess of arms and legs, elbows and knees, and fur and teeth.

Then Bernie heard, "What's going on here?"

Dead silence.

Everyone stopped what they were doing and looked up.

Bree Nottingham, Griselda Plotkin, and Fred, her photographer, all dressed in their party clothes, were peering down at them.

Libby removed Susan's elbow from her mouth.

"Susan killed Lionel," Libby said.

"You mean you've caught Laird's real killer?" Griselda trilled.

"Yes," Bernie said as she grabbed Susan's wrists and pinned them to the floor. "Could you call the police?"

"Wow. What a story." Griselda opened her bag as Libby picked a snarling, snapping Bebe up by the scruff of her neck. "Let me get my pad out." As she groped around for it, she turned to Fred. "What are you waiting for?" she asked him. "Take the shot, for God's sake."

"No pictures," Bree, Susan, Libby, and Bernie cried together.

Bree snatched Fred's camera out of his hands as he was raising it.

"Hey!" he cried. "Give it back."

"No, I will not," Bree replied. "Thank you very much, but Longely's had enough bad publicity for the time being."

And for once Bernie and Libby had to agree with her.

Chapter 42

Libby went over and turned the fan in her father's window to high and sat back down. With Clyde Schiller, Rob, Bernie, and herself crammed in there, the place hadn't cooled down even though it was nine o'clock at night—not that the heat seemed to affect anyone's appetite for the strawberry-rhubarb crisp Bernie had made. It had been two days since "the incident," as Bree had taken to calling it and Libby was still having trouble wrapping her mind around it.

"I still don't understand why you had to take the damned dog," Bernie was saying to Rob as Libby was thinking about Susan.

"She'll look better when her hair's grown out," Rob assured her.

"Her personality will still suck."

"You were attacking her mistress," Rob said. "The dog was just doing her job."

Bernie sniffed. "You're way too soft-hearted, if you ask me."

"Only when it comes to animals," Rob told her.

Libby came to.

"It's hard to think of Susan as a murderer," she said. "She's so . . . so . . ."

"Airy-fairy," Bernie suggested.

"Airy-fairy?" Libby repeated.

"It's a twenties expression. Or maybe it comes from the thirties. I'm not sure. Anyway, it means inane, fatuous. Of course, now it connotes putting on airs."

"How about plain nuts," Clyde Schiller said as he leaned over and took another bite of crisp off his plate. "Lord, this is good."

"Thanks," Bernie said.

The phone rang. Libby looked at everyone. No one was making a move to get it. Given the number of calls they'd been getting from the hyenas, as her father liked to call the reporters, Libby was eternally grateful for answering machines.

"It's probably another booker," she said.

Bernie made a face. "Yesterday I got a call from *Good Morning America*." She took a bit of crisp and decided she'd been right to put a touch of cinnamon in it. "At least Fred didn't get that photograph. Can you imagine if he had?"

Libby closed her eyes and thought about what it would have looked like. "Thank God he didn't."

"That's for sure," Sean said. "We'd never get rid of the bastards then."

He had a tray over his wheelchair, and Libby was glad to see he was slowly eating his crisp. She'd been scared that all the hoopla connected to Susan's capture would exhaust her father but it seemed to have energized him instead. Libby took a little of the whipped cream off the crisp and put it in her coffee as she watched Rob lean forward.

"Bernie, tell me again how you knew about the cyanide."

Bernie licked a dab of whipped cream off her finger.

"It was in one of those books I read. You know, odd facts about food. Like that polar bears' livers are toxic."

Bernie ate another bite of her crisp. "Bamboo shoots have a small amount of cyanide in them, which is why when you boil them you're always supposed to leave the top of the pot off. That way the toxin evaporates. But Susan didn't do that. She left the top on so the cyanide went back in the water. Then she cooked more bamboo shoots in the same water so eventually she'd made herself something that was pretty potent."

"And it tasted the same?" Clyde asked.

"It must have because Lionel drank it right down," Libby said.

Sean shook his head.

"Maybe if Lionel had sipped instead of gulped, he'd be alive today."

Libby tried to make herself comfortable on the edge of her father's bed and not think about what she had to do downstairs in the kitchen.

"Well, he did win the pie-eating contest when he was in high school," she pointed out as Rob looked at her.

"But," he said, "I still don't get why Susan Andrews killed him. Or Geoff Holder, for that matter. What motive did she have?"

Libby indicated her father with a flourish of her hand.

"Dad," she said.

Sean cleared his throat.

"Did you ever read Lionel's book, *Damned to Death*?" he asked Rob.

"Can't say I have. Why?"

"Well, Lionel wrote it—what? A couple of years ago. Anyway, it starts out with this kid who shoots himself playing Russian roulette with his brother and a couple of his friends. Now when this kid shoots himself, everybody, including his brother, thinks he's dead, so they run away.

"Turns out, he wasn't. He was alive but bleeding. He could have been saved if anyone was around, but they weren't, so the kid dies and then comes back as a vampire—don't ask me how that happens—and hunts every-one down to get back at them for what they did to him."

"Okay," Rob said. "But what does that have to do with anything?"

"It was based on something that really happened here. A kid called Josh Andrews shot himself on prom night."

"That was so terrible," Libby said.

Sean nodded.

"Yes, it was. The story went out that it was an accident, but it wasn't. He was playing Russian roulette and he shot himself and bled out."

"Found him over in the park by the river," Clyde said. "His brother . . ."

"Susan's husband," Bernie interjected.

"Yup. He always denied that he was there, but I never believed him."

"I never heard about that," Libby objected.

"You wouldn't have," Clyde said. "It was hushed up. After all, Bud and Josh's father was a Supreme Court judge. Besides that, I think people felt that losing one son and having the other prosecuted for reckless endanger-ment was more than a man should have to bear."

"So Lionel wrote about that incident in his book *Damned to Death*?" Rob said.

"Exactly," Clyde said. "And Bud went in the garage and shot himself a little while after *Damned to Death* came out. And he left a suicide note making it pretty clear why he killed himself—which I never got to read because evi-dently Susan destroyed it before I got there."

"And Susan blamed Lionel for her husband's death," Rob said.

Clyde nodded.

"But there was nothing she could do about it legally. What he'd done wasn't criminal, at least not from the ju-dicial point of view. So when she heard he was coming to town—well, it was a perfect opportunity to even the score. And then with the cooking lesson dealing with the bamboo shoots, knowing Susan, I bet she thought it was a message from the gods to get on with the job."

Clyde reached over and helped himself to another serving of crisp out of the pan. "At least that's what she said in her statement. You know," he said as he took another mouthful of crisp, "I think the walnuts combined with the oats give the whole thing just the right amount of crunch."

Bernie thanked him and got up and started pacing.

"You know what I don't get," she said.

"What?" Clyde said.

"How did Lionel know about Josh's death? Was he there?"

Clyde shook his head.

"I think for Susan that's the worst part of the whole thing. She told Lionel."

"She told him?" Bernie echoed. "Why?"

"Why do people tell other people things after sex? Who knows?"

"She was sleeping with him?" Libby squeaked.

"And Geoff," Clyde said.

Bernie sat back down.

"Boy, for a mousy little thing she certainly got around, didn't she?"

"You know what they say," Sean began, "about . . ."

". . . Still waters running deep," both Libby and Bernie chorused with him.

Sean laughed.

"And Geoff," Rob continued. "What about him?"

"According to Susan's statement, he tried to blackmail her," Clyde told him. "He saw the recipe in the kitchen just like Bernie did, only Susan didn't overhear him talking on the phone. I guess he thought Susan was an easy way to get some money, which as you recall, thanks to Lionel, he was in desperate need of."

"Why did she try to blame everything on Tiffany?" Libby asked.

"She didn't set out to do that," Clyde said. "It just sort of evolved what with people talking the way they were. And she never liked her much. I think she figured better her than me."

Libby shook her head. "I guess we all should be grateful to Bree Nottingham for coming in when she did."

"I'll eat to that," Rob said.

Libby stood up. "Speaking of which, I have a couple of things to take care of downstairs."

Bernie started to rise, but Libby waved her back down. The truth was, she'd rather be by herself. She needed the time alone. When she walked into the kitchen, she breathed deeply and took in the odors of cinnamon and basil and butter and garlic. She felt better already. This was where she belonged. This was where she felt comfortable.

Libby grabbed a sponge and began wiping off the kitchen counters and putting the things Googie and Amber had forgotten away. She was planning next week's specials as she washed the floor out in front when she heard someone knocking on the door. She looked up. Tiffany was standing there. Libby took a deep breath. Her emotions were so jumbled up that she didn't know what she was going to say.

Tiffany motioned to the doorknob and Libby went and unlocked the door and opened it. Tiffany stayed outside.

"You're out," Libby said.

"Since yesterday."

Libby didn't say anything.

Tiffany shifted her weight from one foot to the other.

"I just wanted to come by and thank you before I leave, for everything you've done for me," she told Libby. "And to explain about Orion . . ."

Libby didn't want to hear it.

"There's nothing to explain."

"Yes, there is. I was stupid. I wanted to tell you, but every time I looked at you . . . I mean, you loved him so much. It made me feel so bad."

"Then why did you?"

"It just happened. I was drinking . . . I was dumb . . . I was . . . young."

"That was the first time."

"I guess I was a little bit jealous."

"Of what? You were thin. You went out all the time."

"You just had this nice relationship with your family. Your mother was always teaching you things. I . . . just wished . . ." Tiffany's voice trailed off. She swallowed. "Not that it matters now. Anyway, Orion called and told me about the pie in the face. I just came by to congratulate you and tell you how sorry I am for everything."

"So where are you going?" Libby asked.

"Down to Miami. I think I need to start over." Tiffany cleared her throat. "Will you call me?"

"I . . ."

"Not right away. But maybe in a couple of months when everything has died down."

"I'll think about it."

"Thanks." Tiffany stood there for a moment. "He was never right for you anyway. I always thought you could do better." Then she turned, walked to her car, got in, and drove away.

As Libby watched her go, she could see Bernie and Rob coming up out of the corner of her eye.

"I'm glad you said what you did," Bernie told her.

"You heard?"

"Yup. I've got big ears," her sister said. "And Tiffany's right. You can do better than Orion."

"Perhaps." Libby closed the door and relocked it.

"So where are you guys going?" she asked.

"We came to get you," Bernie told her.

"Yeah," Rob said. "We're going to R.J.'s and we thought you'd like to come along."

Libby shook her head and pulled at her T-shirt.

"I'm a mess."

"So go change," Bernie told her.

"I really don't . . ."

"You're coming," Bernie said in a voice that Libby knew from years of experience brooked no argument. "Now go upstairs and change. Unless you want me to do it for you. And put some lipstick on because Marvin is going to be meeting us there."

"Marvin?"

"Marvin," Bernie repeated. "I just called him."

"You shouldn't have done that," Libby said.

"Well, you weren't going to, were you?"

Libby opened her mouth and closed it again.

Finally she said, "Okay, but I'm not promising anything."

"You don't have to," Bernie told her. "I'll do all the work for you."

"That's what I'm afraid of," Libby told her as she went to put on some new clothes.

Recipes

My friend Amy has made this appetizer for a number of years. The nice things about it is it's quick and easy to prepare. It can be made ahead of time and looks great on the plate. And don't be put off by the word caviar. Red caviar is cheap and can be found on most better supermarket shelves.

Caviar Mousse

6 oz. red caviar
¼ cup chopped parsley
1 tablespoon grated onion
1 teaspoon grated lemon rind
1 pint sour cream
1 cup heavy cream
1 envelope gelatin
¼ cup water
freshly ground pepper to taste

In a large bowl combine caviar, parsley, onion, lemon rind. Stir the sour cream into this mixture. In a separate bowl whip the heavy cream. Sprinkle gelatin over

the water in a saucepan and cook over low heat, stir-
ring constantly, until the gelatin is completely dis-
solved. This takes only a minute or two. Stir gelatin
into the caviar and sour cream mixture. Fold in
whipped cream and add pepper to taste. Spoon into
individual molds or one large soufflé dish. Chill until
set. Unmold onto platter and serve surrounded by
crackers.

The recipes that follow are from my friend Linda
Nielsen, who is a great instinctive cook, as her grateful
friends will attest to. She's one of those people who can
take odds and ends and combine them into something
wonderful.

All these recipes are designed to serve eight. Have fun
with them and don't feel you have to follow them exactly,
except for the devil's food cake and the finger bone cookies,
that is. Here not following the recipes as they are written is
a bad idea because unlike cooking, baking is an exact art.

This is a nice old-fashioned recipe, something your
mother might have made, that works well in the summer
as an appetizer and looks pretty on a buffet table. It's a
great potluck dish because you can make it in the morning
in ten minutes, stick it in the fridge, and bring it to the
party later in the day.

Tomato Aspic

For the tomato aspic you need:
4 cups tomato juice either canned or homemade
2 tablespoons lemon juice

2 tablespoons gelatin
½ cup water

Soak 2 tablespoons gelatin in cold water.
Add lemon juice to tomato juice.
Heat juice but do not allow it to boil.
Stir in gelatin. Stir until it dissolves.
Pour into heart- or ring-shaped mold.
Put into refrigerator and chill until firm.
Unmold and serve on white platter decorated with lettuce leaves.
If so moved you can add ½ cup sour cream and/or chopped green olives or finely chopped celery to the mixture after the gelatin dissolves.

This salad fits nicely into any meal scheme. It works as part of a dinner or, if served with fruit and bread, as a light lunch. You can use regular navel oranges, but the blood oranges have a red color and slightly tarter taste that make them worth looking for.

Mesclun Salad with Goat Cheese, Blood Oranges, and Toasted Almonds in a Balsamic Vinagrette Dressing

½ to ¾ cup blanched slivered or halved almonds
8 cups mesclun lettuce
5 blood oranges
1 log domestic or imported goat cheese

Toast half a cup (or more if you want) of slivered or halved almonds in a pan with a little bit of olive oil, being careful not to burn them. When they are a nice brown, put them on a paper towel or brown paper bag to drain and put aside.

Next wash two bags of mixed baby greens or, preferably, get eight cups worth of mixed baby lettuces (mesclun) at a supermarket with a good produce section, pat dry, tear into bite-sized pieces, and put aside.

Chill log of goat cheese (either domestic or foreign) to make it easier to slice and cut into eight rounds and put aside.

Section five oranges, either regular or blood, and put aside.

Make dressing:
In a cup or a bottle put in 1 teaspoon Dijon mustard, 1 peeled garlic clove, whisk in four parts good olive oil, then slowly add in three parts balsamic vinegar.

Arrange lettuce on plates, put goat cheese on top, arrange orange slices next to them, drizzle dressing over all, scatter with almonds, and enjoy.

A meat thermometer really helps with this one. If you don't already have one, buy it now. It's a good investment.

Midnight Beef
(Black Pepper-coated Beef Tenderloin)

3 lbs beef tenderloin
½ to ¾ cup black peppercorns
1½ tablespoons rosemary

preferably fresh oil
1 tablespoon Dijon mustard.

For this recipe count on ⅓ pound meat per serving per person.
Preheat oven to 500 degrees.
Form the meat into a roll and tie with string or have your butcher do this for you.
Crush peppercorns with a bottle or rolling pin or bottom of a heavy pot.
Finely chop up rosemary.
Mix with peppercorns.
Paint or rub oil into meat.
Coat with Dijon mustard.
Roll meat in pepper and herb mixture.
Place on rack in roasting pan and put in the oven.
Reduce heat to 350 degrees and roast until desired level of doneness.
Test with meat thermometer. For rare the thermometer will read 125 degrees, for medium 130, and for well done 145 degrees.
Let rest for ten minutes, then carve into slices.

Au Gratin Potatoes

About 5 lbs thinly sliced potatoes
2 large thinly sliced onions
1½-2 cups grated sharp cheddar or imported Swiss
1 cup chicken stock
Salt and pepper
A 9- by 13-inch baking dish

Preheat oven to 350 degrees.
Butter baking dish.

Put in layer of thinly sliced potatoes, then the thinly sliced onions.

Sprinkle with salt and pepper, then sprinkle on cheese.

Continue this way until you have three more layers ending with cheese.

Pour in one cup of chicken stock.

Cover pan with foil, bake one hour.

Uncover pan bake another ½ hour.

Finger Bone Cookies
(Kranserkaker)

2 hardboiled cooked egg yolks mashed
2 raw egg yolks
½ lb (2 sticks) butter at room temperature
½ cup sugar
3½ cups flour
Powdered sugar
Maraschino cherries

Preheat oven to 350 degrees.

Combine mashed egg yolks and raw egg yolks in a large mixing bowl. Add butter and sugar and mix well.

Add flour and mix using your hands. (The mixture will be quite firm.)

Take a tablespoon of dough and roll it in your hands to form a narrow roll (the finger). If you want you can put a small piece of maraschino cherry on one end to make the fingernail.

Place on buttered cookie sheet. When finished forming cookies bake them in oven for fifteen minutes or until they are light brown.

Sprinkle with powdered sugar.
Store in covered container when cool.
Sprinkle with fresh powdered sugar just before serving (if you want to).

Devil's Food Cake

1½ sticks butter
2¼ cups sugar
1½ teaspoon vanilla
3 eggs
3 ounces unsweetened chocolate, melted
3 cups cake flour
1½ teaspoon baking soda
¾ teaspoon salt
1½ cups ice water

Preheat oven to 350 degrees.
Butter 3 eight-inch layer pans or a 9- by 13-inch pan.

Cream butter, sugar, and vanilla together.
Add eggs one at a time, beating well after each addition until light and fluffy.
Stir in cooled chocolate. (If it isn't cooled, the cake will be heavy.)
Sift together cake flour, baking soda and salt.
Add above to batter alternately with ice water (i.e., 1 cup flour, stir, ⅓ cup ice water, stir, etc.) until everything is combined. Do not overmix.
Put batter in pan or pans, place in oven, bake for 30 to 35 minutes or until the cake has pulled away from the sides and your finger doesn't leave a dent in the center of the cake. Cool.

Chocolate Mocha Frosting

½ cup soft butter
6 ounces semisweet chocolate, melted and cooled
1 egg yolk
½ teaspoon vanilla
2 teaspoons cognac
1 teaspoon instant espresso or coffee powder

Cream butter until fluffy.
Beat in cooled melted chocolate, egg yolk, vanilla, and coffee powder.

This can be used immediately or refrigerated, in which case it will need to be brought back to room temperature.

To compose: spread icing on cake and place in fridge until serving time. Enjoy!